ELVIS
and the
Blue Christmas
Corpse

Books by Peggy Webb

ELVIS AND THE DEARLY DEPARTED

ELVIS AND THE GRATEFUL DEAD

ELVIS AND THE MEMPHIS MAMBO MURDERS

ELVIS AND THE TROPICAL DOUBLE TROUBLE

ELVIS AND THE BLUE CHRISTMAS CORPSE

Published by Kensington Publishing Corporation

ELVIS
and the
Blue Christmas
Corpse

Peggy Webb

KENSINGTON BOOKS
http://www.kensingtonbooks.com

Kensington Books are published by

Kensington Publishing Corp.
119 West 40th Street
New York, NY 10018

All Kensington titles, imprints and distributed lines are available at special quantity discounts for bulk purchases for sales promotion, premiums, fund-raising, educational or institutional use.

Special book excerpts or customized printings can also be created to fit specific needs. For details, write or phone the office of the Kensington Special Sales Manager: Kensington Publishing Corp., 119 West 40th Street, New York, NY, 10018. Attn. Special Sales Department. Phone: 1-800-221-2647.

Kensington and the K logo Reg. U.S. Pat. & TM Off.

Library of Congress Card Catalogue Number: 2012941700

ISBN-13: 978-0-7582-4143-6
ISBN-10: 0-7582-4143-7

First Hardcover Printing: October 2012

10 9 8 7 6 5 4 3 2 1

Printed in the United States of America

ELVIS
and the
Blue Christmas
Corpse

Elvis' Opinion #1 on Love, Revenge, and Santa Paws

With the Mayan misadventure behind us, you'd think my human family (the Valentines) would be settling down to enjoy a cup of Christmas cheer and a good ham bone, preferably dug up from the back yard by yours truly and seasoned with a bit of Mississippi red clay.

But everybody in Mooreville is "Rocking Around the Christmas Tree." (Not my song, but, hey, I'm a generous, humble dog who appreciates the efforts of other singers—though they pale compared to mine.) The Wildwood Baptist choir (the church of choice for the Valentines) is gearing up for the Christmas cantata, otherwise known as amateur hour. With all that off-key caterwauling, I keep expecting the local choir director to come looking for advice from an expert. That would be yours truly, world-famous King of Rock 'n' Roll in a basset hound suit. But, like everybody else in this little northeast corner of the state, they dismiss me as just another handsome face and go on about their silly business. Which means they don't know G flat from a tasty stick of Pup-Peroni.

Fortunately, I have a human mom who appreciates my many talents—Callie Valentine Jones, owner of the best little beauty shop in town and caretaker to half of Mooreville. Currently that includes my human daddy, Jack Jones, who got caught in a jaguar trap in the jungle and is now happily ensconced in Callie's bed. But not for the reasons you're probably thinking. Callie's taking care of him while he recovers from leg surgery.

Listen, I'm a generous-hearted but portly dog. I want my human daddy to get well quick, but not so fast he has to leave. Callie's got me on a strict diet, but Jack pays that no more mind than he does when she tells him no (as in *no hanky panky*). Which she does with some regularity. While he's here, I get all the forbidden fat-laden snacks I please, plus a goodly number of T-bone steaks. Jack knows who's in his corner and who's not. I'm doing all I can to make sure my human parents get together again. For good, this time.

And speaking of broken relationships, Callie's cousin Lovie still hasn't forgiven Rocky Malone. She claims he left her to become a kidnapped Moon Goddess in a Mayan jungle while he stayed at his dig and searched for old bones. (He's an archeologist, and I'll have to say that a man who loves bones as much as he does gets my vote.) Currently she's out doing the "Jingle Bell Rock" (another song I could have turned to gold, but left in the hands of lesser singers) with another man who's not fit to stir the soup in her pot. (She's the owner of Lovie's Luscious Eats, the best little catering business in the South.)

Then, of course, there's Ruby Nell, Callie's mama, who has finally patched up her feud with Charlie (Callie's uncle and godfather to the entire Valentine family). Ruby Nell has also sent her not-so-true love traveling on a gravel road. That would be Thomas Whitenton, her sometime dance partner and who knows what all. Never one to be "Running Scared," Ruby Nell is up to her neck with Fayrene in plans for a Christmas open house at the séance room on the back of Gas, Grits, and Guts.

Fayrene finally got the séance room built. Thank the lord

and hallelujah, she and her husband Jarvetis Johnson are once again Mooreville's answer to Lucy and Desi. And the mystical addition to our one and only convenience store didn't have to be over Jarvetis' dead body!

So far, the only hitch in Ruby Nell and Fayrene's plan is that Bobby Huckabee's psychic eye is on the blink and they're looking for somebody else who can talk to the dead.

Who needs somebody to talk to the dead when they have a basset hound who used to be the King? Give me a white beard, a little red four-legged suit, and a microphone, and I'll bring down the house. "Santa Paws Is Back in Town!"

Chapter 1

Jazz Funerals, Santa's Elf, and Fa La La La Farewell

The last thing I expected to be doing was dressing for a Christmas party with my almost-lover Champ while my almost-ex Jack sprawls on my bed dishing out love advice. I'm bent over putting on some cute backless Bernardos with rhinestones on the toe when he pipes up with, "Cal, if you plan on snaring a husband, you need to show more cleavage."

"You're a fine one to be giving love advice, Jack. And for your information, I don't *snare.*"

"You snared me."

I'm going to royally ignore that remark. Champ (Luke Champion) is a good man who stays at home to run a nice, safe veterinary clinic instead of gallivanting all over the world getting shot at. I'm not going to let a deep-cover assassin with a Harley Screaming Eagle spoil my evening. Even if Jack did get his leg smashed all to pieces while he was rescuing cousin Lovie.

I just sashay right past the bed where he's taking up his half and mine, too, and start putting on my lipstick. Pretty in pink, which enhances my olive complexion and gives my full lips a kissably soft appearance. Beauty is my business, and I don't skimp when it comes to myself. In addition to expert styling skills, it's my beauty example that has people flocking from all over three counties to make appointments at Hair.Net.

Well, that plus the addition of my new manicurist, Darlene. She's brought Atlanta nail art to Mooreville. Rhinestones on your toes, and all. She did my toenails for tonight. Pink to match my lipstick. I believe in coordinating colors.

Some people clash. Like Mama. Which I won't even get into at this time.

"Cal, before you go, would you plump up my pillows? I just don't feel like lifting my head."

"If you're that weak, how'd you manage to get out of the guest bed and into mine?"

Jack gives me a mournful look then gazes at his crutches like a man with wheelchairs in his future.

He's probably faking it, but I'm too tenderhearted to go around ignoring pain and suffering. What if it's real? I know, *I know*. The doctor said Jack is going to be one hundred percent okay, but I worry.

Besides, Elvis is giving me a few dirty looks. Not the real King but my dog, who politely plopped his ample self onto the bed while I was primping and is now lying there with his head on Jack's chest. He and Jack are two of a kind. Sneaky. They probably planned this pity party.

I spritz on some Jungle Gardenia (for Champ, although it's Jack's favorite perfume) then march toward the bed in a no-nonsense fashion that lets him know I'm all business.While I'm bent over fluffing up his pillows, he's getting a good gander at the body part he said I should bare more of for Champ. Champ, my foot. Jack was only thinking of himself. Which ought to make me mad enough to scream but instead makes me nostalgic.

I try to blame my mood on Elvis. The real singer, not my dog. When I was downstairs making Jack some hot tea, I put

"Blue Christmas" on the CD player, and now I wish I hadn't. The way that man sings can break your heart. No wonder he's still the most popular entertainer on earth, and him dead nearly forty years.

"There." I straighten back up. "Is that better?"

"Just a little more on the left. Please."

I'm bent over Jack—again and for the forty millionth time—when Mama prisses in.

Around Mooreville, it's an insult to your neighbor to keep your door locked when you're home. But it's an equal insult not to ring the bell. Of course, Mama thinks rules don't apply to her.

"I just love a cozy family scene." She swishes into the room trailing a red and green caftan decorated with sequined snowflakes, one of her many Christmas getups. She's topped it off with a dangling pair of purple sequined earrings shaped like feathers. Mama went native in the jungle and hasn't stopped since.

She leans over and kisses Jack on the cheek, then proceeds to fluff up pillows that don't need it one iota.

"Mama, I just did that."

Naturally, she ignores me and keeps fussing over Jack. "Feather pillows pack down quicker than Elvis can run when you say *treat.*"

"Thanks, Ruby Nell." My almost-ex flashes his most winning smile, which I won't let myself even think about, and she acts like a teenager smitten over a rock star.

"Mama, don't you believe in the doorbell?"

"The front door was wide open. Besides, what I have to tell you is important."

"Can it wait? My date will be here in less than fifteen minutes."

"By all means, if you want to hurt Fayrene's feelings, bankrupt my business, and disappoint Charlie, to boot, just go on and forget about us."

Did I tell you? Mama's a drama queen. Still, she's baited a trap and I fall right in every time.

"How on earth does my attending a holiday party hurt Fayrene's feelings? Not to mention bankrupt you."

I don't even add anything about Uncle Charlie. If he wants me to do something, he asks, which is what most sane folks do. In the Valentine, family, though there's a huge streak of the theatrical.

Take Lovie. My cousin can turn a simple stake-out at the famous Peabody Hotel into an event complete with TV cameras while she moons half of Memphis. That was during what the Valentine family refers to as the Peabody murders, which I'm trying desperately to forget. And don't even get me started on her getting kidnapped in the jungle. I don't plan to get involved in anything else that even remotely hints at murder and mayhem. I plan to get on with my life. Starting this evening.

"Never mind." Mama's pursed mouth says she means exactly the opposite. "Just go on about your business. Don't even think about how many orphans you'll let starve."

Jack's laughing his head off.

"Holy cow. Don't encourage her." The doorbell rings, and I'm so grateful for the distraction I nearly trip over Hoyt (my rescued cocker spaniel) trying to get to the door. "That'll be Champ."

"He can wait." Naturally Jack would say that. "We need to hear what Ruby Nell has to say."

"Yoo-hoo!"

Good grief. It's Fayrene. Before I can yell out "Come in," she barrels up the stairs and makes a beeline for Jack.

8

"How are you feeling?" She plumps up his pillows. If they get any fluffier, he'll be airborne.

"Pretty good, Fayrene. Considering." He glances my way in a bid for sympathy. I'm not about to offer it in front of witnesses. It's bad enough I had to offer a bed and have him in my house every minute of every day like God's temptation to weak-willed women.

"I brought you some Christmas cookies, Jack." She plops a plate full of sugar-sprinkled Santas on the bedside table, then proceeds to peel the cellophane cover back and hand him one. "I've been medicating about you every day."

Meditating, I hope, but with Fayrene you never can tell whether her slaughter of the English language is accidental or deliberate.

After Jack finishes bragging on her cookies, Fayrene looks over at Mama and says, "Did you tell her?"

"She's too busy getting ready for a *date*." Mama makes my date sound like an appointment with the guillotine.

"Maybe you should tell her, Fayrene," Jack says. For a man who has to have everybody in Mooreville fluffing his feathers, he looks perky enough to brew coffee without the benefit of the pot.

"Wait a minute." How did Mama and Fayrene end up in my bedroom at the precise moment I'm supposed to be out having a real life with a sane and sensible man? "Jack, did you call Mama and Fayrene?"

"Why?"

"You did! You ought to be ashamed of yourself."

"Carolina, I won't have you talking to a sick man like that." Mama calls me *Carolina* when she gets mad.

"Ruby Nell's right," Fayrene says. "The aftereffects of Jack's surgery could be deathless."

9

Two against one. I might have known. Mama and Fayrene always stick together, even when she's fighting with Jarvetis and Mama sticks her nose into business she knows good and well is not hers.

"Holy cow. I give up." I sink onto the stool at my dressing table and refresh my mascara. It looks like my pretty in pink lipstick will have to go to waste. "Just tell me what's going on."

"There's going to be a fabulous three-day benefit at the mall for the poor little orphans at the Tupelo Children's Mansion." When Mama pours it on that thick, she has a hidden agenda, usually one that involves me. And usually in a way I don't even want to think about. "Charlie's signed us all up."

There's the hook. Uncle Charlie is my deceased daddy's brother, my surrogate father, my best friend, Lovie's daddy, the protector and leader of the entire Valentine clan. What he says goes. Not that he's bossy. It's just that he's so wonderful nobody in this family wants to disappoint him.

I'm getting ready to ask, *Signed up for what*, but Fayrene jumps in to fill the gaps.

"We'll all have booths at the Barnes Crossing Mall. Ruby Nell's calling her Everlasting Monument booth Fa La La La Farewell."

"I'll be offering Christmas discounts on tombstones," Mama says. "And I've written a bunch of new holiday send-offs. How about *Name Inserted climbed aboard a Christmas sleigh and jingled on up to Heaven*? And listen to this. *Name Inserted went dashing through the stars on a one-way ticket to that great Christmas reunion in the sky.*"

Mama's famous for her tombstone sayings. Some of them are a little ambiguous, like the one she did for Jarvetis' third cousin: *Goober Johnson tooted his horn all the way home.* He used to play the trumpet every Saturday night with his band, The Goobers, at the Evergreen Fish and Steak House five miles

10

south of Mooreville on Highway 371. But everybody knows Goober was also a braggart. Which, thanks to Mama, is now engraved in stone for the world to see.

"Charlie's giving away a free jazz funeral," Mama adds.

My uncle Charlie is owner of Eternal Rest, the best funeral home in Mississippi It's in Tupelo, a ten-minute ride from downtown Mooreville, population 652 now that Darlene and her son are here. To supplement my income, I also do makeup and hair for the dearly departed.

"What about you, Fayrene?" Jack asks.

Naturally, he wants to encourage them. The more time I spend getting flustered, the less likely I'll be able to enjoy my date with Champ.

"Jarvetis and I are handing out free samples of our specialty." That would be their pickled pigs' lips. "We'll be offering a jar free with a purchase of ten gallons of gas. And I hear Lovie's going to be cooking on her electric girdle."

If anybody has an electric girdle, it would be my flamboyant cousin Lovie. But for the sake of the family reputation, I sincerely hope she'll be dishing up Lovie's Luscious Eats from an ordinary griddle.

The doorbell rings again, and Lord only knows who's there. This time I beat whoever it is to the door. It's Champ, standing on my front porch looking blond and handsome and entirely sane. A vast improvement over the motley crew in my bedroom.

And speaking of the devil, they're now all lined up on the landing—Mama and Fayrene flanking Jack, who is trying to look as pitiful as possible on his crutches, and Elvis sitting beside my not-quite-husband with his ears perked for trouble.

Ever cheerful, Champ smiles up at them and then me. "Looks like you've got company, Callie. We don't have to leave right away."

"Yes, we do. For the sake of my sanity."

I snag my stylish black alpaca cape from the downstairs coat closet. Champ helps me into it while I endure a hostile audience of four (if you count Elvis, and I always do).

"Carolina, do you think you ought to leave while your husband is burning up with fever?" Mama calls Jack my husband in a deliberate ploy calculated to break me up with Champ.

I won't even dignify her remark with an answer. For one thing, Jack does not have fever. And for another, he's my almost-ex, as she well knows. So does Champ. No need to keep harping on it.

Fayrene puts her hand on Jack's forehead. "Don't worry, hon. If poor Jack catches ammonia while you're gone, we'll call an avalanche."

Champ, who is still not used to Fayrenese, looks slightly shell-shocked, while Jack grins like a possum eating peaches.

"I'll be all right, Cal," Jack says. "Have fun." Just when I'm thinking he's trying to shed all the danger he wears like a second skin and turn noble, he blows that hope right out of the water. "The massage you promised can wait till you get back."

"In your dreams, Jack."

I'm grateful to step into the cool night air.

Southerners never know what to expect in December. Anything is possible, from a heat wave to an ice storm. Thankfully, we're having one of those lovely cold Christmas seasons where you want to spend as much time as you can in front of the hearth with a cup of hot chocolate in your hand and Elvis at your feet. My dog. Though the real thing would be nice.

The party is in Mantachie, an easy fifteen-minute ride north through rural countryside on Highway 371. White frame houses dot the landscape, and all of them are built on lots so big nobody can look out the window and see his neighbor.

The scenery also includes a barn or two, a few soybean fields, and several pastures, some featuring cows. This is one reason I love northeast Mississippi. It's so quiet and peaceful you can easily believe the nightly horror stories coming from the TV news channels don't apply to you.

If you close your eyes and count to twenty, you can drive right through Mantachie and miss the whole town. Same as Mooreville. Though I'll have to admit Mantachie has it one up on us by being incorporated. They have a Dollar General store, a mayor, and city ordinances against firing a shotgun in your back yard, even if you're trying to kill a rattlesnake.

Champ's veterinary clinic is located here. With Elvis and my rescues—Hoyt, the spaniel Elvis views as his competition, and the Seven Dwarfs, otherwise known as cats—I'm his best customer.

Our hostess is also one of Champ's customers, Glenda McAfee, Mantachie's mayor. Her two-story antebellum home is decorated with five Christmas trees, garlands galore, at least fifty pots of poinsettias, and enough lights to guide small aircraft safely home. She matches her house—large, decked out in bright red satin, and flashing enough diamonds to light up a runway.

If she weren't my hostess, I'd offer a little fashion advice. Women of a certain size should not wear red form-fitting sheaths. And when it comes to accessorizing, if you look like you're wearing all your loot from a recent jewelry store robbery, you've overdone it.

Since I'm a guest, I content myself with slipping one of my tasteful business cards out of my black satin purse and leaving it on her hall table beside the cranberry potpourri. Discreetly, of course.

While Champ goes off to the refreshment table, I recognize the mayor's background music as Elvis' *Christmas Peace* album.

"Santa Bring My Baby Back (to Me)" makes me wonder what Jack is doing. Then I feel guilty because, while I'm thinking of another man, Champ has come back from fetching two cups of eggnog. He's kind, handsome, successful, and loves kids and animals—perfect father material. I ought to be ecstatic.

Instead, when he slides his arm around my waist, I feel like an imposter.

"The mayor's gardens are as splendid as her house." Champ leans down so I can hear him over the party crowd. "I'd like to show you around."

A golden-haired, good-looking man in the moonlight would be almost impossible to resist. Champ's been hinting of an engagement since I returned from Mexico, and I'm sure he's looking for every edge, especially since his major competition ended up right back in my house.

Suddenly my cell phone rings. I'm sorry to report, I snatch it from my purse like it's the only life raft on a sinking ship. I plug a finger in one ear and hold the phone up to the other.

"Hello?" *Uncle Charlie*, I mouth to Champ, then disappear into the quiet of the mayor's front porch.

"By now I'm sure Ruby Nell has told you her version of the Christmas charity event at Barnes Crossing Mall?"

"In frightening detail, Uncle Charlie. Are you really giving away a free jazz funeral?"

His rich, booming laughter always makes me feel better. "It was a compromise. Bobby wanted to announce the opening of a new drive-thru window at Eternal Rest."

I can picture it. The newly deceased propped up on satin pillows in front of a picture window, and the grieving viewing him from their car while munching McDonald's hamburgers and talking about how natural he looks. For a dollar you could get a takeout pack of disposable tissues.

"That sounds like Bobby."

A few weeks ago when we returned from Mexico, we were greeted by a huge WELCOME HOME sign Uncle Charlie's assistant had put on the lawn of the funeral home. Relatives of the deceased nearly passed out.

"Naturally, I want to help," I tell my uncle. "I can do a few free makeovers then raffle off a couple of haircuts and a manicure, or something."

"I knew I could count on you, dear heart. Can Darlene man the Hair.Net booth? I need you in another capacity."

"Sure. Free manicures would probably go over better, anyway. What do you want me to do?"

"Santa's down with the flu, and his elf has quit. I'm filling in for Santa, and I want you to be my elf."

"I'll be glad to, but don't you think five nine is a little tall for an elf?"

"It's the spirit that counts."

Uncle Charlie and I work out final details, and after we say goodbye, I sit on the mayor's front porch swing in the dark. By myself. A blessed relief.

All I wanted when I woke up this morning was a normal day. Eat breakfast with Elvis, read the paper with my second cup of coffee, take a nice bath, enjoy making my clients beautiful at Hair.Net, then have a relaxing dinner with my menagerie of rescues.

Already I've had enough drama to start my own private theater.

What next? Lovie as Rudolph the Red-Nosed Reindeer?

Elvis Opinion #2 on Christmas Cheer, Sabotage, and the Art of the Con

You'd think a dog with my good looks and tender heart would be above sabotaging the best human mom any basset hound ever had. But when you're trying to save a marriage, all bets are off. I station my portly self at the front door waiting for Callie to come back from her date.

Champ's Ford Mustang convertible says it all. Listen, he's a nice man and can give a rabies shot so easy even a discerning dog finds no room for complaint. But what woman in her right mind would swap a man who drives a silver Jag and a Harley Screaming Eagle to boot (that would be my human daddy) for a man in a car that won't hold a candle?

The minute my mismatched radar ears pick up the sound of Champ's engine, I howl a few bars of "He Touched Me." Jack comes racing down the stairs like the crutch is a third leg. You might not think a gospel song could get a man moving so fast, but Jack knows his lyrics. It's the idea of another man touching my human mom that has his butt in gear.

We station ourselves on the front porch swing in the dark, and about the time Champ gets within scoring distance of Callie, my human daddy says, "Thank goodness, you're home, Cal. My leg is killing me."

ELVIS AND THE BLUE CHRISTMAS CORPSE

I never saw a man unpucker as fast as Champ. He releases Callie and offers to help Jack inside.

I can smell remorse a mile away, and there's not a whiff coming from Jack. Me, either, for that matter. Listen, a man and his dog have to do what they have to do.

Callie's not too happy with either of us, though. Jack gets bundled back into the guest-room bed with nothing but a cup of hot tea to keep him warm. And for a minute, I think I'm going to have to share my guitar-shaped pillow with that silly stray cocker spaniel Callie went and named after one of my backups. (Hoyt, in case one of my adoring fans wonders.)

But she gets on the phone with Lovie so they can hash over the day's events the way they always do, and I see my human mom visibly relax. Lovie has that effect. Her sense of humor is as big as her heart. If Lovie can't make you laugh and forget your troubles, nobody can.

Still, I go to bed plotting how I'll make up with Callie so she'll let me put on my little four-legged red Santa suit and go to the mall for the charity event. Listen, what better way to ring in the Christmas season than yours truly giving a Christmas concert in Santa's Court? Forget my 1958 comeback concert where I wore black leather. This could turn out to be the comeback concert of the century.

When I had two legs and a head full of slicked-back hair, I turned every Christmas song I recorded into gold. There's no way I'm getting left out of this performance. And I'll pee on the leg of anybody who tries to stop me.

Especially since Darlene's upstart Lhasa apso has been courting Ann Margret behind my back and my former French poodle sweetie has been giving me the cold shoulder. No dog of my intelligence and talent is going to take rejection lying down, no matter how comfortable the silk pillow.

17

Chapter 2

Santa's Court, Jingle Bell Nail Art, and the Tall Elf

Ever since Jack interrupted my romantic moment on the front porch with Champ, Elvis has been greeting me first thing in the morning with his tail wagging and my pink, plush-lined bedroom slippers in his mouth. Call me sentimental, but I think it's the sweetest thing that my dog wants to make sure my feet are warm. I think he's trying to apologize for his bad behavior on the front porch the other night. Elvis actually growled and got his hackles up before I could figure out whether I was really into Champ's kiss or just hoping to be.

If you treat a basset right, he'll reward you by dying for you, if necessary. Of course, nobody around here is going to die if I have a say in it. This is Christmas. I'm just saying I don't feel a bit silly when I get Elvis' little four-pawed Santa suit out of the closet.

"You're taking Elvis to the mall?"

Naturally Jack puts in his two cents. And naturally, he's in my bedroom watching my every move, six feet of handsome and every inch tempting.

"Yes. The kids will love him."

"They'll love you, too."

"A tall, skinny elf? Are you kidding?" Still, Jack's comment pleases me. More than it ought to, really. If he doesn't hurry up and get well and leave this house, I don't know what I'm going to do about my runaway inconvenient attraction.

Jack's black-eyed stare lets me know he's not kidding. I have to distract myself with the business of making sure his meds are all lined up on the bedside table and his cell phone within easy reach. Things he's perfectly capable of doing for himself. Still, kindness is my motto. This world would be a better place if more people spread it around. Especially at Christmas.

Finally Elvis and I head to the door, and Jack calls after us, "Be careful."

Of what, I wonder, but I don't stop to engage in further conversation. The less time I spend around my ex, the better for my peace of mind. In that light, it's a good thing Uncle Charlie booked all the Valentines for this event.

The Barnes Crossing Mall is a sprawling complex of stores that started out in the middle of a pasture on the northwest side of Tupelo. Anchored by Sears on one end and Belk's on the other, it features a food court in the middle and a movie theater tacked to the east side. Shortly after the mall was built, Walmart erected a store across the street, and then shops, service stations, restaurants, drugstores, a medical clinic, and a grocery store sprang up faster than Elvis can con Jack out of forbidden treats. (Don't think I don't know. I just pretend not to. Why spoil their fun?)

Elvis and I arrive well before the mall opens, park in the east lot near the double glass doors near the center court, and go in the entrance reserved for participants in the charity event. The mall is not officially open for another forty minutes and is empty except for volunteers. Mama and Fayrene aren't here yet, but I'm happy to see that my new manicurist is already in the Hair.Net booth.

Darlene Johnson Lawford Grant is wearing her usual boots and jeans, a green sweater decorated with silver sequined snowmen, and the diamonds she kept from both her ex-husbands. With perfect makeup and nails, her hair a long silken sweep of blond, she will attract a large crowd. I give her the thumbs up, and Darlene gives me the victory sign.

Though at first I had my doubts about hiring her, especially after I found out she won't paint your nails till she consults your horoscope, I've come to applaud my choice. My clients love her, and they enjoy getting their nails professionally done without having to drive to Tupelo.

At the rate Darlene is helping fill my coffers, I'll soon be able to add a tanning bed to Hair.Net. My hope is to turn my beauty shop into a south of Mooreville Riviera. Now as I head toward the dressing room to find out what kind of elf costume awaits, Elvis jerks the leash out of my hand and bolts.

"Elvis, come back here," I yell, but obviously his mismatched ears have suddenly lost the ability to detect sound. It's not long before I see why.

"Elvis! You old chow hound." Lovie has arrived, all hundred ninety pounds of her engulfed in sequins and jingle bells and the mingled scents of sugar and cinnamon. Food will get my dog every time.

I jog over to my cousin and best friend in the universe and give her a hug.

"Got your electric girdle?" I ask, and she deadpans, "Always." We slap hands and chant, "God bless, Fayrene."

We're laughing *with* her, not *at* her. Thank goodness, the Valentines were brought up to know the difference.

"Do you need me to help you unload?" I spot Lovie's van parked just outside the glass double doors to the mall's east entrance near my Dodge Ram.

"Are you kidding? With this come-hither figure, I'll soon

have more male muscle than I can shake my National Treasure at."

She's talking about her tattoo—NATIONAL TREASURE, one word on each hip. In a weak moment I don't even want to recall, we both got tattoos on Beale Street. I refuse to talk about mine. Suffice it to say, I'm not shaking it at anybody. Especially Jack.

"You'd better give the National Treasure a rest, Lovie. Santa's Court is rated PG."

"Maybe just a forbidden shake every now and then. Gotta keep in practice." She dumps an oversize red-sequined tote bag into her booth. "I'm a little nervous, Cal."

If you didn't know Lovie the way I do, you'd scoff at the idea. But underneath all that bravado lurks a vulnerable woman who has a hard time believing she's good enough. My secret theory is that's the real reason she broke up with Rocky Malone.

"Ah, Lovie." I hug her again. "Don't you know? You're the best cook in the South. People are going to snatch up your cookbook so fast your head will swim. Especially with part of the proceeds going to charity."

A copy of her first cookbook peeks out of the top of her bag—*Lovie's Luscious Holiday Treats*.

"Maybe I should have left *Luscious* out of the title."

"You want people to make an instant connection with your catering business. People love your cooking."

"That they do, dear heart." Uncle Charlie strolls up, leans over to pet Elvis, then hugs us before he surveys the mall's center court. "I don't see Ruby Nell and Fayrene."

"You know Mama. She probably had to change clothes six times before she was satisfied. It's a wonder she didn't call me this morning to change her hair color."

Mama changes hair color more often than I change my air

freshener. Currently her hair is still raven from her attempt at being a senorita in the Mayan jungle.

"We'd better get in costume, then." Uncle Charlie says.

I leave my dog in the booth with Lovie, which is a polite way of saying a herd of stampeding elephants couldn't have dragged him away from her sugared doughnuts.

"Watch him for me till I get back. And no sweet treats. He's on a diet."

Elvis and Lovie both give me innocent looks, but I'm not the least bit fooled. The minute my back is turned she'll be feeding him, and he'll be eating like he didn't have a full bowl of dog chow this morning plus the stick of Pup-Peroni Jack sneaked to him.

I can't be too hard on Elvis and Jack, though. Holidays are made for breaking rules. But I swear, as soon as the holidays are over I'm really going to clean up their act. Mine, too, but right now I can't think about how to get Jack off my mind.

Uncle Charlie and I have arrived in the dressing room, and I have to use all my energy trying to figure out how I'm going to get nearly six feet of me into a little green costume made for someone who's five feet tall.

Holding up the costume, I'm appalled at the amount of leg it will leave bare.

"Who was the elf before me? A Wizard of Oz munchkin?"

Uncle Charlie emerges from behind one of the three curtained-off cubicles. "I don't know his name. All I know is that he was here for years."

Uncle Charlie already has his red pants on over his khakis and is busy stuffing the waistband with pillows. It's going to take several. He's as fit and trim as any sixty-three-year-old gentleman you'll ever meet. Which figures when you consider that he was once a Company man, like Jack.

"He wore a skirt?"

"I'd imagine he wore pants. That's probably a costume used by the elf before him."

In the Dark Ages, I'm guessing. In addition to having a too-short skirt with jingle bells on the bottom, my costume has a moth hole in the seat of the green underpants. I'll have to remember not to bend over.

I step behind another curtain and into the costume, then proceed to tug at the skirt. Fortunately, the fabric is slightly damp and stretches to add about an inch to the bottom, enough so I won't give mothers heart attacks and young kids an unexpected education. I glance at my watch to see if I have time to run to the fabric store in the mall and get six-inch-wide ribbon for the skirt, but it's too late. I'll just have to make do.

When I step outside the curtain I do a double take. In his coat and boots and faux white beard, Uncle Charlie looks like the real deal. Of course, in their red, fur-trimmed suits, all Santas look alike.

"Ho ho ho," he says, and I applaud. He's headed toward the door when I spot the rest of his costume lying on a metal chair.

"Wait. Your gloves." When I pick them up, I notice they're even wetter than my skirt. "These are damp, Uncle Charlie."

"Probably a leak from the air conditioner or something. There's construction going on all over the mall."

"I wonder why they didn't wait till after Christmas."

"Who knows? The mall's old. Maybe they had an emergency situation." He offers his arm. "Ready, dear heart?"

By the time Uncle Charlie and I get to Santa's Court, I'm tickled pink to see people lined up two-deep in front of the Hair.Net booth to sample Darlene's free jingle bell nail art. Mama's Fa La La La Farewell booth has attracted a crowd, too. And Fayrene is knee deep in people who'll soon find out that pickled pigs' lips are not an exotic new delicacy but taste as much like the barnyard as they sound.

Over at Uncle Charlie's Eternal Rest Funeral Home booth, poor Bobby has no one itching to talk about kicking the bucket and receiving a free jazz funeral. My first thought is to call Jack to drop by the mall so Bobby will have somebody to talk to. Then I remember that Jack can't drive yet. Maybe I'll call Champ.

The star of the center mall, of course, is Lovie. Her griddle is smoking, her deep-fry cooker is sizzling, and you can't stir her crowd with a peppermint stick. Everybody wants a taste of Lovie's Luscious Eats.

I drop by her booth to pick up Elvis, then proceed to the back entrance of Santa's Court. It's a roped-off area with two security guards in elf costumes up front trying to keep order among the screaming kids and their tired-looking mothers. Somebody ought to tell those two guards that *disgruntled* is not the proper demeanor for Santa's elves.

The centerpiece of the court is Santa's throne, an elaborate metal structure spray-painted gold and adorned with faux jewels, plush, red-velvet cushions, and a string of Christmas bulbs that will light up when the opening ceremonies begin.

When Uncle Charlie takes a seat and says, "Ho, ho, ho," you'd think Elvis himself had risen from the dead. The kids go into a screaming frenzy. Of course, with this age (two to six), they could be screaming for no reason at all.

Walking carefully so I won't open the show with a flyaway skirt, I make my way through fake snow, plastic reindeer, faux trees hung with Christmas ornaments, and cardboard-cut-out elves. I'd make three of these little inanimate Santa's helpers.

The kids waiting for a turn on Santa's lap don't notice. Partially because I head into the crowd to hand out candy canes but mostly because I have Santa Paws on a leash. (Let me tell you, Elvis is hamming it up.) With two Santas in the building, the screaming has reached near-hysteria, even if one of the Santas is canine.

A man with a face as wrinkled as a peach pit struts my way. In jeans and leather jacket, he'd look like an ordinary mall shopper except for his size. His head comes up barely past my elbow.

He makes no bones about looking me up and down, and Elvis makes no bones about his disapproval. Hearing that low grumbling growl, I lean over and try to soothe my dog's ruffled feelings.

"Be nice, or I'll call Champ to take you home." Elvis gets the picture. When I straighten up, he's a model of canine decorum. Translated, that means he's not drooling and using my legs as a salt lick.

"You're some tall elf." The strange little man holds out his hand. "Hi, I'm Corky Kelly. I just dropped by to wish you luck."

I take an educated guess. "Former elf?"

He doesn't laugh; he giggles. I know the difference. Lovie and I have spent hours down on Mama's farm or sitting cross-legged in the middle of her bed or mine eating popcorn and giggling.

"Retired elf." A look of longing crosses his face. "I miss it, though."

"Stick around, Mr. Kelly. I'd love for you to give me some pointers.""

"Wish I could, but I'm meeting my nephew across town at Danver's. One of the perks of being retired. Leisurely lunches with family and friends."

I don't notice Elvis is missing until Corky strolls off. It's just like my dog to pay me back for a public chastisement by slipping his collar and leaving me holding an empty leash. Panicked, I'm about to start calling his name when I hear him. Front and center in Santa's Court, head thrown back, his throat working on a series of long howls.

Good grief. My dog is onstage, probably thinking he's singing "Blue Christmas." Listen, I know you think I'm crazy, but this basset acts like he's a world-famous entertainer. He grabs every opportunity to perform.

The kids are laughing and clapping, which only encourages him. Elvis spins in a little circle, shows his audience a curled-up lip and a bit of teeth, then keeps on howling.

"Somebody grab that dog!" The screech comes from Mayor Earl Getty's wife, Junie Mae.

Mayor Getty himself, who is standing in Santa's Court fiddling with the microphone, tries to grab my dog, but I'm too fast for him. I leap into action and have Elvis back on his leash before he can pee on Junie Mae's snakeskin pumps.

He hates being called a dog. I remind him that Junie Mae is one of my best customers. She drives all the way from Tupelo to Hair.Net and has a standing request for me to make up her up like Marilyn Monroe when she's ready to pass on to Glory Land. When she delivered postmortem instructions, she said, "For once, I want to take the spotlight from Robert Earl."

I have Elvis back under control before anybody has time to think our shenanigans are anything except part of the act. The kids start clapping, and Mayor Getty, who knows opportunity when it mows him down, is quick to take the credit.

"A little added attraction," he says.

"Behave yourself," I tell my dog; then I make sure his collar is a notch tighter, too tight to slip out of but not tight enough to be uncomfortable.

Meanwhile the mall's PA system is blasting "Jingle Bells," the crowd is getting restless, and Mayor Getty is tapping away at the microphone the way he always does.

ELVIS AND THE BLUE CHRISTMAS CORPSE

At the front of the crowd, Junie Mae looks like an Easter marshmallow in her too-tight pink suit with the faux-fur collar and little matching pillbox hat. And I mean that in the best of ways. I like marshmallows.

"It's working, hon," Junie Mae calls out.

The crowd laughs. Every time the mayor makes a public appearance, he taps and she yells the same thing. Theirs is almost a George Burns and Gracie Allen routine.

With Elvis firmly on his leash, I station myself beside a Christmas tree in the corner of Santa's Court. Mayor Getty glances at Uncle Charlie and me to mouth, *Ready?*

We both nod, and he says, "La-dies and gent-le-men."

"Wait!" Somebody in the crowd yells. "Stop!"

It's the mall's manager, Cleveland White, his long legs pumping toward Santa's Court, his wild red hair sticking up, his florid face redder than Santa Claus' suit.

What now? I'm holding my breath, right along with the crowd, when Cleveland announces, "Rudolph is not here yet."

On a collective exhale, we all turn to see a half reindeer, half man loping in our direction. The only way we know he is Steve Boone, owner of Tupelo Hardware, where Elvis bought his first guitar, is that he's carrying his head. It has pointy antlers and a bright red nose.

Junie Mae grabs his furry left flank as he lopes by. "Psst. Put your head on."

Steve heaves the big shaggy costume head over his, and Rudolph the Red-Nosed Reindeer steps into Santa's Court.

Mayor Getty clears his throat to start over. "Welcome to the North Pole! On behalf of the city of Tupelo and the Barnes Crossing Mall, I give you Santa Claus and his court!"

Elvis barks while Rudolph grabs Uncle Charlie's gloved hand and leans over to whisper something to him. Suddenly

27

the throne lights up, Rudolph's nose starts flashing, and he flies through the air with the greatest of ease. Meanwhile, Uncle Charlie starts to "Shake, Rattle and Roll."

Something is horribly wrong. While I'm frozen in fear, the crowd goes wild. Am I the only one who knows this is not part of the show? When Uncle Charlie topples from the throne, I shake off my paralysis and race his way. The clapping now becomes cheering.

Holy cow! Everybody still thinks they're being entertained. Everybody, that is, except Lovie, who is shoving her way through the crowd.

An overwrought mother with rambunctious twin boys says, "You can't cut this line." Lovie would have ignored her if she hadn't added, "You hog."

"Kiss my grits, heifer." Lovie keeps on trucking. Thank goodness.

Uncle Charlie and Rudolph the Red-Nosed Reindeer are lying on the floor, and they are not moving.

Chapter 3

Unexpected Christmas Show, Final Curtain, and Ruldoph the Red-Nosed Deer-ly Departed

Frantic, I kneel beside Uncle Charlie and start CPR. Where is the manager? Can't the guards trying to restore order see that nobody is attending to Rudolph? Is there no doctor in this crowd?

Plowing her way through the bedlam, Lovie screams, "Daddy! Daddy!" When there is no response, she says a word that would strip paint.

"Lovie, get down here and take over."

Poor Rudolph is still lying unattended a few feet away. I race to him and try to find a pulse on the side of his neck, an impossible task through his reindeer costume. There's only one thing to do: jerk off his head.

Seeing Rudolph beheaded, little kids start screaming and overwrought mothers start trying to drag them away from Santa's Court. Harried security guards hustle to remove the mothers and children from the center mall, but the manager is nowhere to be seen.

With two fingers against Rudolph's neck, I'm praying for signs of life when Mama barrels into Santa's Court. She takes one look and yells, "Ruldolph is dead!"

The already distraught kids start crying while now-crazed

mothers send looks our way that could kill. They act as if Lovie and I have personally knocked off the red-nosed reindeer.

I try CPR on him, but I think Mama's right. Poor old Steve Boone, a.k.a. Rudolph, has caught the first Christmas sleigh to Glory Land. There's nothing more I can do.

Terrified now, I race over to kneel beside Lovie. I don't care if my short skirt causes everybody in the mall to see Christmas. For those of you who don't know, that was Grandmother Valentine's name for private parts that shouldn't be seen in public.

Mama is cradling Uncle Charlie's head in her lap, patting his face. "Charlie? Charlie?" It's the most forlorn voice I've ever heard.

I haven't seen Mama lose her pizzazz since Daddy died. A parallel I don't even want to think about.

"Lovie, do you want me to take over?"

"I think he's coming around."

Uncle Charlie draws a hitching breath, and Mama starts crying.

"Thank God, Charlie. We thought you were gone."

"What happened?" he asks.

Lovie's too shaken to speak, and so am I. But I'm not so addled I don't remember the sequence of events. Elvis' frantic barking. A warning. Dogs smell disaster a mile away.

Ruldolph taking hold of Uncle Charlie's glove. His *wet* glove.

Electric power lighting up Santa's throne. Ruldolph flying and Santa jiving.

Suddenly I'm inspecting Uncle Charlie's gloves. The right one where he grabbed Rudolph's hand is seared. It looks like power passed through him and grounded in the poor unfortunate reindeer.

"Lovie." I point to the blackened glove. "Look."

She bends closer and takes a sniff. "Steve Boone got fried like a sausage."

Bound for her to equate dying with food. Lovie equates everything with food. Fun. Music. Sex. You name it.

In the distance I hear sirens. Present circumstances considered, it's the sweetest sound I've ever heard.

By mid-afternoon Uncle Charlie's lying in a hospital bed, his skin white as a bar of Ivory soap, his eyes shut, and his face showing lines I didn't even know he had. Mama, Lovie, and I are hovering around him like he might grow wings at any minute and be raptured right on up to Glory Land. If you're Southern Baptist, which we are, the idea of being raptured is supposed to send you down the hall rejoicing.

"If I could get my hands on whoever did this," Lovie says, "I'd beat the tar out of him with a baseball bat."

So much for rejoicing. And my cousin didn't say *tar*, either. She said a word I wouldn't want my future children to hear. If I had any prospects of them. Which I don't.

"I'd tie him up behind my tractor and drag him through a briar patch."

This from Mama, who looks so fierce I don't doubt her for a minute. And for your information, she can still drive the John Deere tractor on her farm.

"I'd like to take my steel-toed boot and kick somebody to Kingdom Come over this," Lovie adds.

With the mood she's been in since her kidnapping in the jungle and her disappointment that Rocky wasn't the one to rescue her, just about anybody would do.

"I'm right there with you, Lovie. I'd give him a whack with the stiletto heel of my Jimmy Choos."

That's tough language coming from me. I'm so nonviolent I

catch spiders in the house with tissue paper and release them in the back yard. And I don't even like spiders. I can't abide the thought of little hairy arachnid legs crawling all over me.

If anything could rouse Uncle Charlie, it would be our wild-eyed plans for revenge. For once, though, he doesn't tell us, "Now, now, dear hearts" or sit up to quote Shakespeare. Maybe he's in too much pain, but we'll never know. With his burned hand swathed in bandages and whatever magic potion the nurses rigged dripping into his veins, he's probably not himself. And even if he was, he wouldn't worry us by complaining.

A hatchet-faced nurse comes in and tries to shoo us all into the hall, but not before she gives my jingle bell elf costume the once-over. I can't tell if she's trying to decide to have somebody haul me off to jail for indecent exposure or to the loony bin.

"I'm an elf."

"Yeah, well, I'm Frosty the Snowman. Jingle yourself out of here."

It could have been worse. I could have told her Elvis was waiting for me in the parking lot.

I jerk Lovie out into the hall before she can say a word she didn't learn in church. We lean our weary selves against the wall. Thank goodness, the nurse pays us no more attention. She has her hands full with Mama, who is refusing to leave Uncle Charlie.

"Nurse Ratched can argue till Kingdom Come and Aunt Ruby Nell won't budge."

"I'm glad I'm not as stubborn as Mama."

"Who says?"

I don't want to think of all the reasons Lovie could be right. Instead, I dig in my purse for a pack of peanuts, rip into the bag, and share it with Lovie. We've had no lunch, and this is a poor substitute, but it will have to do. Nobody is willing to leave Uncle Charlie to go in search of a vending machine, let alone the hospital cafeteria.

When the nurse leaves, we barrel back inside. Mama looks mad enough to spit nails.

"What made that witch think I'd leave Charlie? Somebody murdered Ruldoph the Red-Nosed Reindeer. Plain and simple."

"The victim's not a reindeer, Mama. And you don't know it was murder. The cops are treating it like an accident."

We had talked to them briefly at the mall, then later in the hospital waiting room while doctors were running tests on Uncle Charlie. Mama knows this as well as I do.

"Flitter, I know murder when I see it. I'm an expert."

For your information, she's certainly no expert. She just happens to have been at the wrong place at the wrong time on more occasions than I care to recall. But when she makes up her mind, it takes an act of God to get her to budge. Or Uncle Charlie.

"Whether it's murder or an accident, I can guarantee you the wretch will pay for it." Only Lovie didn't say *wretch*. She said a word that would grow hair on Santa's beard.

"This talk of murder is ridiculous." I hope I'm right. "Who would want to kill Steve Boone? Everybody liked him."

I picture the mild-mannered owner of Tupelo Hardware greeting customers with a smile and a handshake, never getting flustered, even if you ask for a thingamajig he has to climb that big, tall library ladder to find. Poor Steve.

"Maybe they were after Charlie." Mama moves closer to the bed and grabs his good hand.

"Nobody's after me. It was an accident." Uncle Charlie sounds so much like himself I nearly wet my pants in relief. "Ruby Nell, you can quit crying now."

"Do you think I'd cry over you, you old fart? I'm allergic to this new mascara. That's all."

For all Mama's bravado, she bunches with us around Uncle Charlie like baby chicks trying to hide under the wings of a mother hen. When I think how close we came to losing him, I want to curl up in a corner and cry.

All Lovie can say is "Daddy," over and over. I finally pull myself together long enough to ask, "How do you feel?"

"I've been better, but don't anybody start getting ideas about replacing me as the family boss."

"Dream on, Charlie." Mama's trying to sound tough, but she's just as scared for him as the rest of us. "Nobody's the boss of me."

He grins, a very good sign. "Callie, you and Lovie have to find somebody to replace me. We can't disappoint the children."

"You just concentrate on getting well, Uncle Charlie. We'll handle everything."

"You bet your sweet patootie we will." This time Lovie really did say *sweet patootie*. When she thinks the occasion calls for it, she moderates her language around Uncle Charlie.

"Callie, just find a new Santa, and Lovie, you quit worrying. Now, I want everybody to go back to the mall and help salvage the charity event."

I can tell Uncle Charlie wants to say more, but he's worn out. There's no telling what all the electricity passing through him fried and messed up and rewired. I can't bear to think of the Valentines without a hundred-per-cent-functional Uncle Charlie. If Elvis were here, he'd be a calming influence, but he couldn't come in because of hospital rules.

"Flitter, Charlie, if you think I'm leaving this hospital room you're full of malarkey." Mama shoos us out of her way then drags the chair closer to the bed. "I'm staying right here to make sure nobody kills you. And that includes Nurse Ratched."

He doesn't argue, which just proves his weakened condition. I'm glad she's staying, though. As much as I protested that this was only an accident, I feel cold all over. Not a good sign. The last time this happened, Lovie was in the jungle kidnapped and a killer was planning to deprive me of my last breath.

When Lovie and I get back to the parking lot, Elvis is waiting in my pickup truck, a Dodge Ram with a big bad hemi engine, my alter ego. Lovie and Mama rode in the ambulance with Uncle Charlie, and my cousin's van is back at the mall. Fortunately, Mama carpooled this morning with Fayrene, so I don't have to worry about getting her car back to the farm.

Lovie scrunches herself into the passenger side of the truck, hefts Elvis onto her lap (much to his delight), and proceeds to give orders.

"Drive by my house."

"Uncle Charlie said go to the mall."

"I'm spending the night with you, and I don't want to be in my house trying to get my stuff in a suitcase in the dark."

I don't ask if she thinks a killer's on the loose. I don't want to know.

"That's great, Lovie. You don't need to be by yourself. Besides, I'm having dinner with Champ tonight, and you can play nursemaid to Jack."

"Should I throw in my French maid's uniform?"

Considering it has no top and very little bottom, my answer is an emphatic *no*.

My cousin's house on Robins Street is a pink, doll-like cottage with stained-glass windows. It's the last kind of house you'd expect for Lovie. With her big personality and ostentatious red hair, you'd expect her to live in a place that matches. But she loves this confection of a house, and I do, too. It's in a charming little gentrified neighborhood surrounding Milam, the school where Elvis set teenage hearts aflutter. The King, not my dog.

And speaking of dogs, I tell mine, "You have to stay in the truck, Elvis." Lovie's postage-stamp yard is filled with ancient magnolia trees teeming with busy-tailed squirrels. We have too much to do for my basset to sidetrack us chasing his favorite target.

I follow Lovie into her house and down the hall to help her pack. Her bedroom is royal purple because she's the Queen of Everything, according to her. Of course, Mama claims the same title, so it's a toss-up who is currently wearing the crown.

Lovie, it looks like, because I spot one hanging lopsided from her bedpost. While I'm still catching my breath over the amount of bling in her room—sequined picture frames and mirrors, rhinestone jewelry overflowing the top of her dressing table, plus the honest-to-gosh tiara—she grabs a big pink suitcase from the top shelf of her closet and starts tossing in clothes.

"Maybe we could ask Bobby to fill in for Daddy."

Lovie's not thinking straight. Who can blame her? I'm not thinking much better myself.

"Somebody has to man the Eternal Rest booth." I pull open a bulging drawer and put an assortment of socks into her bag. "Besides, Bobby will have to be at the funeral home when they bring Steve Boone's body in."

"I guess the reindeer wins the free jazz funeral."

I throw a pair of purple fuzzy sleep socks at her. Still, laughter through tears is the Southern way, and I'm glad to see she's coming back to her old perky self.

"Uncle Charlie's going to be all right, Lovie."

"I know. Daddy's indestructible."

We hope. The doctor still hasn't told us the extent of his internal injuries.

"Listen, Lovie. I'm certain Steve's death was an accident, but I don't want to ask anybody to be the new Santa till we find the manager and make sure he unplugs the power to the throne."

"We'll find him if I have to hunt him down and hog-tie him."

Lovie heads to her state-of-the-art kitchen. She never goes anywhere, even my house which is only fifteen minutes away, without packing a goodie bag. With enough snacks to sustain small countries through a three-week siege, she locks up, then tosses her suitcase into my pickup.

Meanwhile, Elvis is giving me the cold shoulder and I'm trying to get back in his good graces. He turns his plump backside to me.

"Listen, this is not personal, Elvis. I'm in a hurry, that's all."

"For Pete's sake." Lovie pulls a doughnut from her goodie bag and has him eating out of her hand. Literally. "You just have to know how to treat a man."

"Speaking of which . . . have you talked to Rocky yet?" Her silence says it all. "You need to return his calls. He's crazy about you."

"Too late. Somebody else is on a quest for the Holy Grail."

"Good grief, Lovie."

I'm not even going to ask. Her Holy Grail is her you know what, and if somebody is trying to claim it, he's just one in a long line of bad men who've been on the quest before him.

With Uncle Charlie in the hospital, Jack in my bed, Mama crying *murder*, Elvis overloading on sugar, and Lovie mixing up sex with religion, I'm lucky I have enough sense to drive. I barrel down Gloster Street toward Barnes Crossing Mall determined that one thing will go right today. I'm going to find the manager if I have to crawl on all fours through the mall and sniff the floor like Elvis.

Elvis' Opinion #3 on Foolish Rules, Sugared Doughnuts, and Old Sparky

If it weren't for the mellowing effect of Lovie's sugared doughnuts I'd be back down at the hospital putting a few karate moves and some serious hurt on a certain eagle-eyed guard.

Lovie was in such a hurry to get inside to see Charlie, she didn't shut her door hard enough to engage the latch. All I had to do was nose it open.

I'd have been home free if the uptight guard hadn't caught me tying to sneak inside and break the hospital's foolish "no pets allowed" rules. Don't they know rules don't apply to the King?

That silly, misguided guard read me the riot act. I shot right back at him with a howling rendition of "Baby I Don't Care." He hustled me out of there, anyhow. A lesser dog would have taken a chunk out of his leg, but being the gentlemanly hound I am, I restrained my baser urges. I didn't want my human mom to get tossed out alongside me. Listen, she's got enough trouble on her hands keeping everybody in line now that the Valentine godfather is down.

Now I nose over and offer Callie half of my doughnut, but she says, "Not now, Elvis." If I were that wimpy Hoyt, I'd think I was in the doghouse. But, listen, this is yours truly. Without me, Callie would be a bundle of nerves and uncertainties. Fortunately, she knows it. When I sit in her lap at night and she rocks me in that big old rocking chair she's hoping to use with future babies, I call tell she understands that my mission in life is to help her find her true self, and as a result, her true happiness.

Another mission is to help her solve her problems. Currently, that's replacing Charlie as Santa Claus. While we whiz past blazing Christmas stars on the light poles along Gloster Street at a speed that's going to get my human mom a speeding ticket unless I can sweet-talk our way out of it, I try to figure out how I'm going to approach her to suggest I take his place on the throne. I'm a natural. The kids adore me, and I already have the Santa suit.

This is going to be harder than you'd think. She and Lovie are batting names back and forth, while I bide my time.

"I'd ask Champ, but he did some major surgery on a chow and two Siamese cats yesterday. He'll have his hands full at the clinic this weekend."

"Jack would be fabulous."

"You always think Jack is fabulous, Lovie. You're as bad as Mama."

"Well, he is."

"I could say the same for Rocky."

"I don't want to talk about it."

"Then leave Jack out of this conversation."

The very mention of my human daddy's name makes my human mom go all melty-voiced and sad-eyed. I put my handsome head in her lap and my sugar-coated muzzle against her belly. Absently, she rubs my head with one hand. Always a good sign.

"Besides, what kind of Santa has to hobble on a crutch?"

When my human mom says that, I know the direction of her mind. And her heart.

"I didn't say anything, Cal."

"Good. Don't."

Lovie eats a doughnut and offers me another one, but a dog with a hidden agenda knows when to decline forbidden sugar.

"I'd suggest Jarvetis," she says, "but take him away from his redbone hound dog Trey and Gas, Grits, and Guts, and I don't think he could get up enough nerve to say *ho, ho, ho.*"

"You're forgetting his mambo with Fayrene in Memphis."

"That was an aberration, Callie. He's usually so quiet you barely notice him."

"Okay. So you're right this time. But not about Jack."

Lovie just grins. She knows the lay of the land between those two. And she's pulling for Jack as hard as I am. I'm glad she's going with us to Mooreville.

We arrive at the mall in the nick of time. There's a line of hungry folks at Lovie's booth and they're getting surly. Meantime, over in Santa's Court, there's a sign that says, TEMPORARILY CLOSED. SANTA'S FEEDING HIS REINDEER.

Callie hurries over to relieve the security guards, who have been pressed into service to hand out candy canes. I don't know who made that mistake. The guards' scowls are enough to give little kids nightmares about lumps of coal in their Christmas stockings. Fortunately, Callie and yours truly hurry to the rescue.

While she soothes the little kids with sweet talk and a little something for a sweet tooth, I mosey my splendid Santa self over and climb onto the throne. This takes Herculean effort and four attempts. But when Callie sees me sitting there in my natural royal glory, she says, "Get down from there, Elvis."

Well, so be it. What does a King need with another throne? Besides, I have a nose for trouble, and there's plenty afoot at the mall. Let somebody else risk sitting in a throne that turned into Old Sparky (the state penitentiary's electric chair). I have other plans for my many talents.

Finding the mall manager, for one. That'll be a snap for a King in a basset hound suit. Listen, my nose is more than a noble proboscis on a handsome face.

And who needs surveillance equipment when they have a set of mismatched radar ears. Somewhere in this crowd is somebody who knows what really happened in Santa's Court today. And yours truly—dog detective extraordinaire—intends to find out.

I get my chance at sleuthing when Jarvetis Johnson comes over to Santa's Court with his grandson, a little person named David. Otherwise known as my second-best source of forbidden treats (Lovie being the first). Now that Darlene is doing nails, her son is a fixture at Hair.Net. I'm happy to report he doesn't mind sharing his ice cream cone with a famous dog.

While Callie's occupied with her favorite cherub, I slip off down the mall, ears and nose at the ready. The only thing of interest I find is a bite-size chunk of hamburger bun that still smells of meat, plus Bobby Huckabee in the food court drinking a latte. He's all eyes for his companion, none other than Darlene.

When I say all eyes, I'm talking about his green eye as well as his psychic blue eye. It figures. She consults the stars and he consults the dead.

Darlene whistles at me and I trot right over, mainly because she's taken the top off her drink and is offering me a lick of cream off her fingers.

"This is our little secret," she says. "Okay, Elvis?"

Wild horses couldn't drag her tête à tête with Bobby out of me. Fayrene thinks Darlene's had too many husbands, but personally, I say, go for it, girl. Nothing's more fun than a "Whole Lotta Shakin' Goin' On."

Anyhow, Darlene doesn't have to worry about me. I'm a loyal-to-the-bone dog who knows how to keep a secret.

Unless somebody bribes me with a ham bone seasoned with just the right amount of Mississippi mud. Now that's my kind of eating.

"Elvis!"

What's this I hear? My human mom calling my name.

Busted.

I hurry my ample self out of the food court. But I don't show my face right away. First, I hide behind a garbage can till I can get my mojo working and do a little judicious eaves-dropping.

"Poor Cleveland," Callie is saying to Lovie. "He's beside himself that he threw the switch to the throne."

"I hope he believed us when we said we don't blame him for what happened to Daddy and poor old Rudolph."

"The main thing is that he's promised there will be no power to the throne tomorrow."

Sounds like the coast is clear. Putting on my cutest basset grin (which, I'll have to say, is a poor doggone substitute for the smile that in my other life sent fans into a fainting frenzy), I sashay out from behind the garbage can, then act all sur-prised and hound-dog-eyed to see Callie and Lovie packed up and ready to go home.

"Elvis, is that cream on your muzzle?"

I lick Callie's ankle then do a little swivel-hipped turn and howl a few bars of "If Every Day Was Like Christmas." You might think distracting her is a naughty thing to do, but if you could hear her laugh, you'd change your tune. It's a cross be-tween sleigh bells and jingle bells.

She picks me up and totes me out to her Dodge Ram like I'm the most important dog in the world. Which I am.

"Let's get you home, boy, before everybody in the mall mobs you for your paw print."

She waves at Lovie, who is heading to her van, then calls out, "See you in Mooreville."

I wonder if Jack is waiting with a little snack of Pup-Peroni.

Chapter 4

Home Cooking, Unwanted Safety Tips, and Murder

Thank goodness, I get to dress for this date in peace. Elvis is outside playing with Hoyt and the Seven Dwarfs while Lovie is in the kitchen with Jack playing poker. It feels so good to have my cousin and my almost-ex both in the house that for a moment I forget who I'm dressing for.

I put on the final touches, a spritz of perfume, just the perfect shade of lip gloss, and a cute pair of Sesto Meucci boots I got on sale after Thanksgiving, then head down the stairs to tell them goodbye.

Jack does a double take. "You're not wearing that top, are you?"

"Why? What's wrong with it?"

"The way to the vet's heart is not a tight red sweater. It's some good chicken and dumplings."

This from the man who only yesterday advised me to *lure* Champ with *more cleavage*.

"You're just angling for a home-cooked meal."

"No." He tips his chair back, looking every bit as cocky as he is handsome. "I'm just trying to get you out of that sweater."

I might have to kill him. And Lovie's being no help at all. She's sitting there laughing.

"Don't encourage him, Lovie."

Fortunately, her cell phone rings. She snatches it up like her National Treasure is on fire and whoever is on the other end of the line is fixing to fan the flames.

"Wayne." She's all but cooing. She's only mentioned Wayne Hunter to me once, and in a way that always spells trouble. You couldn't get me out of this kitchen if man-eating African lions were roaring my way.

"That sounds wonderful," she says into her phone. She makes four syllables of *wonderful*. This is bad.

Even worse, she races up the stairs, moving faster than I've seen her move since we crash-landed the hot-air balloon and got chased by a bunch of mad pigs.

"What next?" I ask, and Jack says, "Let her have her fun, Cal. Maybe it'll take her mind off Charlie."

Mama told him about the accident, of course. Or maybe it was Uncle Charlie. He and Jack are closer than father and son. And I think it's more than bonding because of a mutual background with the Company.

I sit down opposite Jack, then put my hands in my lap so I won't be tempted to smooth back the lock of dark hair that won't stay out of his eyes.

"Do you think what happened at the mall was an accident, Jack?"

"Maybe. I just want you to be careful."

"Careful is my middle name."

"I thought it was trouble."

His crooked grin gets me every time. Fortunately, Lovie is back. Unfortunately, she is carrying her French maid's uniform.

"Holy cow, Lovie. What are you doing with that thing?"

"My fiancé likes it."

"Since when has Wayne been your fiancé?"

"Since I decided to push him in that direction."

"Lovie, maybe you ought to slow down. You've been out with him, what? Five times? When you're on the rebound, it's no time to be getting serious with somebody else."

"Speaking of rebound . . ." Lovie raises one eyebrow, and I blush to the roots of my glossy, natural brown hair. I'm not about to admit that I'm on the rebound or that my situation with Jack and Champ is anything like Lovie's with Rocky and Wayne. Because it's not. She goes through bad boys like bags of popcorn, and I've only ever in my life been in love with one man. And he happens to be sitting across the table from me keeping his mouth shut for once. Thank goodness.

When the doorbell rings, I almost faint with relief. It's Champ, looking really, really appealing in a cashmere coat that sets off his shoulders to a tee. My mouth ought to be watering.

When Jack comes up behind me and says, "Come on in," I realize I'm standing there like a doorstop thinking about who my mouth waters over and why.

Champ says, "Good evening" all around, then, "All set, Callie?"

I reach for my wrap, but Jack already has it. He takes what feels like two weeks draping it around me. Then with his hands on my shoulders and his body heat burning through the back of my cape, he proceeds to treat Champ to a long-winded lecture.

"Be careful tonight. There'll be lots of Christmas shoppers out, and some of them will be driving like maniacs."

"I know. I've had my license a while."

Lovie and I giggle at Champ's dry wit, but Jack remains poker-faced.

"Stay away from the mall. After what happened today, I don't think Callie should be near there."

"On that, we agree," Champ says.

"If you have to get coffee, go to Starbucks on West Main. And be sure Callie has decaffeinated. Caffeine keeps her awake at night."

"Do you have an instruction manual, Jack? Maybe I ought to read it before we go." Champ is grinning and taking all this bad advice in stride, which just shows the kind of good man he is.

"I'll print one up."

I wouldn't put it past Jack. I wiggle from his grasp and steer Champ out the door before my almost-ex thinks up any more absurd reasons why I shouldn't be going out.

"Have fun!" Jack is standing in the doorway looking like he means every word. Which I know good and well he does not. He ought to be an actor.

So should I. Here I am in the car with a really good-looking, really great guy who is probably going to propose, and all I can do is wish I were at the hospital checking on Uncle Charlie or at my house making sure Jack takes care of his leg.

"You look gorgeous in that red sweater."

So much for Jack's advice. "Thank you."

"Is there anything in particular you'd like to do tonight?"

"Actually I'd like to go to the library." Nobody is going to get down on their knees at the library. Unless it's to beg for a current bestseller they've been waiting on for three months. "I need to check on some things without having a bossy audience."

"The same audience who's going to write an instruction manual called *Taking Care of Callie*?"

"One and the same."

"I always did like libraries." Champ heads straight toward the corner of Madison and Jefferson Streets. Any woman in her right mind would fall madly in love with this man.

The Lee County Library on the corner of Jefferson and

ELVIS AND THE BLUE CHRISTMAS CORPSE

Madison is a square brick structure with tall, narrow windows, typical of the architecture of the seventies. A mural of all things Mississippi—mockingbird, magnolia and Tupelo gum trees, Civil War battle scenes, Native American scenes—occupies the east wall. A twelve-foot Christmas tree with glowing lights sits in front of the mural. I mist up when I see it.

"Callie, what's wrong?"

"I am just thinking about poor dead Ruldoph and wondering if somebody really was after Uncle Charlie."

"I figured that's why you wanted to come here. How can I help you?"

"I want to find out the names of everybody who has played Santa at Barnes Crossing Mall."

"Done."

"Thank you."

We walk toward a bank of computers, and Champ finds two unoccupied, side by side. Grateful, I slide into my seat. "This is not much of a date for you. I'm sorry."

"Callie, being anywhere with you is fun."

Blinking back tears that have been threatening since Uncle Charlie got shocked off Santa's throne, I try not to feel guilty. Fortunately, I get caught up in the search. Old newspaper articles from the *Northeast Mississippi Daily Journal* show the opening of Barnes Crossing Mall and their first Christmas court. Front and center is Santa.

"Champ, are you finding what I'm finding."

"Only one Santa?"

"Yes. If there is a killer loose, was he after the original Santa or Uncle Charlie?"

After we leave the library, we head to Starbucks—on West Main, as Jack instructed, I notice. Feeling guilty that I've deprived Champ of his evening, not to mention his chance for a romantic Christmas proposal, I don't talk about murder anymore. Still, as soon as we finish our coffee, we head home.

Thank goodness, I don't have an audience when I get there. Still, I don't linger on the front porch, and I don't invite Champ inside for a cup of coffee. I need a serious conference with Lovie. In spite of my assurances to everybody concerned that Steve Boone's death was an accident, my instincts are screaming otherwise.

The minute I walk inside, I know I am not alone. It takes a while for my eyes to adjust. Jack is sitting on the sofa in the dark, barely visible by the light from the electric candles in the front windows.

"Did you have a good time, Cal?"

What's this I hear? Uncertainty? That is so un-Jack-like I forget to turn on the overhead light.

"Champ's a really great guy."

"I can't argue with that."

Speechless, I unbutton my cape. Jack leaps off the sofa and helps me, taking his own sweet time.

"I made hot chocolate from scratch. Want some?"

Hot chocolate is my favorite winter drink, and he knows it. I follow him into the kitchen, but when I head to the cabinet for cups, he pulls out a chair at the table.

"Sit down. You've had a hard day." I sink into the chair, happy to let a man on a crutch wait on me. Lulled by his chivalrous act, I fantasize how things might have been—me wrapping presents, Jack putting the star on the tree, and little baby Jones cooing in a cradle nearby.

He sets a cup in front of me and I take a sip. If chocolate is nectar for the gods, I guess I'm a goddess. I think it was invented for me. Nothing makes me feel better than the warm, sweet creamy taste of 60 percent cocoa with just a touch of cinnamon and red pepper. Well, *almost nothing,* but I'm not getting into that.

"Jack, this is very pleasant."

"Yes, it is." He studies me over the rim of his cup. "What did you and Mr. Wonderful do this evening?"

Strike *pleasant.* "Nothing that would interest you."

"It couldn't have been much. You're home early."

"For your information, some people respect that I'll be up at the crack of nine so I can play elf all day."

I march off in such a miff I leave half a cup of good hot chocolate on the table. But I'm not about to go back in the kitchen. Too many memories of cozy late nights with my almost-ex and too much chance he'll make another smart remark that feels like the truth.

I dress in pajamas, then hole up in my bedroom with the door shut to wait for Lovie. What's taking her so long? I can hear Jack whistling as he hobbles up and down the stairs. My conscience twinges that I'm not helping him with his evening meds and refilling the pitcher of ice water he keeps beside his bed.

What can I say? I'm not perfect. Except for my hair and my style. And maybe the way I take care of everybody.

Elvis hops onto the bed with me. Dogs can sense when you need comfort. I stroke his warm fur.

"Were you a good doggie while I was gone?" He licks my hand. "Were you nice to Hoyt and the cats?"

"Say *yes,* Elvis," Lovie says as she bursts through the door with the fanfare of a three-ring circus. She throws herself onto the bed and kicks off her boots.

"Wayne volunteered to be Santa at the mall. He's fabulous."

The way she says *fabulous,* all long and drawn out like a

sigh, I don't think she's taking about his prowess as Santa Claus.

"Call him and tell him no thanks."

"The mall manager promised there will be no power to the throne tomorrow. Besides, I already told Wayne yes."

She probably told him *yes* more times than I want to know. "I'm in no mood to hear about your love life."

"For Pete's sake, Cal, who pulled your chain? As if I don't already know."

"It's not what you're thinking, Lovie. I spent the evening at the library with Champ."

"Kinky."

"For your information, we didn't kiss behind the stacks."

"Why not?"

"I had more important things on my mind. Like using their computer so Jack wouldn't be snooping around seeing what I'm doing."

"Don't tell me. I don't want to know." Lovie hops off the bed and jiggles out of her clothes and into a nightshirt that asks *Who died and made you queen?*

She might be acting like somebody who doesn't want to hear the latest bulletin, but she's not fooling me, even when she heads into the bathroom to brush her teeth.

I trail right along behind her and prop myself in the door frame. "Jack's cautions tonight were over the top, even for him. I got to thinking maybe he suspects something about the mall accident he's not telling."

"Why spoil the mood with murder?"

"Whose mood?"

"Mine." Lovie stows her toothbrush, then plops onto the bed, pulls up the covers, and turns her back to me.

I count silently to ten. By the time I've reached five she pops upright, sits cross-legged, and says, "All right. Tell all."

"I found a list of everybody who has ever played Santa Claus at Barnes Crossing Mall."

"You're assuming today's events were attempted murder and the alleged killer was after Santa and not Rudolph."

"The electricity came from the throne, and you can't see Santa's Court from the power switch. The killer couldn't have known Rudolph would be clutching Santa's hand, grounding the killing jolt."

"Have you caught Aunt Ruby Nell's murder-on-the-brain syndrome? Nobody is going around killing Santas at Christmas."

"I'm serious, Lovie. Wayne shouldn't come tomorrow."

"Are you planning to be in Santa's Court?" She's got me there. "I thought so. Since Wayne's going to be in the family, he might as well start now."

"I notice you're not flashing a ring."

"Yeah, but I flashed everything else."

"I'm not even going to respond to that."

"Okay." Lovie lies down and turns her back to me. " 'Night, Cal."

"Furthermore, I'm going to keep my list of Santas to myself."

"I'll live through it."

"Let's hope so."

I make my voice as dark as possible. I make it so gloomy I sound like Bobby. I might as well go ahead and tell Lovie that Santa is in *danger from a dark-eyed stranger*, Bobby's favorite prediction.

Which has come true more times than I care to think about.

Elvis' Opinion #4 on Wish Lists, Wayne's Act, and Christmas Cookies

Listen, if you think I spent the evening playing with the silly stray cats Callie rescued and calls the Seven Dwarfs, you've put too much whiskey in your eggnog. The only one I can halfway stand is Happy, and that's because she has sense enough to let a basset hound snooze in the sun in peace. The rest of the stupid cats think bouncing on the basset is a game. Let me tell you, I know how to send them running. And I'm not talking about a polite warning growl. I'm talking big bad dog here. Snarls and an impressive show of teeth followed by a howling rendition that tells cats "There's No Tomorrow."

But only when Callie and Jack are not looking. Though he tries to hide it, he's as tenderhearted as she is. I don't want my human parents to think their favorite dog has a dark side.

Anyhow, I managed to get by with a show of temper without getting busted, and by the time Callie returned from her so-called date, I had my belly full of dog chow, plus a side helping of scraps from Jack's hamburger, and was snoozing innocently on my guitar-shaped silk pillow.

Before you get to thinking the dog's life is cushy, just remember that I once played a gold-plated piano (a gift from Priscilla), could buy all the steak I wanted, and had the world at my feet. Now I'm lucky if I can get the Valentines to fetch and carry for me. Still, "Que Sera Sera." I could have come back as a potbellied pig.

The next morning I wake up to the smells of coffee and bacon and eggs, plus buttermilk biscuits. Today is going to be a good day.

But what's this I hear? Jack and Callie arguing in the kitchen.

"I'd rather leave Elvis here, Jack. Why don't you want to keep him?"

"You're twisting my words, Cal. I love Elvis."

"Then let him stay home today."

"Since you insist on going to mall and I can't be there to protect you, Elvis is going with you."

"For your information, I don't need protecting."

She does, though, and today that's up to me. Lovie left early so she could go to the hospital to see Charlie, then hurry to the mall and give her fiancé last-minute instructions on being Santa Claus. Fiancé, my left hind paw. Lovie will no more marry her latest hot fling than I would walk "Five Hundred Miles" to hear some of these upstarts who call themselves entertainers. With their grungy hair and torn blue jeans, they look like railroad tramps. Listen, I could tell them a thing or two about the importance of sequined jumpsuits with capes that make you look like Captain Marvel come to save your soul. Image. That's the thing. Of course, you have to have the pipes, and I'm glad to report I still do.

"Maybe you can handle everything," Jack says. "But you're not going to win this argument. You're taking Elvis."

A little intervention is in order here. Grabbing my four-legged Santa suit in my mouth, I hustle down the stairs, then sashay my ample butt into the kitchen, looking cute. If I didn't have a mouthful of red cloth, I'd treat my human parents to a snazzy rendition of "Here Comes Santa Claus."

At the sight of me, my human mom melts, and before you can say "Pass the buttered biscuits," I'm on the way to the mall as Santa Paws.

Though I'd love to give the kids a thrill with another Christmas concert, today my job is bodyguard. Starting with Lovie's so-called fiancé.

This Wayne character has more charisma than I'd counted on. He calls my human mom "Miss Callie," which fluffs up her feathers and improves her opinion of him. "Don't Ask Me Why." He's already in his Santa suit when we get to the dressing room, and believe me, I priss my scintillating self in there with my human mom. I don't care if Lovie's current Mr. Wonderful did say he'd wait for Callie outside the door.

While Callie's getting into her elf costume, I put my famous nose to the ground. There are more fresh scents in here than those of Charlie, Callie, and Wayne. Trust me. The strange odors I'm picking up are more naughty than nice, and I don't think those people were in here "For the Good Times."

I sashay my little Santa self behind the curtain to warn Callie. "I Got a Feelin' in My Body" that doesn't have a doggone thing to do with Christmas cheer.

"Not now, boy." She leans down to scratch behind my ears and adjust my little Santa cap. "We'll get a treat after the first break."

Usually my human mom is more in tune with my moods. I chalk it up to stress.

When we exit the dressing room, the mall manager is standing outside with Wayne. He sees my human mom and says, "Don't worry about a thing. The power to the throne is off. There will be no incidents today."

I wouldn't call murder an incident. But let me tell you, it's not happening on my watch today. I strain as far out as I can get on the leash and run ahead, sniffing for trouble.

Well, bless'a my soul. What's this I smell? Cookies.

A sweet-looking gray-haired lady is holding a basket full of cookies sprinkled with colored sugar and shaped to look like Santa, Frosty the Snowman, and Ruldoph the Red-Nosed Reindeer. She bends over and says, "My, my. Aren't you the cutest thing!"

I lick her legs. If I had one my famous silk scarves, I'd drape it around her wrinkled little neck. She smells like baby powder and old age. A comforting combination.

"This is Elvis." I hear pride when Callie introduces me. Always a good sign.

"Well, I'm Opal Stokes. Can I give this cutie pie a cookie?"

My human mom is quick to say yes. Thank goodness, Christmas cheer rules the day.

Miss Opal passes out cookies to the children while Wayne does his act as Santa. And a fine act it is. Take it from one who knows. Like Charlie, you can't tell this man from the real North Pole version. Maybe I'll have to rethink my opinion about his future as part of the Valentine family.

Suddenly I feel the call of nature. Doing my little whirling dervish dance that tells Callie "Take me outside now," I get her attention. As we race toward the exit, I see at least fifteen mothers racing toward the toilets with little kids in tow. Looks like their urgency for the bathroom has suddenly become bigger than their urgency to tell Santa their wish list. Their squinched-up faces tell me they're in the same situation I am. Emergency.

But as Charlie, who is fond of quoting Shakespeare, would say, "All's well that ends well."

Lovie's booth is packed all day, Darlene has painted more jingle bell nail art than my friend Trey (Jarvetis' best redbone hound dog) has fleas, Bobby finally has two people show up to talk about the free jazz funeral, and nobody in Santa's Court gets shot at, knifed, or fried on Santa's throne.

After we leave the mall, we head to the hospital to see Charlie, where I have to cool my paws in the truck again. It's worth the disgrace of being treated like an ordinary dog to see Callie's smile when she gets back in the truck. Ruby Nell is with her.

It turns out Charlie is feeling much better. We take Ruby Nell back to the farm, a beautiful spread south of Mooreville where I love to chase rabbits while my ears blow in the wind.

"Mama, you should stay home and rest tonight."

"All I need is a change of clothes and my car. I'm not fixing to loll around on my royal you know what and leave Charlie in the hands of Nurse Ratched."

"But Uncle Charlie said for you to stay on the farm."

Callie might as well save her breath. Ruby Nell will never "Surrender." In fact, she says, "Flitter," and that's her last word on the subject.

When we finally get home, I belly flop on the cool kitchen tiles and listen to Callie and Lovie tell Jack about the day. He gets a big kick out of the tale of the great toilet rush. His booming laugh is better than a used T-bone with a little meat clinging to it. It makes me want to out-Crosby old Bing himself with a mellow turn of "White Christmas."

"All those toilet emergencies sound suspicious to me." This from Lovie, who not only laughs first at a good joke but is usually the one telling it. "I think that crazy old lady was serving tainted cookies."

"Holy cow, Lovie. Opal Stokes is one of the sweetest people I've ever met. She adored Elvis." Liking dogs is a sign of good character. My human mom knows this.

"You thought that about Beulah Jane Ball, too, and she was going around the Elvis Festival knocking off Elvises."

"Could there be a tad of professional jealousy talking?"

"Professional jealousy, my foot." Only Lovie didn't say "foot." She used a word that would curdle eggnog. If Charlie were here, he'd say, "Now, now dear hearts."

Fortunately, my human daddy is getting ready to step into the Valentine godfather's big shoes. I can smell his intent a mile away.

"Why don't you two go into the den and turn on the six o'clock news while I make a big pot of my famous hot chocolate?"

"Should I be jealous of your cooking skills, Jack?" Lovie's laughing when she says this, so I know there's "Peace in the Valley" once more. Not that there was ever any danger of a real rift between Callie and Lovie. The cousins are a team, and lord help the man who tries to come between them.

"Lovie, you make me a big pot of your chicken and dumplings and I'll share my Mayan chocolate recipe."

"Done."

Lovie and Callie link arms and head to the den, but I stay behind in the kitchen. Listen, this is the place that smells the most like Christmas—the cinnamon Jack puts in the hot chocolate, the fragrant pine and holly berries Callie arranged in earthenware jars, the bayberry candles in the center of the table. With all this cheer in the air, Jack is sure to sneak me a little treat.

Chapter 5

Bad News, Big Surprise, and Deck the Mall with Christmas Corpses

By the time the evening TV news anchor Cody Lacey comes on, Jack is in the den with a tray, holding a pot of steaming hot chocolate that smells like heaven, a rawhide bone for Elvis, and my pottery Christmas cups that feature a snow scene with cedar trees and red birds. The cups are from a set of holiday dishes Jack bought for me our first Christmas together. I thought it meant he was building a future with me. Turns out he only got them because he knows I love pretty dishes.

It also turns out I don't have time to dwell on the cups because a more pressing matter is at hand. *Pressing* being the operative word. Jack squeezes in between Lovie and me, proceeding to take up his part of the couch and mine, too. Still, he feels solid and warm and safe, and after the events at the mall, I'm sorry to report that I don't feel the least inclination to get up and move to another chair.

Besides, he made the chocolate, which is delicious, and I am not a petty, tacky person.

"This is really great, Jack," Lovie says, and he thanks her, then winks at me. But I'm not going to let one dark-eyed wink make me forget his preference for a Harley Screaming Eagle over a baby cradle.

Fortunately, I don't have long to dwell on the past because Cody is standing in center court at the mall talking about Uncle Charlie.

"Tupelo's iconic funeral director, Charles Sebastian Valentine, nearly lost his life right here in Santa's Court. He was filling in for Nathan Briggs, the mall's regular Santa, when a jolt of electricity passed through his gloved hand and into Steve Boone, who was in costume as Santa's favorite deer. Steve, a.k.a Rudolph, was declared dead on the scene."

This news sounds like something you'd hear on one of those TV sitcoms.

Jack squeezes my hand. "I think you ought to turn in your elf suit, Cal."

"Why now? What do you know that I don't?"

"Nothing."

Considering his dangerous history, I doubt that. Suspicions flaring, I turn my attention back to the TV. Onscreen, Cody is now interviewing Nathan Briggs.

"Cody," he says, "I'm feeling one hundred percent better. And I can assure you that I will be back on Santa's throne tomorrow."

"See?" I tell Jack. "There's nothing to worry about. Nathan will probably bring his own elf. My days in a jingle bell suit are over."

"A pity."

"Why? You just said you didn't want me going back."

"Yeah, but I always did love to ring your chimes."

"Just because I shared your chocolate doesn't mean I'm sharing anything else."

"I'm not going anywhere, Cal."

I hope he's talking about the restrictions of his banged-up leg, but I don't think so. The way Jack is looking at me, I think he means he's not going anywhere else. Period. Ever.

I get the shivers, but not so he will notice. I don't want that big muscled arm around my shoulders, making me believe in love and happily ever after with a dangerous man. Besides, he's made it perfectly clear he doesn't want children. My fondest dream.

My cell phone rings, and the moment between my almost-ex and me is broken.

It's Bobby Huckabee, saying he has Steve's body at the funeral home ready for my finishing touch.

"I have to go to Eternal Rest."

"The red-nosed reindeer?" Lovie says, and when I nod, she adds, "I'm going with you."

"Stay here and relax, Lovie," Jack says. "I'll go." I can't say I'll be sorry to have Jack around while I'm applying pancake to a man who may or may not have been murdered. Usually I'm very much at peace prettying up the recently deceased, but souls felled before their time don't rest easy.

Jack swings his cast into my truck with the confidence of a man used to having perfect control over his body.

"Why are you going, Jack? I do this all the time by myself. The dead don't scare me."

"Me, either, Cal. It's the living I'm worried about."

"You know something you're not telling."

"Not guilty." He puts his arm along the back of the seat and caresses my neck. "Can't a man spend a little time alone with his wife?"

"Ex."

"Not yet."

"For your information, we won't be alone."

"I don't think the Christmas corpse is going to notice what we do."

"What we'll *do*, Jack, is that I'll be applying pancake and you'll be keeping your hands to yourself. I'm almost engaged."

"Almost is a big word, Cal."

Actually, he does keep his hands to himself, but Jack is the only person in the whole universe who can do nothing but sit on the sofa under the shell-shaped sconces watching me work and still make me feel as if I've been undressed and kissed on every inch of my skin. Even when I'm working on a corpse.

By the time we get home, I'm too worn out to protest when he kisses me good night. Fortunately, he's makes the kiss brief, then goes to his own bed without trying to sweet-talk his way into mine.

I'm sorry to report it would have been ridiculously easy.

I get up early and dress in a jogging suit and running shoes so I can sneak out of the house without waking anybody. I need a morning run to clear my head. Leaving Lovie and Elvis snoring, I tiptoe past the guest room where Jack is sleeping. I hope. It would be just like him to be wide awake, listening to every move I make.

It's one of those cool, brisk December mornings when the grass is frosted and scents are intensified. Inhaling the heady fragrance of cedar and pine, I sprint through my front gate and past Mabel Moffett's and Fayrene's houses. Overnight, Santas have sprung up on their rooftops, and North Pole scenes have appeared in their front yards. Rounding the corner into the cul de sac, I spot Frosty the Snowman on top of TV weatherman Butch Jenkins' house.

The only house in the neighborhood not lit up like La-Guardia belongs to Mooreville's newest resident, Albert Gordon. Either he hasn't decorated yet or he's the kind of person who likes to celebrate holidays quietly. Since he's retired military and lives alone, to boot, I'd guess the latter.

I make a mental note to take him a tin of Lovie's chocolate cherry Christmas cookies.

By the time I return to my cottage I feel ready to face whatever the day brings. My little house welcomes me with a pinecone wreath on the door, pine garlands strung on the front porch railings, and electric candles glowing in every window. I have everything except my tree. Usually Uncle Charlie digs up a small cedar on the farm and balls the roots in burlap so he can replant it after Christmas. I don't know what I'll do this year. Like Miss Scarlett, I'll have to think about that tomorrow.

Jack is in my kitchen in his pajamas pants, sans top, propped on his crutch and making scrambled eggs Mexican style. My favorite.

"Hey, Cal. I thought you'd be hungry. I know I am."

"Eggs sound great." Ignoring how one look from him can cause goose bumps, I make myself act breezy. "I'll wake up Lovie so we can get a quick start." With the old Santa back on the job, I'm looking forward to being in the Hair.Net booth today.

"She's already gone."

"So soon?"

"Cleveland called and said Nathan Briggs had a relapse. She's gone to help her fiancé get into his Santa suit." Jack sets the plate in front of me, steam still rising from the eggs. That's not the only place it's rising. "It's just us, Cal."

I grab my fork and dig in. Between bites I say, "I'd better hurry. If Wayne is Santa, that means I'm still an elf."

Jack runs his hand over my hair, which he knows I absolutely love, then gives my neck a little squeeze before he sits at the table and starts eating the eggs. As if he has not set me on fire.

"Be careful today. Take Elvis."

I'm not going to argue with him today. I'm only too happy to get out of my own house, where temptation lies around every corner. Reminding myself that Jack and I tried to be a couple once and failed, I hurry to Barnes Crossing Mall to find Wayne already suited up and inside the dressing room putting on his boots.

"These boots are wet," he says.

"So is my costume. I guess they haven't fixed the leak yet."

With construction workers all over the mall, you'd think fixing one small leak wouldn't be a problem. I don't have time to dwell on it because I have to get dressed and hurry to Santa's Court. As my jingle bell skirt falls into place, I think about how close Jack is to ringing my chimes.

I don't have time to think about that, either. Elvis is poking his nose into every corner of the dressing room, and the hairs on the back of my neck are starting to rise. Not a good sign. If you want to know the truth, I probably have more psychic ability than Bobby, even though both my eyes are the same color.

"What's up, boy?" When Elvis looks up at me and whines, I'd swear he is humming "Fools Rush In." I squat down to give him a reassuring pat. "We'd better hurry, boy. The kids will be getting restless."

The sign on Santa's Court says it opens precisely at ten-thirty. Since the only fanfare was on opening day, and the mall manager is nowhere in sight, it's up to me to make sure we start on time.

Still, I can't forget my premonition. Glancing around, I try to see if anything is amiss. In spite of Rudolph's untimely end, there's a huge crowd of children already screaming in ear-splitting decibels. The Christmas cookie lady is back, and when she sees me, she gives a big smile and waves. I wave back, then check to see if Wayne is in his place on the throne.

He gives me a thumbs-up sign. Once again I'm startled at how realistic he looks, as if he's been the mall's regular Santa for years.

Everything looks normal. Even Elvis is behaving. Always a good sign.

"Ready?" I ask. When Wayne nods, I turn the CLOSED sign to read SANTA'S COURT IS NOW OPEN, then unsnap the velvet rope guarding the entrance. Within seconds I'm mobbed by little kids all vying to be first to spill their secret wishes to Santa.

Selecting a cute, curly-haired cherub in a ruffled, red-velvet dress, I take her by the hand and lead her through the entrance.

"What are you going to tell Santa, honey?"

"I don't want no baby bruvver for Thrithmath."

"Well, honey, just think what fun you'll have when your brother is old enough to play with you."

"No! Thend him back."

As I guide the reluctant big sister onto the red carpet, Santa's throne lights up like a Christmas tree. This can't be happening again.

I jerk the little girl into my arms and stumble backward as Santa Claus topples from his throne. He's not moving, not a twitch. I can't get over there to help him because I'm too busy having my hearing permanently damaged by a screaming toddler who hates baby brothers and now is going to hate Christmas.

But I don't have to take his pulse to know: Wayne was dead when he hit the floor.

All bedlam breaks loose. Lovie races over, screeching Wayne's name, the mother snatches her little girl from me, and Santa's Court starts filling with paramedics and police.

Holding onto Lovie, I watch as Wayne's sheet-draped body is carried out on a gurney.

"I can't believe this." Lovie looks shell-shocked.

Neither can I. First, Steve Boone and now Wayne. With one Santa Claus and the favorite reindeer both dead, nobody in his right mind will be calling the first death an unfortunate accident.

A detective who looks younger than my favorite tennis shoes—Carter, his badge says—approaches me and says, "Ma'am? I'd like to ask you some questions."

Holy cow. Since I was the one closest when Rudolph and Santa died, I'm up to my neck again in murder.

"Did you see anything suspicious?"

"No." In this crowd, what would constitute suspicious?

"Did Steve Boone or Wayne Hunter act agitated before entering the court?"

"I couldn't tell about Steve. He was late arriving. But Wayne was in a jovial mood."

"Did the alleged victims have contact with anyone before they came into Santa's Court?"

"I don't know about Steve, but Wayne and I were at the dressing room together right before we entered Santa's Court."

"Do you have a beef against either of them?"

"*Me?*" Holy cow! All I wanted was to help give the orphans a good Christmas. It looks like I've ended up on the hot seat for murder.

The only good thing I can say is this line of questioning shakes my cousin out of her love-lost stupor. She storms over in her steel-toed cowboy boots and snatches me away from Detective Carter like I'm a newborn and he's the bubonic plague.

"That's enough. Can't you see she's traumatized? There's been a death in the family."

"Excuse me, ma'am? Now, who are you?"

"Santa's fiancé." Lovie starts shivering and bawling so loud you can hear her all the way to the Alabama state line. If I didn't know her so well, I'd think she was in deep mourning. But this is not Lovie being heartbroken: this is my cousin reprising her role as the Wicked Stepmother in her fifth-grade production of "Snow White and the Seven Dwarfs."

Detective Carter looks like he'd rather be anywhere except in the faux North Pole with an unlikely elf and a grieving almost Mrs. Claus. He tells me not to leave town, then pats Lovie on the arm and wanders off like somebody lost in a snowstorm.

Meanwhile, the cops are busy putting up yellow tape, and the manager is hanging a sign that says SANTA'S COURT IS CLOSED UNTIL FURTHER NOTICE. If anything can snatch dreams of sugar plums right out of the heads of little kids, crime tape ought to do it. For once in my life, I'm glad I'm not a mother.

How do you explain to a three-year-old that you lied about the man in the red suit? That in spite of Santa dying right before their eyes, he will still clamber down their chimneys to bring gifts you'll be paying for over the next six months? Even worse, how do you tell them that somebody out there hates Santa Claus?

Lovie is quiet as she watches Santa's Court become the crime scene. I link arms with her.

"This is awful, Lovie. Somebody out there hates Christmas and that cop thinks it's me."

She says a word that would raise blood blisters. "If the killer thinks I'm going to sit back after he's snatched a perfectly good fiancé before I could get to the altar, he's got another think coming."

She roars through the mall like a summer tornado. And I'm grateful to sail along in her tailwinds. Listen, this is Lovie we're talking about. I'd much rather see my cousin in revenge mode than falling to pieces over a man she never loved in the first place.

Trust me. I know.

Chapter 6

Yellow Tape, Santa Haters, and Cancelled Christmas

As we storm through the mall, Christmas charity booths are being abandoned faster than Elvis can steal a ham bone. Bobby has already left the Eternal Rest booth and Fayrene is packing up the Gas, Grits, and Guts paraphernalia. Mama, who is still staying in the hospital with Uncle Charlie, never even opened Fa La La La Farewell today.

I feel sorry for poor Cleveland White. He's racing from one vendor to the next, mopping his face with a large white handkerchief and trying to talk them out of abandoning the mall's biggest Christmas event, no doubt.

Whipping out my cell, I call Darlene to give her an update. Since the Hair.Net booth was not located in viewing distance of Santa's Court, she had no idea what was happening. And neither did her customers.

"People are still lined up here three deep," she says.

"Good. Keep the booth open as long as we've got a crowd. I knew they'd love your nail art."

" 'Natch. But it's the star predictions that's drawing them in."

"Don't tell me you're reading horoscopes."

"Everybody wants to know the future."

At the rate people are getting knocked off, looks like some of them won't even have a future.

"Just don't make any iron-clad promises. Okay, Darlene?"

When we get to the parking lot, Lovie and I stop to plan.

"We can't go home," I say. "Jack's there." Meaning he would try to keep me from wading up to my neck into police business. He'll find out soon enough, but at least I'll have a head start.

"My house. And we'd better tell Aunt Ruby Nell and Fayrene."

"Why? The last time they were involved in a murder investigation, I had to wear war paint, dance half-naked under the moon, and kill a chicken."

"If somebody is really out to kill all the Santas, Daddy needs to know. He could still be in danger."

She's right, of course. Telling Lovie I'll meet her at her cottage, I sprint toward my pickup holding Elvis' leash with one hand and punching in Mama's speed-dial number with the other. No need to call Fayrene. Mama never does anything without letting her know.

After I explain what happened to Wayne and tell her that Lovie and I are going to put our heads together, I say, "Stay in the hospital with Uncle Charlie so I'll know you're safe."

"Flitter."

"Mama, what does that mean? Flitter's not even a word."

I might as well save my breath. Mama has already hung up. No telling what's she's fixing to do. I don't even want to know.

Elvis and I get to Robins Street just as Lovie is pulling into her driveway. For once I don't tell Elvis to wait in the truck. I'm in no hurry to head out after a killer, and besides, I feel safer with my dog at my side.

When we get inside, Lovie already has the coffee on. She emerges from the kitchen with a platter of doughnuts, three kinds of cookies, a bag of potato chips, three Snickers bars for her, and a Hershey bar with almonds for me. She knows it's my favorite.

"Good grief, Lovie. It looks like you've prepared for a siege."

"Never go into battle on an empty stomach."

"I don't plan to go into battle. Just do enough sleuthing to find out a few things and keep my family safe."

"We can tend to our own little red wagons, thank you very much." Mama sweeps into the living room with Fayrene right behind her. I'm so upset I didn't even hear her drive up.

"I told you to stay at the hospital, Mama."

"Since when do I take orders from my daughter?"

"Never."

"Precisely." Mama flops down beside me on Lovie's blue velvet sofa and proceeds to grab my Hershey bar. I wouldn't tell her it was meant for me if you hog-tied me and threatened to cut my hair with a hacksaw. That's how stubborn I am when I'm upset. I admit. It's a flaw. But not fatal, and not one of many.

While Mama and Fayrene snack and commiserate with Lovie over the loss of Wayne, I pull myself together. With Uncle Charlie in the hospital, I'm the only one left to head up the Valentine family. Mama's too flighty, Lovie's too hot-headed, and Jack's got a shattered leg.

Why did I even include Jack? I guess it's because he's half in the family and half out, and it's all up to me whether he goes or stays. Maybe I ought to be the one asking Darlene to predict my future by the stars.

I go into the kitchen and pour coffee for everybody. No need to ask who wants cream and sugar. The good thing about friends and family is that everybody knows how you like your coffee.

I set the tray on the coffee table then return to my seat beside Mama. She winks at me and I wink back. Two stubborn peas in a pod, looks like.

"Who do you think this killer is after?" Mama asks.

"That's anybody's guess," I say. "He could be out to get the mall's regular Santa. Or maybe he was after Lovie's fiancé."

"If he was out to get Charlie, he'll get him over my dead body." Mama looks fierce.

"Everybody loves Daddy."

Lovie's right. Up to a point. I know things about Uncle Charlie's past that nobody in this room does. But I'm sworn to secrecy. One word about his involvement—and Jack's—with the Company, and there's no telling who would die.

"Rudolph and Santa were killed by electricity passing through the throne. And Rudolph died only because he had reached out to grab Uncle Charlie's hand when the power was turned on." I hate to think how close I was standing. "I think Santa's the target."

"Yeah, but which one?" Lovie has a Snickers bar in each hand. Who can blame her? It's not every day you lose a fake fiancé.

"I did a little sleuthing earlier," I say, "and found out that Nathan Briggs has been the mall's only Santa since it opened."

"What about Charlie?"

"As far as I know, Uncle Charlie and Wayne are the only substitutes Nathan has had. That narrows our search to the people who had a history with the Santas."

Since Mama is halfway through my Hershey bar, I have to content myself with a second helping of cookies. I'm not usually this hungry. But there's something about the combination of Christmas and murder that makes me crave chocolate and sugar.

"The dead Santa or the two live ones?" Fayrene has a point.

"All three," I say. "Mayor Getty was in the court when Uncle Charlie got hit with voltage."

"Flitter, Robert Earl adores Charlie. Besides, he's elected mayor by a landslide every time he runs. That many people can't be wrong about him."

"What about Cleveland White?" Lovie asks. "He threw the switch."

"He's a deacon at Calvary Baptist Church," Fayrene says. "That obliterates him."

I hope she means *eliminates*, but this time I'm not too sure.

Lovie says a word that would boil water. "I've had more than one deacon after my Holy Grail."

"Hush up, Lovie. At least pretend to be mourning for your fiancé." This is the kind of conversation that calls for caffeine. I pour myself a second cup. "Besides, Cleveland turned on the power to the throne. Nobody would be foolish enough to murder Rudolph the Red-Nosed Reindeer and Santa so openly."

"I don't think the killer's Cleveland," Fayrene says. "I'm not picking him up on my ESPN."

Ever since Fayrene met Bobby, she's claimed to have psychic powers via ESPN.

Lovie nearly chokes on her coffee. I give her a discreet kick under the coffee table, then search my purse for paper and pen.

"I'm going to put Robert Earl and Cleveland on the list anyhow. Lovie, grab the phone book and look up the addresses."

She jerks the phone book out of a drawer in the end table, and out flies a thimble, two spools of purple thread, a dog-eared copy of *Gone with the Wind*, and an adult toy I'm not even going to name.

Without the least blush, Lovie shoves her questionable belongings back and says, "I'm not disguising myself as a maid."

"Good grief. Nobody said anything about disguises."

"I did." Lovie tells me the addresses of the mayor and the mall manager. "Who's next?"

"Corky Kelly. Former elf. He was there the day Steve was killed. Does anybody know him?"

"I don't have a clue," Mama says, and Lovie shakes her head no.

When Fayrene pops out of her chair, she can barely contain her glee. She loves center stage. "He's been to Gas, Grits, and Guts a few times. There's no scantification for Corky to be a suspect. I've heard several people prefer to him as 'good old Corky.' "

Lovie's now holding her hand over her mouth. I can just hear what she'll say later about the malapropisms for *justification* and *refer.*

"Besides," Fayrene adds, "They say he's the perfect neighbor, always lending a hand."

"That doesn't rule him out, Fayrene. Lots of serial killers are called the *perfect neighbor.*" Mama has a point.

"Maybe Opal Stokes tried to kill the Santas with her cookies," Lovie says. "When that didn't work she had to finish the job with a jolt of electricity."

"That's far-fetched, but I'll put her on the list. I can't imagine her being involved in murder."

"Guess where she lives?"

"Holy cow, Lovie. I'm in no mood for guessing games."

"Four twenty-three Mockingbird Lane. In Audubon. And you know what happens there every Christmas?"

"The unanimous Christmas thief!" Fayrene is all but prancing. She's talking *anonymous,* of course. Every year Audubon reports more thefts of Christmas decorations than any other residential section of Tupelo.

"Surely that sweet little lady is not a Christmas thief," I say.

"What about the shenanigans of those sweet little old ladies in the Elvis Presley fan club?" Lovie enjoys gloating when she's right. "Maybe Opal hates Christmas so much she's graduated from theft of plastic Santas to murder."

"You're convicting her without evidence, Lovie. Just because she made cute Christmas cookies." Still, my cousin may be onto something.

"Get that look out of your eye, Cal. I'm not about to break and enter."

Lovie has a point. The first time she ended up watching a geriatric Grandma and the Big Bad Wolf, and the last time she ended up mooning half of Memphis.

"We're not breaking and entering this time. We're going in the front door."

"Fayrene and I will ensure your success with a Christmas Mayan ceremony with feathers," Mama says.

Remembering how their ceremonies turned out in Mexico, I yell, "No!"

"You don't have to be so touchy, Carolina. We're just trying to help."

"I know, Mama. But I think your best bet is to go back to the hospital so you and Uncle Charlie can look after each other." Nobody's going to get to Uncle Charlie through the hospital security, but I don't tell Mama that. She likes to feel needed. "I just wanted you to be aware of what's going on, that's all."

"Flitter, you just don't want my help, Carolina."

"I'm sorry. I didn't mean to upset you. If you and Fayrene

insist on a ceremony, go right ahead. Just please don't do it in Audubon."

Fayrene is already on the phone calling Bobby to meet them at the séance room and to bring some *hubbubs*. I don't even want to know.

Elvis' Opinion #5 on Cherubs, Super Basset, and Radar Ears

Fayrene's *hubbubs* are cherubs. It takes a dog of my dazzling intelligence to know. It also takes a basset of great diplomacy and patience to sit on Lovie's Oriental rug yawning while my human mom and Ruby Nell discuss my fate.

Ruby Nell offers to take me back to Callie's house, but my human mom is afraid Ruby Nell will spill the beans about her proposed nefarious activities with Jack. The last thing she wants is Jack storming around on his crutch trying to keep her safe. Callie prides herself on being independent.

And she is. Most of the time. What she doesn't know is that I'm the reason she feels secure at night when Jack's not around; I'm a major attraction at Hair.Net (and therefore partially the cause of her booming business), and I'm the one she consults when she's making decisions.

I loll around biding my time till my human mom finally announces, "Elvis will go with Lovie and me. He'll be fine in the truck."

To show you what a great actor I am—contrary to what some of those lightweight movies the Colonel made me do would indicate—I don't jump up and howl a swivel-hipped rendition of "Got My Mojo Working," then snarl, "And, baby, I'm not waiting in the truck."

Listen, Lovie may be able to fool the cookie lady with her disguise as a buck-toothed, gray-haired census taker. And Callie can pretend to be a man in a drooping black mustache and one of Charlie's old tweed coats that Lovie had hanging around in the closet. But it's yours truly who will save the day.

If I could swap this four-legged red suit for a red cape, I'd show you Super Dog at his finest. Forget leaping over tall buildings in a single bound. With my talents for detection combined with my formidable fame, I'm a dog to be reckoned with.

And I can guarantee, the reckoning won't take place on the cold front seat of Callie's pickup truck.

Look out, Mockingbird Lane. Here comes the King.

Chapter 7

Frosty the Stolen Snowman, Mrs. Claus, and the unHoly Cow

Since Lovie's van has LOVIE'S LUSCIOUS EATS printed on the side, we're barreling across town toward Mockingbird Lane in my truck. The radio is blaring "All I Want for Christmas Is My Two Front Teeth," and in the distance I hear the train whistle.

It happens every time I go through crosstown (the intersection of Main and Gloster, the two major streets in Tupelo). No matter what time of day, I get caught in traffic backed up for blocks by the GM&O. One of the beauties of Tupelo is that it's a small, charming town. The downside is that like most small Southern towns founded a hundred and forty years ago, it was built around railroad tracks. Nobody ever said, "Gee, we've got trains going right through the center of town. Reckon we ought to do something before we get too big for our britches?"

My cousin reaches over and turns up the heater.

"Good grief, Lovie. It feels like August in here."

"Stress makes me cold."

"I know. But I'm sweating like I've run the Boston Marathon." Uncle Charlie's too-big hat slides down my forehead. "Grab my hat before I run into the train and kill us all."

She plucks it off, and my hair comes loose from my French twist to curl around my cheek. "I don't know why I had to be the man."

"Because I have too much hair to hide under a hat. Besides, a thirty-eight double D would never pass. Even under Daddy's coat."

"You have a point."

"Two, in fact."

"Good grief, Lovie." I don't remind her why we're in disguise. It's good to see that she can joke around in spite of practically being Santa's widow. "When we get to Opal's, I'll look around while you talk."

Lovie shines at small talk. And she's nearly as good at fiction as Mama.

"I'm going to ask her what she put in those cookies."

"Don't you dare. We weren't supposed to have seen her at the mall. Remember?"

"I'm lucky to remember my own name. Poor Wayne."

"I'm sorry, Lovie. When he gets to Eternal Rest, I'll make him look natural." That's always the family's request, unless the deceased has made prior arrangements and wants to sleigh up to Glory Land looking like George Clooney.

"It's too bad he didn't die before Rudolph."

"Lovie!"

"He would have won the jazz funeral. Wayne loved music."

Sitting between us, Elvis takes that as a cue to start howling. I'll swear it sounds like a doggie version of "Silent Night."

The last car on the train finally passes by, and I take a short-cut past the middle school to Audubon. Suddenly I'm in bumper-to-bumper traffic. With school out for the holidays and every teenager who can drive on the roads—plus harried moms and dads searching for the latest toy little Jimmy saw on

TV—there's no chance Lovie and I can sneak into this neighborhood undetected.

But looking on the bright side—and I always do—how can anybody remember us in this crowd?

I make a right turn through the brick-columned entrance to Audubon and nearly run into a van full of seniors. With their gray heads sticking out every window of a van with METHODIST SENIOR SERVICES painted on the side, they're gawking at a beige, seventies-style ranch house where Santa and his reindeer have landed on a roof entirely covered in lights.

And so has Jesus. His arms are outstretched, pointing the way to the front lawn, where Joseph and Mary preside over an assortment of animals. The faux Holy Mother and Joseph are probably trying to herd their menagerie away from the North Pole scene on the other side of the lawn so they won't freeze to death in the mountain of fake snow. After all, the elves and Mrs. Claus are wearing mufflers.

"Holy cow!"

"And holy pig, to boot," Lovie says. Sure enough, there's a pig in lights among the assorted holy herd. "Didn't I tell you this place was a paradise for the Christmas thief?"

"Yeah, Lovie, but that doesn't mean we can connect the dots between theft and murder." I ease my truck around the van, while Elvis stands on his hind legs to watch out the back window. He probably can't believe his eyes, either.

"Hey, slow down."

I inch to a crawl past a two-story Georgian brick house so Lovie can get a better look at the blue lights strung around every window, tree, and bush. Trying to climb the west wall is a gigantic, hairy bigfoot.

"What next, King Kong?" We're acting like tourists instead

of sleuths. At the rate we're going, we'll never get to Opal's house. I pick up the speed, then turn left onto Mockingbird Lane. "Lovie, keep your eyes peeled for four twenty-three."

It turns out there's no need for her vigilance. Opal's house sits among the lights and nativities and North Poles like a toad. It's a squat brown brick house with a line of meatball-shaped shrubs along the front and a porch that doesn't even have a swing. No lights, no fake snow, no Christmas tree in the window. Not even a Christmas candle burning.

"I'm about to change my mind about that sweet little old lady."

"There's no telling what she put in the cookies."

"Get off her cookies, Lovie. We've got other fish to fry." I twist my hair up and secure it with pins, make sure it all fits under Uncle Charlie's hat, then adjust my mustache in the rearview mirror. "How do I look?"

"I wouldn't give you my phone number."

"I don't want to look like every woman's heartthrob. I just don't want to look like a twenties gangster."

"Then ditch the mustache."

"Gladly. It itches, anyhow." I peel it off and stow it in the glove compartment, then give Elvis one of the rawhide treats Lovie always has in her kitchen. "That should keep you busy while we're gone, boy."

Next I caution him to stay in the truck. Listen, don't tell me dogs can't understand what you say. Elvis is more attuned to nuance than some people I know. I'm too polite to name names, but still, years in my beauty shop have given me a hands-on education in human nature.

Armed with official-looking notebooks and a half-baked plan, we sashay up the front walk and ring Opal Stokes' door-bell. We hear a loud crash that sounds like something heavy being dropped on the floor. Then a wavery voice calls, "Just a minute."

The minute stretches nearly to Christmas before we hear footsteps. Opal opens the door, smiling, but she has the look of a woman who is up to something. Her bun is askew, her green cotton duster is buttoned wrong, and she's missing her glasses. Still, she watches us with eyes as lively as a jaybird's.

Lovie punches me and I step on her toes. This little old woman looks like nobody's fool. If we're not careful, she'll be onto us.

"Census takers! May we come in?" Lovie is as cheerful as a party balloon. If she gets any perkier, she's going to levitate.

Opal makes no move to open the door. "I thought the census was last spring."

"It was! We're just tying up a few loose ends."

"Well, I don't like to think of myself as a loose end." Opal still has not invited us inside.

A police cruiser drives by, too slow for my peace of mind. What if somebody who saw us at crosstown reported two suspicious-looking women, one wearing a man's mustache? Futhermore, I wonder how I'm going to remind Lovie that she is not in cheerleader costume but the garb of a senior citizen.

"Act old," I say under my breath, then cover my snarl with a cough.

"Bless you." Lovie pats me on the back as the cruiser disappears around the corner. "Mrs. Stokes, I know census takers are about as popular as a striped polecat, but it's been a long day, Edgar's allergies are acting up, and my feet are killing me. If you'll just let us in, I promise to be quick."

"Well, in that case. But make it snappy." She swings open the door with all the good cheer of a woman preparing for a hernia operation. Her grumpy attitude is a vast change from the sweet-tempered little lady who gave out cookies at the mall and called Elvis a "cutey pie."

Lovie and I exchange looks as we follow Opal into a den straight out of the sixties: café curtains at the windows, early American plaid sofa and chairs with maple end tables, and a twenty-one-inch TV in a console. The only decorations are a pottery vase filled with faded plastic daisies and two pictures on the wall, one Joan of Arc and the other Eleanor Roosevelt. Crusading women. What does that say about Opal Stokes?

Lovie whips a notebook out of a green oversize tote. "This is the long form, but we'll start with the routine stuff. How many live here?"

"One. I've been a widow for sixteen years, and if the government doesn't know that by now they ought to quit asking."

"Well, I couldn't agree more, Mrs. Stokes. Do you own your home?"

"You bet your britches I own it. Taught school for thirty years and paid for it myself. Not that that's anybody's business. Including the government. The next thing you know, they'll be asking details about my gall bladder operation."

Opal glares at Lovie and me as if we have personally deprived her of her gall bladder. She focuses her stare on me.

"You don't look old enough to shave? How old are you, young man?"

I go into another coughing fit, and Lovie slaps me on the back.

"He's twenty-one. Poor Edgar. When his allergies are like this, he can hardly talk."

"I guess not." Opal sits there staring at me. Apparently nobody ever told her about Southern manners.

"I wonder if he can go into the kitchen and get a glass of water?" Opal glares at Lovie as if she's lost her mind, but my cousin is unflappable. "That way I can finish up this census and we'll be out of your hair."

"Praise the lord!" Opal raises her arms and waves her hands, feisty as all get-out. I'll bet she was a pistol when she was younger. "The kitchen's down the hall and through the last door on your left. Glasses are in the cabinet left of the sink. Don't break anything."

I hurry out, grateful I won't have to endure Opal's scrutiny any longer. Since I don't know how well insulated this house is and what Opal can hear, I go into the kitchen, grab a glass, and turn on the tap water. While it's running, I rummage through her other cabinets. Coffee, tea, flour, cornmeal mix, sugar, Ex-Lax. Laxatives?

What other surprises does Opal have in her kitchen? Remembering the body Lovie and I found in Bubbles Malone's chest freezer, I peek into Opal's upright. No bodies, thank goodness. Just two frozen chickens, and they look like they died from natural causes.

How much longer can I stay in the back of Opal's house without her charging in to make sure I'm not breaking glasses and stealing her silver? I check out both doors leading from the kitchen. One is to the panty, the other to her basement.

A quick scan shows nothing unusual in the pantry, so I tiptoe down the basement stairs, descending into what appears to be a black hole. I hope I don't fall and break my neck. Anything could be lurking in the dark, including spiders. If one lands on me, I'll scream. Then, as they say in the old film noir classics Lovie and I are partial to watching, the jig will be up.

If I'm going to keep landing in the middle of murder, I've got to arm myself with a flashlight. Forget the gun. I have one, but so far all I've been able to kill is a perfectly good pair of Jimmy Choos.

At the bottom of the stairs I find a cord hanging from a bare bulb. Holding my breath, I give it a yank. The basement lights up, revealing all Opal's secrets.

A scream bubbles up in my throat, and I cover my mouth, hoping nobody heard me. Santa is here, ten of him to be precise, along with Frosty, six Rudolphs, eight tiny reindeer times three, enough elves to keep Santa's workshop going for the next twenty years, four Christmas sleighs, Mrs. Claus, and so many strings of lights that if they were all burning you could see Audubon from Mars.

But these Christmas decorations aren't waiting their turn on the neighborhood rooftops and front yards. They are beheaded, dismembered, burned, gouged, and scratched.

Opal Stoke's basement is a torture chamber for Audubon's stolen Christmas decorations.

I yank the light cord and hurry up the dark stairs before I meet the same fate. Two days later, at least, I gain the kitchen and lean over the sink wondering if I'm going to be sick or be killed.

"What's taking so long in here?"

Good grief! Opal has appeared in the door and is glaring at me. Lovie is right behind her, looking frantic and making slashing motions across her throat.

Purse-lipped and gimlet-eyed, Opal looks around her kitchen. My hands are shaking when I turn off the water tap.

"If you're searching for the family silver, you're out of luck, mister. That sorry husband of mine lost it in a poker game."

"What a shame." Lovie can make a quicker recovery than anybody I know. I'm still hanging onto the edge of the sink expecting Opal to frisk me for stolen property.

"If the old jackass hadn't died, I'd probably have killed him."

"Would you look at the time?" Lovie feigns great interest in her watch. "We have to be going."

She starts dragging me out of the kitchen. But Opal, the Santa Slayer, grabs my arm.

"Not so fast."

Is she going to pull a gun? Call the cops? Push us down the basement stairs for some Christmas torture?

For once I wish I'd come armed. Lovie didn't even bring her baseball bat.

My cousin looks like she's getting ready to haul off and sock Opal when the former sweet little old lady lets go of me and storms toward the pantry. She jerks open the door and vanishes inside.

"Two against one," Lovie whispers. "We can take her."

"Hush up and run. You're going to get us killed."

But being paralyzed with terror is not conducive to a fast getaway. Just as we're getting our numb limbs to obey, Opal bursts back through the door, holding a mop. "You're not fixing to leave here!"

Holy cow! She means business. As she surges forward wielding her weapon, we both freeze. I can feel Lovie's intent from a mile away. She's getting ready to kick an old woman.

"Don't you have any manners?" Opal yells, then thrusts the mop into my hand. "Clean up that water you spilled."

I don't know whether to giggle or run. Lovie punches me in the ribs, and I start mopping. Lovie's hand is over her mouth, and her shoulders are shaking. If she bursts out laughing, I'm liable to bop her over the head with the mop.

"You missed a spot." Opal points and I set to work. Agent 007 would disown me. Some spy I turned out to be. I give Lovie a look that says, *Do something*.

She jerks the mop out of my hand, slaps my back, and yells, "Good job, Edgar." Then she hands the mop to Opal and tugs me toward the door. "Hurry along now or we'll never meet our day's quota."

We hustle toward the front door with the Santa Slayer hot on our trail, yelling, "Wait a minute." I wouldn't wait if Brad Pitt was standing behind me buck naked. "You forgot your notebook."

Lovie backtracks, scoops it off the sofa, and we hotfoot it toward the truck. I barrel inside, expecting to be greeted by a cold, wet nose and a big, slurping doggie kiss.

Wouldn't you know? Elvis is missing.

Elvis' Opinion #6 on Rescues, Obedience, and the Art of the Con

I don't know why Callie bothers to lock the truck doors. The minute she and Lovie are out of hearing range I smash my paw down on the unlock button, and I'm almost out of here.

All I have to do now is wait for one of my fans to come along and spring me. If a fan doesn't show up, anybody in a Christmas mood will do. Listen, the day a handsome basset in a four-legged Santa suit can't con his way out of a Dodge Ram pickup truck is the day I turn in my blue suede shoes. All it takes is one look into my melting brown basset eyes, a crooked grin, and a little spin from my days as a world-famous singer in a gold jumpsuit, and I'm on the way to see what's cooking at 423 Mockingbird Lane.

"T-R-O-U-B-L-E", that's what my senses are telling me. Don't think I didn't know it was Opal Stokes' cookies that sent me on an emergency mission to the mall's grassy outdoor potty paradise. There's no such thing as coincidence. Any dog worth his Pup-Peroni knows that.

Wait! What's this I see "Tip Toeing Through the Tulips?" A teenager with an iPod sprouting from her ears and a foxy beagle on a leash. That little beagle cutie would have me singing "Rock-a-Hula Baby" if I weren't still enamored of a certain pheromone-loaded French poodle.

The beagle yelps when she sees me. *Naturally.* In addition to being the King, I'm the sexiest dog alive. The teenager pulls the plugs out of her ears, and I go straight into my act. When she claps and says, "How *cute,*" I put my front paws on the door and whine—the pièce de resistance of the doggie con.

"Poor thing," the teenager says. "Did somebody forget about you?" I do my best mournful howl, and she opens the truck door.

I bound out like I'm headed to the "Promised Land." Being the gentlemanly dog I am, I pause long enough to take a little bow in their direction, then streak toward the back yard like there's a heated dog house and a big dish of Kibbles 'n Bits in my immediate future.

Once I'm out of sight, I put my famous nose to the ground. Listen, I'm the only one in the Valentine family who picked up the scents in the costume changing room, and I intend to see if one of them belongs to Opal Stokes.

What's this I smell? Rabbits in Audubon? Squirrels I expected, but not the Easter bunny. These critters must be getting smarter. They must have found out that it's illegal to shoot a gun in the city limits. No wonder they're migrating from Ruby Nell's farm south on 371 to a neighborhood with Jesus on the roof.

All sorts of smells assault my noble nose. I'm just getting ready to sort through them when my human mom calls, "Elvis! Where are you?"

Drat. Busted. If she didn't sound so panicked I'd ignore her for a while. I'm onto something big here.

But when she calls my name again, she sounds like some lonely soul singing "It Won't Seem Like Christmas (Without You)." When it comes to a choice between being a star detective and comforting my human mom, Callie wins every time.

I ditch my detection and show my handsome self around the side of the house. Before I get back on her good side with a little turn of "I'll Be Home for Christmas," she scoops me up, runs to the truck, and peels out like we're being chased by an ill-tempered Doberman pinscher.

She doesn't even scold me.

I'm not long finding out why.

"Holy cow, Lovie. I thought that mean old woman was going to kill us."

"And you said she was *sweet*. I never did fall for that cute little old cookie lady act."

"She keeps Ex-Lax in her cabinet. It appears she put more than sugar in her cookies."

"I knew it."

"And you'll never guess what I found in her basement." Callie starts recounting a scene of Christmas mutilation that makes me glad she caught me before I finished my snooping. Listen, I may be a premiere dog detective who goes the second mile, but I draw the line at sacrifice.

"It figures," Lovie says. "Anybody who would put a laxative in Christmas cookies would steal and torture the neighbors' Christmas decorations."

"But all that still doesn't make her a killer."

"Why not? Some people get the Christmas spirit. Opal gets Christmas rage."

"But does she get mad enough to kill? And if she does, how would a former school teacher know how to turn Santa's throne into an electric chair?"

"Just because I'm a caterer doesn't mean I can't re-wire a lamp."

"You're right, Lovie. Did you make a connection between Opal and either one of the victims?"

"Wayne was one of her students."

"You're kidding me! But why would she want to kill your fiancé?"

"I don't have a clue. Why would she put Ex-Lax in cookies and hand them out at Santa's Court?"

"If she hates Christmas so much she chops off the heads of plastic Santas, she's bound to hate little children, too."

"The thing I can't figure out, Cal, is how Opal would know Wayne was Santa? Only you and Jack and I knew."

"Plus, when he got dressed, he looked like every other mall Santa." Cal strips off Charlie's hat and shakes her hair out of the pins. "Did you say anything about Wayne to Cleveland?"

"No. I only let him know we had a Santa substitute and he didn't have to worry."

"I still can't picture Cleveland as the killer. Did Opal know Uncle Charlie or Nathan Briggs?"

"I was just getting ready to ask her that when she jumped up and raced toward the kitchen like her coattail was on fire."

"A few seconds earlier, and she'd have caught me in her basement. Why didn't you warn me?"

"Next time I'll light a cigarette and yell, *Fire*."

"You don't smoke."

"That's not the point. We need to work out a signal. I don't intend to die at the business end of a mop."

"Good grief, Lovie. You weren't the one she was after. Besides, there's not going to be a next time. We need to turn this investigation over to professionals."

"Who? The cops? The way they were questioning you in Santa's Court, you're at the top of their suspect list, Cal. I can just see how they'll react to information you've gleaned snooping in Opal Stokes' basement."

"You have a point."

This admission makes my human mom slump. I edge over and lay my head in her lap. Listen, if there's anybody in the world who can keep Callie from having a "Blue Christmas," it's yours truly.

Of course, Lovie always does her part, too. Usually with a six-pack of Hershey bars and a barrel full of sass. Currently she's jerking off her granny wig and perking up.

"Let's change clothes at my house, then drive by the hospital, Cal. We need to tell Daddy about Wayne before he hears it on the six o'clock news."

"That's a good idea. But don't tell Uncle Charlie he was your fiancé."

"Why not?"

"That would only upset him. He likes to think he can take care of everybody in the family."

"Poor Wayne. He probably never would have made it into the family, anyhow."

My human mom is wise enough to keep quiet. I know what's on her mind. The same thing that's on mine. Wayne was simply another of Lovie's diversions. Deep down she's still hoping Rocky Malone will leave Mexico and start digging for *real* treasure.

Lovie gives me a treat at her house—bacon-flavored Milk Bones. She knows when a loyal dog deserves a reward. When Callie finally parks her truck in front of the hospital and says, "Wait in the truck, and I *mean* it, Elvis," I don't argue.

Listen, I may be the best canine detective in the world, but I'm not a lick of good if I miss my sleep. And it's past my nap time.

I watch until Callie is safely inside the hospital, then I give that suspicious guard who's looking my way a snarl and curl up on the warm spot Callie left behind. Even a famous dog has to have his rest.

Chapter 8

Gentle Murder, Graceland Send-offs, and Fatal Attractions

Uncle Charlie's color is better, but he still looks fragile. On the way up to his room, Lovie asked if I'd be the one to tell him about Wayne.

"You can do it so much more gently than I can, Cal."

"Sure," I told her, but I don't know how you can be gentle when you're breaking the news about murder.

I flounder my way through, but Uncle Charlie takes the latest Christmas murder in stride. Lovie is the one who takes things badly. I'm not used to seeing my unflappable cousin cry.

She lets Uncle Charlie hug her, and even leans on his shoulder a while, which is unusual for her. Lovie has always believed her daddy is disappointed that she's not a boy. She tries so hard to act like she doesn't care, she's finally convinced herself it's true. "Why don't you stay here with me tonight, dear heart?" he says to Lovie. "The death of a friend is hard. You could use the company and I could, too."

"I think I will if Cal doesn't mind."

"Of course not." I tamp down on my enthusiasm. It won't do to let Lovie see how excited I am that she's finally dropping her tough girl attitude and letting her real feelings show. "Besides, I need to stop by the funeral home to make sure

Bobby doesn't need help getting ready for Steve Boone's wake tonight."

"He called to say he has everything under control, but I'd feel better if you'd check, dear heart."

I hug Lovie and Uncle Charlie, tell them to call if they need anything, then hurry through the parking lot. I spot my truck, but no Elvis. If he's gone missing again I'm going to scream. I barrel toward the Dodge Ram, resisting the urge to scream, "Elvis!" I've had enough drama today without everybody in the parking lot thinking I've gone stark raving crazy.

Yelling that famous name in Tupelo can cause a stampede. Half the folks here think somebody else is buried at Graceland while the King leads a simple life in the hills, venturing out only once in a blue moon. Some even declare to have spotted him at the Piggly Wiggly.

I say a little prayer, then jerk open my truck door. Elvis stands up, stretches, yawns, then gives me a slobbery dog kiss. I know this is not George Clooney—or for that matter, Jack Jones—but I was never so glad to see anybody in my life.

"Elvis! You obeyed!"

He twirls around and takes a bow. I swear, he looks like somebody on center stage, which in a way he is. I've spoiled him into thinking everything in my life is all about him.

Still, isn't that what you're supposed to do with animals and people you love? I give Elvis one last cuddle, then hop into my truck and turn the keys in the ignition.

But suddenly everything that has happened in the last few days crashes around me. I can't go another step. Leaning my head on the steering wheel, I just breathe.

Elvis nuzzles my arm, but I still don't move. When he whines, I say, "This has been a long day, boy. And it's not over yet."

Satisfied, he flops onto the passenger side, while I take another deep breath before heading to Eternal Rest. It's a wonderful old Victorian house on Jefferson Street in the heart of downtown Tupelo. When Uncle Charlie converted it into a funeral home, he used a Graceland theme minus the shag carpet. Mama's influence, no doubt. Still, the bereaved take a great deal of comfort in knowing Uncle Charlie sends their loved ones off in grand style.

Thankfully, the parking lot is empty because nobody has died this week except Santa and his reindeer.

Holy cow, I sound like Mama. I must finally be coming undone.

After doing another deep-breathing exercise, I let myself in the front door, then take Elvis off his leash. This is a second home to him. He has the run of the place unless there's a funeral or a viewing in progress. Of course, there have been a few times when Elvis escaped our vigilance and showed up in the chapel to howl "Amazing Grace" along with Mama. She does the music for all Uncle Charlie's funerals, though she's usually not howling.

Today I don't have to worry, though. Eternal Rest is empty except for Steve Boone, who is lying in state in the blue parlor on my left. I don't have to check to know that he looks good. When I make up the dead they look like they could pose for the cover of *Harper's Bazaar*.

Leaving Elvis to wander toward the kitchen, probably looking for crumbs, I head toward Bobby's office. It's downstairs, near the embalming room and across the hall from the room I use to work my makeup magic on the deceased.

Bobby's door is ajar, so I don't knock. Instantly, I regret that decision. Bobby's standing with his back to the door and his arm around the waist of a curvaceous blond. Will wonders never cease? Both of them are bent over his desk with their heads together, mumbling something.

I'm sorry to report that I lean forward, straining to hear, but only for a split second. My better nature reasserts itself, and I creep backward and pull the door almost shut. Then, calling on acting skills learned when I was a cabbage in Mr. McGregor's garden in a second-grade play, I keep a straight face and give the door a sharp rap.

There are footsteps inside, and Bobby comes to the door. He's followed by none other than my manicurist.

"My goodness," I say. "Darlene!" I know, *I know*. Not very cabbage-like of me, but it has been a long day and my savoir faire is slipping.

"Oh, hi, Callie." All smiles, Darlene opens the door wider, while I stand there speechless and Bobby looks on, red-faced. "Come on in. Bobby and I were just looking at today's horoscope."

He tugs his tie and expels a long breath. Poor Bobby. Listen, if he and Darlene are trying to get something going, I'm glad. He's so shy he can barely string two words together unless he's around Mama and Fayrene. They think he's a true psychic and consult him all the time. He's practically garrulous around them.

"What's the prediction?" I stroll into the office and sit in an overstuffed beige chair in front of a bookcase bulging with books. I'm so tired I might just fall asleep.

"Clear sailing ahead," she says. "Good thing, don't you think, considering the two Christmas corpses in Santa's Court? What do you see, Bobby?"

"I don't know. My psychic eye is acting up."

Poor Bobby. Usually he says, "There's danger from a dark-eyed stranger." Today I'd be inclined to agree with him. I've had Opal Stokes' little beady brown eyes on me enough to feel the danger.

Darlene pats his arm. "Don't worry. Before you can say *Pass the eggnog,* you'll be getting psychic signals right and left." She grins at me. "Sometimes you have to stretch your imagination a little to line up what the stars say with what Bobby gets first-hand, but he's always right."

I half expect him to shuffle his feet and say, *Ah, shucks.* When he says, "Thank you, 'Lene," I nearly pass out from surprise. Considering that he calls Vanna White on *Wheel of Fortune* his best friend, his progression to a nickname for Darlene shocks me as much as if Lovie had left off using all the words she didn't learn in Sunday School.

"I've gotta run." Darlene grabs her purse and blows us a kiss. But I don't miss that she's sending it more in Bobby's direction than mine. "Mama and Daddy have David at Gas, Grits, and Guts, and Mama's going to have a conniption fit if I'm late."

"Thanks for your help at the charity event, Darlene. I couldn't have done it without you."

"It was fun. But I'm glad it's over. Wow! Two murders in three days. Thank goodness the bazaar's not open Sunday."

"Take Monday off, too, if you want. It's always a slow day at Hair.Net."

"And miss all the fun? No thanks. I'll see you there."

She whizzes out the door with Bobby watching until she disappears.

"Well," he says, then plops behind his desk like a man who has suddenly discovered his legs are made of straw.

"She's very nice, Bobby. I'm happy that you two are developing a friendship."

"Yes."

I wait for him to say more, but when nothing is forthcoming, I rub my hands together as if I'm trying to wash away events of today. "Do I need to help you do anything to get ready for Steve's viewing?"

"I'm all set."

"How about the jazz funeral?"

"His family declined."

"Not everybody appreciates a creative undertaker. Mama's going to be busy taking care of Uncle Charlie, and Lovie and I have our hands full, so call the substitute organist and caterer."

My phone rings, startling me almost out of my skin. "Before I forget, Bobby, call me if you have any trouble." I press my cell phone to my ear. "Hello."

"Callie, when are you going to get home to see about Jack?" It's Mama.

"What are you doing at my house, Mama?"

"Since when is it a crime to check on my son-in-law?"

"Ex."

"Flitter."

"You didn't tell him what I'm up to, did you?"

"What do you think I am? Senile? Get yourself home, Carolina. I need to leave so I can stay with Charlie."

"I'll be home in fifteen minutes. Besides, Jack can take care of himself, and Lovie's staying with Uncle Charlie tonight."

"I'm not leaving till you get here. Furthermore, you're bringing Jack to Sunday dinner after church. He looks like he's starving to death."

"Good grief, Mama, I'm not even going to dignify that with a comment. 'Bye now." I shove my phone back in my purse and stand up.

"Be careful, Callie," Bobby says.

"It's been a bad day. If you tell me there's danger from a dark-eyed stranger, I'm going to scream."

Bobby actually grins. "My psychic powers are on the blink, but I know there's a murderer loose."

Coming from him, that's the equivalent of a State of the Union address.

"I'll be careful, Bobby. Thanks."

I give him a little hug simply because he looks like he needs it. And to tell the truth, I do, too.

Then I round up Elvis and head to Mooreville to face the music. Translated, that means face Mama and Jack at the same time; they're a powerful duo when they're in cahoots with each other.

As it turns out, Mama's red Mustang convertible (what else?) is not in my driveway, and I don't even feel like an ungrateful daughter when I say, "Hallelujah." Elvis thumps his tail as if to say, "Amen."

My dog bounds out the door to greet Jack, who is waiting for me on the front porch swing. Or was he waiting for Elvis? I hang back while Jack greets him as if my basset is a soldier arriving home after a three-year tour of duty in a dangerous third-world country. My conscience pricks me, and not for the first time.

But I refuse to think about divorce at Christmas. Especially since my lawn is newly covered with wire reindeer moving their spindly legs and flashing their tiny blue lights.

"Jack, who put the reindeer out?"

"I did. Ruby Nell helped."

Now I *do* feel like an ungrateful daughter. "Why did Mama leave?"

"I told her to go on home, Cal. She needed the rest." I ascend the steps and Jack drapes his arm not-so-casually across my shoulders. "It looks like you do, too. How does hot chocolate sound?"

"Hot chocolate, a long hot soak in the tub, and then an evening in front of the fire watching a holiday movie classic, preferably something with Jimmy Stewart."

Jack grins at me and we say, "It's a Wonderful Life" at the same time.

For once I'm glad Jack is in my house. I'm glad I don't have a date. I'm glad I don't have company.

In the gathering dusk, we walk inside, arm in arm, while the Christmas reindeer on my lawn sparkle like tiny blue stars.

Chapter 9

Up on the Rooftop, Mooreville Mayhem, and Santa Barbecue

I'm happy to report that I wake up alone in my bed (which means Jack behaved last night and so did I), that the Sunday morning news reports nobody connected to Christmas got maimed or burned or electrocuted during the night, and that my little herd of wire reindeer is still grazing on my front lawn.

Furthermore, Jack is in the kitchen on his crutch making ham and eggs, and he's wearing his Sunday best.

"What's this? Eggs Benedict and a necktie? Am I in the wrong house?" I pour myself a cup of coffee and add real cream.

"If I'm going to church, I'm don't want to embarrass Ruby Nell."

"You're going to *church?*"

"Call me one of the C and E crowd." That's the Christmas and Easter crowd, but I never thought Jack would even be part of that. "Besides, Ruby Nell invited me to Sunday dinner. If I remember, that's not to be missed."

Mama's matchmaking, of course. And Jack seems only too happy to play along. Or is he serious? Still, it doesn't matter. I'm not going to let a bit of Christmas spirit sweep me into making another mistake with Jack.

After a breakfast that feels like old times, we climb into my truck, and I drive down Highway 371 south to the white-frame Wildwood Baptist Church across from Mama's farm. This takes less than five minutes. Mooreville is convenient that way. If I drew a circle around my house and drove ten minutes in any direction, I could see everybody I know in this community.

The church was built by my Granddaddy Valentine, and most of the stained-glass windows are in memory of my relatives. When Jack and I sit on an oak pew sharing a hymnal, it's almost like being at a family reunion. Up front, Mama pounds out "Joy to the World" on an antique mahogany upright with ball-and-claw feet. It wouldn't be Christmas without Mama at the church piano and the congregation of Mooreville's finest singing carols off key.

After services, Lovie joins us at Mama's, where she reports that Uncle Charlie is being discharged from the hospital this afternoon.

"I'm glad he's almost out of Nurse Ratched's clutches," Mama says, and then she serves the roast beef.

We sit around her table in the dining room, which features the scandal of Mooreville—a giant poster of one of Modigliani's elongated, naked women. Mama got it at the Metropolitan Museum of Art six years ago when Lovie and I took her to New York.

To say Mama's flamboyant is to say Elvis could sing—a mighty understatement.

I'm not going to pretend it doesn't feel good to have Jack beside me sharing one of Mama's Sunday dinners. I'm just going to say that I refuse to dwell on it.

Fortunately, I don't have to. The sudden racket at the door is not a tornado trying to tear the house down: it's Fayrene, bursting with bad news. She bustles in wearing a sweat suit the exact shade of a dollar bill. She's partial to clothing the color of money.

"While I was sitting in my living room listening to the Sunday morning broadcast of the Sermon on the Mound, Jarvetis discovered our rooftop Santa was missing. They even took the one at Gas, Grits, and Guts."

"Did you call the sheriff?" I ask.

"Lord, *no.* I left Jarvetis opening up the store and came straight to Ruby Nell." Silly me. I don't know why I even asked. "I'm about to have a heart prostration attack."

Fayrene pulls out a chair and plops down beside Lovie while Mama fetches a glass of iced tea and a plate. Lovie passes the potatoes, Elvis smacks his lips over a roll Fayrene accidentally drops under the table, and Jack whips out his cell phone. As he leaves the room, he starts talking to no telling who. With his connections, it's probably somebody who has formed a Mooreville Mafia.

Sunday dinner at Mama's has turned into a three-ring circus, which happens with more frequency than I care to think about. I'm losing my appetite, but I can't say the same for Lovie. She's digging in as if this is the only side of beef in Mississippi and she's at the Last Supper.

But I try to look on the bright side. At least Mama's former dance partner showed his true colors during what we now call the Memphis mambo murders, and Thomas Whitenton is no longer invited to the Valentine family dinners. That's one less thing to worry about.

Jack strolls back in, pocketing his cell phone. "Allegedly, the thief is Albert Gordon. He made a sweep of the neighborhood, snatching Santas."

"How do you know?" Mama's back in her seat, holding court at the head of the table.

For once, Jack ignores her. I'm the only person in this room besides him who knows why. On this issue, my almost-ex and I are on the same team. It won't do for Mama to know about his dangerous connections with the Company.

"I thought he was just a quiet old retired military man who recently moved to our neighborhood," I say. "He's never acted like he would hurt a flea."

"People are not always what they seem, Cal."

"You can say that again, Jack." But, of course, he doesn't. I thought I'd married an international businessman and look what I got. Somebody who goes into deep cover all over the world getting shot at.

Mama gives me the evil eye, but I ignore her. Thank goodness, Lovie gives me *the look*, which means she's going to rescue me.

"How was Albert identified as the thief?" she asks Jack. I owe her.

"While everybody in Mooreville was in church, he was in full camouflage stealing Santas. Roy Jessup spotted him."

The owner of Mooreville Feed and Seed. If I recall there was a huge inflatable Santa by the front door.

"It's a wonder Roy didn't stop him," I say. I cut Roy's hair, and he's not known for being wimpy.

"They had a tussle, but Gordon got away."

I've had about enough of dealing with people who hate Christmas decorations.

"If he took my blue reindeer, I'm going to let Elvis take a poop on his lawn."

"Apparently he only took the man in the red suit." Jack

winks at me. "Roy told the sheriff Gordon's threatening to have a Santa barbecue."

"When?" Fayrene asks, as if this is the Fourth of July and that crazy old man is planning a neighborhood picnic.

"It's not going to happen, Fayrene. The sheriff's out looking for him now. He was last seen heading toward the Itawamba County line." Jack turns to me. "Don't even think about sticking your cute nose into this."

Major mistake. Even Mama knows better than to tell me what to do. I kick Lovie under the table and she kicks me back, our secret signal that we'll do whatever we please, no matter who says no.

"Who, me?" I say.

"Yes, you. If Albert Gordon is lighting Santa's fire, it's a matter for the law."

Lovie rolls her eyes at me, but I can't roll mine back because Jack is watching me. Then she winks, meaning she has a plan, which always includes me. Hating Christmas is enough to put Albert Gordon on the murder suspect list, and I intend to check him out. What Jack doesn't know won't hurt him.

"I can't believe Albert Gordon would do such a thing," Mama says.

"You know him?" I don't know why I'm surprised. Mama has more secrets than the CIA.

"Not personally. But he was in Special Forces with Charlie in 'Nam."

"I don't know why you're sticking up for him, Ruby Nell," Fayrene says. "He stands at the store counting his change out loud like I'm some kind of pretty thief. And he wouldn't put a penny in the March of Dimes jar if the devil was after him with a pitchfork. Bobby says his aurora is black as sin."

107

Aura, I'm hoping, but I guess he could have somebody named Aurora stashed somewhere. I'll do anything to find out short of being a *pretty* thief.

"I'm not sticking up for him," Mama says. "All I'm saying is I'm surprised."

"I'm not. You can bet your bottom britches I'd be at that barbecue, but I've got bigger fish to eat." Trust Fayrene to get her metaphors wrong.

"Like what?" Mama wants to know.

"Darlene's trying to steal Bobby Huckabee."

Lovie's eyebrows go up. I haven't had a chance to tell her, and she's wondering if I already know, and if so, why I haven't shared the news with her. I can read her like a book.

"They'd make a cute couple, Fayrene." Mama loves romance and takes every chance to promote it.

"Hush up, Ruby Nell. I'm not about to lose my psychic over my daughter's foolish needs to be admired by the opposite sex."

"Well, I never thought about it that way."

"Lucky for you, you don't have to think, Ruby Nell. You've got me and my futile mind."

If Lovie chokes on her roast beef, I'll have to do the Heimlich. I push my plate aside, and Mama pipes up with, "Where do you think you're going, Carolina? I haven't even served dessert."

"I'm going with Lovie to get Uncle Charlie." Turning to Jack, I smile. "Stay and visit with Mama as long as you like. I'm sure she'll drive you home."

"Cal . . ." He shoots me this dark look that says he's not a bit fooled. If he'll care to remember, I've been taking care of myself ever since he walked out the door—and a long time before that, to boot.

"Take care of Elvis while you're at it, Jack. They won't let him in the hospital."

Lovie grabs two pieces of pecan pie to go, air kisses in Mama's direction, then hotfoots it out the door. Jack sends *I'll deal with you later* looks in my direction, while Elvis lowers his head to his paws and moans. He ought to be on stage. He's acting as if I'm leaving on an African safari, never to be seen again.

Let's just hope the *never to be seen again* part doesn't come true.

When I get to Mama's front yard, Lovie is waiting beside her van.

"Are you ready to pick locks?" I ask.

"Are you thinking what I'm thinking?" We look at each other and say, "Albert Gordon," at the same time.

I tick off the reasons we're going to break and enter. "He has a history with Uncle Charlie, he hates Christmas, and he's got all kinds of scary training. Motive and means, wouldn't you say?"

"Let's go." Lovie unwraps a piece of pie and stuffs it into her mouth. "We'll get Daddy out of the hospital first, then we'll break the law."

"Why don't I get Uncle Charlie while you snoop around Albert's? I'll join you there."

"Daddy will wonder where I am, and besides, I don't want to be at Albert's alone."

"The sheriff's probably chased him to Kingdom Come by now."

"Or maybe not." Lovie starts unwrapping the other piece of pie. "Do I look like a woman who wants to get killed all by herself?"

"No, you look like somebody who ate your pie and mine, too."

"You should have spoken up sooner."

When I spot Mama at the window, spying, I say to Lovie, "To the hospital, and hurry." Then I hop into my Dodge and try not to peel out. *Act normal*, I tell myself, though I'm not sure I even know what normal is anymore.

Elvis' Opinion #7 on Bad Music, Good Rump Roast, and Left Behind

If you think I'm the kind of dog who sits home every Sunday while the humans go to church, you're full of "Kentucky Rain"—or Kentucky straight bourbon. I ride along in Callie's truck wearing a pink bowtie clipped to my collar like the gentlemanly basset hound I am.

She won't let me go into the church, though, which is fine by me. If you think that caterwauling coming from the choir sounds bad in the truck, imagine what it would be like up close and personal.

While I wait, I have my methods of entertainment. Sometimes I look out the window and see how many rabbits I can count in the woods behind the church. Sometimes I think up ways to get the attention of the cows grazing in the pasture on my right. Have you ever seen a panicky cow run? Now there's some Sunday morning fun. Usually all I have to do is get up on my hind legs, do a little vocalizing, and watch the bovine "Bossa Nova Baby."

In case you haven't already guessed, my vocalizing consists of howling a verse or two from one of my solid-gold hits. Today it's "When the Saints Go Marching In." Callie always leaves the windows cracked so I can get fresh air, and it's easy for a dog of my talent to project to the back of the coliseum. Or in this case, the back side of the pasture.

Sometimes it projects into the church, too, but Callie's too tenderhearted to chastise me. She knows a dog has to have his fun.

By the time the Baptists come out, usually sweating from a weekly dose of hellfire-and-damnation fervor, I'm curled up on the front seat taking a little nap. A dog has to rest up for his Sunday dinner, especially when Ruby Nell is doing the cooking.

We get more than we'd planned for at Ruby Nell's this Sunday, and I'm not talking about food. Fayrene spoils the "Wonderful World of Christmas" with reports of Santa stealing, and the air is so thick between Callie and Jack you could ride it like the "Night Train to Georgia" (not my song, but, hey, I'm a generous dog).

To top it all off, Lovie's aura says she's up to something, and when she's out for trouble, it always involves my human mom. Adding insult to injury, Jack's so upset about being in a cast and having to sit around while Callie's up to her pretty neck in murder he slips me only one bite of roast beef. It's not big enough to satisfy a silly cat, let alone a hound of my discerning culinary tastes.

As if all that weren't enough, Callie leaves without me, and all I can say about that is she'd better hide the Prada boots she got at the after-Thanksgiving sale. I'm a dog to be reckoned with, and I'm in a pissing mood.

Chapter 10

White Lies, Baseball Bats, and Big Trouble

By the time Lovie and I get Uncle Charlie out of the hospital and settled into his apartment above Eternal Rest, it's nearly dusk. Winter afternoons seem to fly by, and dark always comes before I'm ready for it.

He looks very good, almost normal. Though I'm certain Jack has already told him what's up with the Santa killer, I don't mention Albert Gordon.

And I certainly don't mention our plans. He'd be just like Jack, anxious to keep us out of police business and therefore out of danger.

Uncle Charlie and Jack are not only as close as father and son, but my uncle trained Jack for the Company. Charlie Valentine may be everybody's favorite silver-haired undertaker and look like he wouldn't hurt a flea, but he's led a dangerous and checkered past.

Of course, I'm the only one in the family who knows about Uncle Charlie's dark side besides Jack. And he's technically not even a member of the family.

Thinking about family secrets and a Christmas killer on the loose makes me long for a big cup of eggnog and a vacation, which is not likely to happen anytime soon. The holiday season is one of my busiest at Hair.Net.

"I hate leaving you here by yourself, Uncle Charlie. Are you sure you'll be all right?"

"If the killer is after me, he's liable to find more trouble than he bargained for." He winks at me.

"For Pete's sake, Daddy, you sound like John Wayne doing Rooster Cogburn. Maybe I ought to see if Bobby will stay with you."

I wish I could tell Lovie what Jack told me: Uncle Charlie was the Company's best marksman and can shoot a dime out of the air. I really hate keeping secrets, especially from Lovie.

"Don't worry, dear heart. If trouble comes looking for me, the cops are only six blocks away."

Mollified, she kisses him on the cheek and we head out the door. In the parking lot of Eternal Rest, she says, "My house."

"Why?"

"Cat burglars don't wear red sequins."

I see her point. Shine a light on me and my Christmas sweater could be seen clear to the Pontotoc County line. And Lovie's wearing jingle bells. When she moves, her sweater decorations sound like Santa swooping past with his eight tiny reindeer.

I follow my cousin to her pink cottage, where we discuss our plans while we ditch church garb and put on some of her black sweatpants and tee shirts. Since she outweighs me by a ton and I'm a gazillion inches taller, all I can say is, "Thank goodness for elastic waistbands."

"Eat chocolate," she says. "That's why I have so much fun and you're always worried about something."

"I'm not worried. Just cautious."

"Let me put your mind at ease."

She pulls her baseball bat from underneath her bed and swings it. If a Santa thief had been standing in her path, he'd be missing body parts. Might I add, she played first base in high school, and she was known for knocking the ball out of the park.

"I feel safer already."

"Smart ass," she says, then detours by the kitchen and comes back armed with a bulging brown paper bag.

"Goodness gracious, Lovie. What's all that?"

"Every stakeout has food."

"We're not going on stakeout. This is a simple break and enter."

"You'd starve to death without me."

She sashays out the door, and I'm right behind her wearing baggy, high-water pants that I hope don't fall off. It's full dark now with the threat of rain. Not a star can be seen among the dense cloud cover, and not even a sliver of moon.

"It's a good night for skullduggery," Lovie calls through the dark.

"Let's rumble."

We sound like characters in one of the black-and-white film noir classics Lovie and I enjoy. Giggling, I crank up my truck and head out for an evening of breaking the law.

According to plan, Lovie and I enter my neighborhood from the east side so we won't pass by my house. Jack and Elvis can pick out the sound of my Hemi engine from two blocks away. He'd put two and two together before I could say "shoe sale." Crutches or no, he'd be after me before I could get past Albert Gordon's gate.

Also as discussed, we turn off our headlights on the approach to TV weatherman Butch Jenkins' house and park in the shadow of three giant oaks in his yard. Being careful not to slam my car door, I mince my way across the pitch-black yard to Lovie and run smack into her.

Only it's not Lovie, it's a holly bush with enough prickles to almost make me say one of Lovie's colorful words.

"Where are you?" I whisper.

"Over here."

"Are you laughing?"

"Yes."

"I may have to kill you."

"Get in line." Lovie switches on a miniature penlight, and I follow the tiny beam toward a hedge that separates the Jenkins' yard from Albert's. "You first."

Believe me, Lovie's not being polite. This intimidating, prickly-feeling hedge looks like it could swallow small dogs and skinny hairdressers. Still, I brave on through. At what cost to my hair and Lovie's clothes I don't even want to ponder.

"When I get home I'm going to look like I've been to war."

"If you get home, Cal."

Lovie sounds as dark as Bobby. Furthermore, she's on the other side of the hedge.

"Come on through, Lovie. It's not so bad."

"Maybe not for you. Try being a bale of cotton."

"Good grief. Reach for my hand." I stretch my arm past thorns the size of redwoods and grab hold of her. Digging in my heels, I tug. Lovie pops through the hedge in one piece, but I can't say the same for her clothes. Judging by the ripping sounds, I'd say she now has a hole in her pants as big as the Grand Canyon. I don't even want to know where.

Instead, I scuttle across a backyard where I have no business while she stomps along behind me saying words that would ignite bonfires.

If Albert hears her, our goose is cooked. Or is that our geese? Holy cow. I think I'm going crazy.

Suddenly a big hulk looms out of the darkness. "Psst, Lovie. Up ahead." I grab her arm and she switches off her light and her mouth at the same time. We both come to a dead halt, *dead* not being a prophetic word, I hope. If there was ever a time to practice being a cabbage, now is it. I stand so still I can practically hear the sweat inching down my face.

"You should have brought a weapon," Lovie whispers.

"Too late now."

If that very large man turns in our direction, we can forget about finding out who wants Santa dead. We'll be boogieing on up to Glory Land full of bullet holes. Or worse.

"Distract him, Callie." In the dark, I feel Lovie inching away.

"Wait. What are you doing?"

"I'm going to get behind him and knock his brains out."

"He's dangerous. I say we stay put."

"And wait for him to get the jump on us? *Distract*, Callie."

Distraction comes, all right, but it's not from me. Next door, the Jenkins' little cocker spaniel makes enough ruckus to wake the dead.

Lovie says a word that would make them keel right back over.

Through the darkness Butch's wife Wanda calls out, "Sadie, baby, what is it?"

Sadie baby is too close to the hedge for comfort. If she gets brave enough to scramble through, Lovie and I might as well prepare to spend Christmas in jail.

Grabbing hold of my cousin's arm in case she decides to use this distraction for her foolhardy plan, I hold my breath.

"Is anybody there?" Wanda yells.

"Does she expect a thief to answer?"

"Hush, Lovie. She'll hear us."

"Not unless she has X-ray ears."

Suddenly the Jenkins' yard lights up like the White House Christmas tree. It's Wanda's floodlights, pouring across the hedge.

Tackling Lovie, I drop onto my stomach and see the incredible hulk in Albert's yard in full, living color. It's Santa, the jolly old man in red who appears on the rooftop at Gas, Grits, and Guts every Christmas. If I weren't afraid Wanda was going to hear me and call Sheriff Trice, I'd laugh myself silly. Here we are, out to catch a murderer, and both of us are cowering at the feet of a plastic Santa.

"Wanda!" It's Butch, calling to his wife. Let's hope he's not headed into his back yard. "What's going on out there, pumpkin pie?"

"It's just Sadie. Go back to watching *True Blood*, sweet pooky dookums."

Lovie pinches me and I pinch her back. I can tell by her strangled sounds that she's about to explode with laughter. Who would have thought? Mooreville's mild-mannered TV weatherman and his equally shy wife have a hot thing going.

The back door slams—Butch and Wanda going back inside, I hope. I do a slow count to three, and just when I'm getting ready to rise, Wanda screams, "I said, who's there?" Meanwhile her nosey cocker spaniel sniffs closer to the hedge and barks like she's on the trail of bears.

The only good thing I can say about this situation is that I didn't bring Elvis. He considers every dog in the neighborhood his competition and takes every opportunity to prove his superiority. Not that he's a fighter, but he does like to lord it over the lesser dogs.

From this perspective—shivering and cowering on the cold ground—I see that Fayrene's Santa has company, a pile of Santas with firewood laid in a circle around them. Proof positive that Albert Gordon is planning a big bonfire.

"Lovie, look."

"All we need are marshmallows."

Bound for her to think about food at a time like this. A hundred-and-ninety-pound bombshell—and every inch of her generous-hearted—Lovie is going to have a hard time getting back up.

I'm in tiptop shape, but if Wanda doesn't soon turn off the floodlights, even I will have a hard time rising off the ground. My left leg has a cramp, and my right's not feeling too perky.

Mercifully I hear her little dog yip as she scoops her up. Her back door slams, her yard goes dark, and I wait for total silence.

Finally I nudge Lovie. "Come on. That was a close call. Let's get this over with."

"Thank God I didn't bean Santa."

"It could be worse. We could be in handcuffs."

She grunts, and I roll to my knees, then spring up and sprint toward Albert's covered back porch. The screen door is open, so I slide through and lean against the wall. Guess who isn't leaning with me?

"Lovie?" No answer. Holy cow! I backtrack and nearly stumble over her. She's still sprawled on the ground in pitch blackness.

"Get the backhoe."

"Good grief, Lovie." I grab her hand and tug. She rises like Lazarus from the dead, and we race toward the porch. If early events are any indication, this evening is not going to turn out well.

Lovie props her baseball bat against the wall, sticks a hairpin into Albert's back-door lock and sets to work. My part in all this is playing lookout while I pray for protection from Mother Nature, Mother Theresa, and motherhood.

Lately, my cousin's had more practice picking locks than I care to think about. We're inside Albert's house in record time. Fortunately, he has left lamps burning, so Lovie doesn't have to use her penlight. Still, I grab her arm before she goes bulldozing through his kitchen.

"The curtains," I say, then drop to all fours. They're wide open. All Wanda and Butch have to do is look out their window to see us.

"If you think I'm getting down on my belly again you're crazy. I felt like a beached whale."

"Then stick to the shadows and come on."

"Where?"

"How should I know? If you'll care to remember, I'm not a professional crook."

She says a word that would defrost icicles, then creeps around the walls and vanishes through an open door. I crawl along behind her and find her standing in the middle of Albert's den. Lit by the glow of a desk lamp is an arsenal big enough to blow Mooreville off the map.

"Holy cow." The den curtains are closed, and I can walk around like a normal person to take stock. There are .44 Magnums in here and double-barreled shotguns and .38 pistols and weapons with names even a country girl who grew up on a farm south of Mooreville doesn't know. But you can bet your boots I intend to find out.

If I live to get to a computer.

"Lovie, are you thinking what I'm thinking?"

"Yes, this is a dangerous man. We need to get the hell out of Dodge."

"Wait." On a bookshelf I spot three framed photos of a grim-looking, dark-haired man I assume is Albert posing with his Special Forces buddies. Uncle Charlie is in two of the photos, the prominent horseshoe-shaped scar on his right forearm a dead giveaway.

"Lovie, look." I hand the photo to my cousin. In both pictures, Uncle Charlie's face is scratched out.

"Looks like Albert Gordon hated Daddy."

"The question is why? See what you can find in his desk."

While Lovie's riffling through Albert's desk, I hustle over to his file cabinets.

"What are we looking for?"

"Good grief, Lovie. I'm not Quantico. You'll know it when you see it."

I spot Albert's medical records when I hear a sound not found in nature. Whirling around I see Lovie sitting in Albert's chair with her feet propped on his desk eating a bag of potato chips.

"What in the world?"

"These were in his desk just going to waste. Since he's deprived me of my evening's entertainment, he owes me. Besides, I'm starving to death."

Considering she ate enough of Mama's roast beef to tide her over till New Year's Day, I doubt that. Still, I wouldn't let her stay for dessert, so I keep my smart remarks to myself and focus on the task at hand.

Albert's medical records go all the way back to his days in Special Forces. One in particular catches my eye. *Post-Traumatic Stress Disorder*, it reads.

"Hey, Lovie, do you think post-traumatic stress disorder could make Albert hate Christmas?"

"If I had it, I'd hate everything." She rams another handful of chips into her mouth. "Except food."

Suddenly a boom rocks the house and chips fly every which way.

"Hit the decks," Lovie yells.

I don't have to be told twice. Every window in the room lights up like Fourth of July fireworks. I don't know whether to scream or run.

Elvis' Opinion #8 on Love, Revenge, and Bachelor Buddies

Ordinarily, I enjoy being home alone with my human daddy, just two buddies hanging out. Jack always fixes us a bunch of snacks, and we pile up on the couch to watch the news or whatever sport happens to be seasonable.

Tonight, though, for all the attention Jack's paying me, I might as well be trying to get back into the "Crazy Arms" of that two-timing French poodle, Ann Margret. Listen, I'm a dog with my ear to the ground. Don't think I don't know she's come down with a "Fever" for Darlene's uppity Lhasa apso. William thinks he's the Dalai Lama. *Dalai Lama* my crooked leg! If he's ever had a lofty thought in his head, I'm Michael Jackson. And we all know I don't need a moon walk and a white glove.

Anyhow, ever since Ruby Nell drove us home, Jack's been trying to find out where Callie and Lovie are. Usually my human mom has him humming "Gentle on My Mind." But when she's with Lovie, Jack's always trying to figure a way to build a "Bridge Over Troubled Water."

He's in the kitchen now talking to Ruby Nell on the phone. I sidle in there and lick his ankle, a dog with a purpose. Number one would be getting a little smackeral of something good, preferably with sugar and grease.

Number two would be eavesdropping. Forget about southern manners. I've got as many as the next dog. But when it comes to protecting my human parents, I'll stoop to any low.

"I just wanted to make sure you got back safely after you brought me home," Jack is saying, and he means it, too. He thinks she hung the moon, and she thinks he walks on water. (Contrary to what some of my biographers wrote, I'm smart enough to know a hackneyed phrase when I say one. But do you think I give a "Flip, Flop, and Fly"? I got to be a worldwide icon and my biographers didn't. I've earned the right to talk any way I want to.)

"You're such a sweetie to check on me, Jack!" Ruby Nell is saying. "Naturally, I got home all right. I'm an expert driver." If Ruby Nell is a good driver, I'm Johnny Cash. If she gets one more speeding ticket, she's liable to be singing the "Folsom Prison Blues."

"With all the ruckus going on around Mooreville, I'm going to send Cal to spend the night with you when she gets home."

That's Jack's cagey way of finding out if Callie is already there. He has a snowball's chance in you-know-where of *sending* my human mom anywhere, and he knows it.

"I won't be here, hon. I'm heading out to spend the night at Charlie's."

"Is he okay?"

"To hear him tell it he is, but I'm not taking any chances."

When Jack pockets his cell phone, I seize my chance for food. I amble my handsome self center stage, meaning right in front of the kitchen cabinets and do my bringing-the-house-down version of "Don't Be Cruel."

That gets a laugh from Jack, but nary a bite. "Just a minute, boy."

Before I can say "Pup-Peroni," he's on the phone with Charlie. You might think "It Ain't No Big Thing" when he finds out Callie and Lovie aren't there, but let me tell you, "It's a Matter of Time" before somebody's head rolls. And the mood Jack's in, just about anybody's will do.

If he didn't have that cast, he'd be on his Harley and on my human mom's trail. As it is, he says a word Lovie would appreciate.

Listen, I know this is the time when a dog of my intelligence and compassion should try to make his human dad feel better. But you try being compassionate on an empty stomach, and see how much fun it is.

Holding my spot in center stage, I throw back my head and remind Jack not to "Put the Blame on Me." Listen, I'm a short dog with four feet and no opposable digits. I can't help it if these humans get into more trouble than I can get them out of.

And I know you're not supposed to end a sentence with a preposition, either. Learned that in the fifth grade at Lawhon Elementary while everybody else was making fun of my overalls. Now they're trying to outdo each other with I-knew-Elvis-when stories. But "That's Life." Learned that from old Blue Eyes himself.

I reckon I still have the stuff, because Jack bends down to scratch behind my ears, then hustles around fixing me a hefty snack of Milk Bone *and* Pup-Peroni.

"Don't tell Cal."

Does he think I'm "Crazy"? (I don't mind borrowing from Patsy Cline, either. That woman had some pipes.) As soon as I finish eating, my lips are sealed.

Since he can't get out of the house, Jack starts popping corn. Another tasty treat. If I hold my ears just right he'll let me have my own bag.

Sure enough, he takes one look at cute little me and puts another bag into the microwave. One pop out of the bag, and the kitchen window lights up like Mooreville's fixing to be raptured.

Before I can say, "There's No Room to Rhumba in a Sports Car," Jack is on the phone with the Lee County sheriff.

Don't let his cast fool you. My human daddy is still the man in charge.

Chapter 11

Lethal Games, Angry Neighbors, and Annie Get Your Gun

While Lovie and I cower on the floor of Albert's den, the ruckus from outside sounds like the Second Coming. With my face in Albert's dusty old rug and my hands over my head, I wait for I don't know what all to befall me.

"Lovie?" No answer. Holy cow, has she been kidnapped? "Lovie, are you okay?"

She says a word that will likely get her barred from the Pearly Gates—unless I can get there first and do some fast talking. But at least I know my cousin is still her sassy self.

Lifting myself on my elbow, I risk looking around. Everything is normal in here, meaning Albert's file cabinet is standing wide open, potato chips are everywhere, and his guns all look like they're pointed straight at me.

Outside the racket goes up several decibels. I begin to make out voices.

"That's my Santa. Grab him!" That's Fayrene.

"Are you kidding me?" That voice belongs to Roy Jessup of Mooreville Feed and Seed. I'd tell him Fayrene was not kidding, but I'm in hiding. "If you stick your hand in that fire, you'll bring back a burned nub."

Sirens scream. Probably Mooreville's Volunteer Fire Department to the rescue. Maybe even a Lee County squad car or two. Visions of jail dance in my head.

"Lovie, let's get out of here." In one fluid move I'm off the floor.

"Not so fast, missy."

Holy cow and pig and stockings, too. Albert Gordon looks exactly like his Vietnam photo as he faces me in full camouflage. A lethal-looking weapon is pointed at the chest of my cat burglar suit, which might as well be a red-sequined sweater for all the good it's doing me now. I'm going to have to start wearing a flak jacket.

The only good thing I can say about this situation is that I've never seen Lovie get off the floor so fast. You'd think she was the cousin who jogs three miles every day instead of the one who has three sausages and biscuits for breakfast, then one more with butter and jelly.

While I'm still staring into the barrel of a gun whose gauge I don't even want to know, Lovie grabs my arm and drags me into the kitchen faster than Elvis can chase my seven formerly stray cats. Albert is right behind us.

"Quick, Lovie. The back door."

She says a string of words that would stop a platoon of Army tanks. Through the glass panels, I can see why. The back door leads to a giant bonfire, a flock of angry neighbors trying to rescue burning Santas, Sheriff Trice, and two deputies, plus a troop of firemen trying to contain the blaze.

Lovie jerks me toward a door that goes no telling where. A hallway that leads to a bedroom, it turns out, but even I know better than to hide under the bed. If there's one thing all this unexpected sleuthing has taught me it's *never let yourself get cornered*.

"Come out, come out, wherever you are," Albert calls.

Holy cow! He's playing cat and mouse for keeps, and he's right on our trail. Thank goodness he apparently didn't see us duck in here. I hear loud footsteps as he stomps off in the opposite direction.

I try to shove open a window while Lovie stands guard with her baseball bat. I don't tell her it would be no match for Albert's gun. Let her live her last few minutes in ignorant bliss.

The window's stuck. This is an old house with at least three previous owners since I've lived in the neighborhood. The latch looks like it's covered with so many coats of paint it would take an act of God—or Jack Jones—to get it loose.

Putting my shoulder against the window, I give another big shove. Meanwhile, somebody at the back of the house pounds on the door while somebody else discharges a gun.

Forget shoving and pushing. I jerk off a perfectly good Donald J. Pliner ankle boot and proceed to ruin the heel by smashing the windowpane. Glass flies everywhere, including on me, but I have bigger worries than whether or not I'm going to bleed to death.

"Freeze!" Sheriff Trice yells.

I don't intend to stick around to find out whether I'm going to be shot by Albert or arrested by the sheriff.

Knocking the rest of the glass out, I yell, "Lovie, dive!"

With my long legs, I step right through the window. But I can't say the same for Lovie. She's stuck, the top half of her viewing freedom and the bottom half saluting whatever lies behind.

"Quick, Lovie. Reach for me."

I grab her hands and pull, but as hard as I tug, I can't get her to budge. In the bedroom I've just vacated, it sounds like Armageddon.

Any minute now, Lovie's going to say something noble like,

128

"Save yourself, Cal. Run!" But of course, I'd never leave my cousin.

What she really says is, "If you don't get my big ass out of here, I'm never sharing another secret with you as long as I live."

So much for noble.

I brace one leg against the side of Albert's house and give another tug. Lovie pops through with the ease of a cork shot from a champagne bottle. As she lands in an undignified heap on the ground, I'm looking straight through the shattered window into the grinning face of Sheriff Trice.

"I thought you could use a little help from this side, Miss Callie." He tips his hat and winks. Behind him, I spot a deputy I don't know leading Albert off in handcuffs.

"Aren't you going to arrest us, too?"

"I never saw you. Have a nice evening." With another tip of the hat, he's gone.

"Jack's doings, no doubt," Lovie says from her throne on the ground.

"How do you know? Maybe Sheriff Trice just likes me."

"It was my royal backside he had his hands on. Get me up from here."

"If you're going to start issuing orders, you ought to wear a crown." I help her up for the last time, I hope.

"Next time I will."

"Furthermore, I don't think Sheriff Trice's assistance has anything to do with your Holy Grail. Or your National Treasure, either."

"Don't be too sure about that."

The next thing I know Lovie will be trying to overcome her grief as Santa's almost-widow by flirting outrageously with our tough "Walking Tall" sheriff.

If I don't do something, and fast, she's going to end up trying to be Lee County's answer to Mrs. Buford Pusser. But I can't think about that right now. I'm too busy running from trouble and getting punctured by Albert's prickly hedge. As I hotfoot it across Butch Jenkins' yard hoping his little dog doesn't come out and finish off what's left of me, I pray to every goddess I know, including Martha Stewart.

Tonight I've been shot at, slashed with thorns and flying glass, and almost arrested. All I want is a nice bath, a cup of hot chocolate, and Elvis.

Well, who doesn't want Elvis, but I'm talking about my dog. And I'll have to say, with his cute little wiggle and his funny basset grin and his silly, howling imitation of "Blue Christmas" he's a wonderful substitute.

Not that I can go home after tonight's fiasco. It's bad enough that Jack tries to keep tabs on my dates. If he sees my cuts and scratches, there's no telling what he'd do.

Lovie and I have almost reached my truck when I hear Wanda calling her dog. "Sadie, baby. Where are you?"

Maybe I should have prayed to Oprah.

I freeze, hoping Wanda won't turn on the light. Suddenly I spot Sadie baby, streaking around the side of the house.

"If that little dog barks, we're done for."

"Not yet." Lovie shoulders her baseball bat. "The next person who comes after me is asking for a big headache."

About that time, Sadie baby sidles up to me and pees on my designer boots. If Lovie laughs, I'm going to give her a cheap Christmas present.

Fortunately, she doesn't, and Sadie trots peacefully back to the front porch, where Wanda says, "Did Mommy's widdle baby do her widdle potty?"

"All over my cousin's boots," Lovie deadpans.

"They were old." I flounce into my truck and slam the door.

"Phew." Lovie slams the other door. "Don't turn on the heater."

"Roll your window down and don't say another word."

Lovie's nobody's fool. She knows when I've reached my limit. She's over there on the passenger side with her lip zipped, which happens only once in a blue moon. The only racket she makes is the rattling of her paper bag as she rummages for food. Chocolate, it turns out. I could smell it a mile away.

"Aren't you going to offer me a bite?"

"You said not to say another word."

"Smarty pants." I reach, palm up, and she breaks off a chunk of Hershey's with almonds, our comfort food of choice. Though after all we've been through tonight, it would take a six pack to settle my nerves.

My cell phone rings, and I nearly jump out of my borrowed baggy cat burglar suit. It's Mama.

"Jack's looking for you."

"Mama, what happened to *hello*?"

"Where are you?"

"In my truck."

"Going where?"

"To Lovie's, if you must know."

"Is that any way to act while I'm still making my Christmas gift list? Besides, since when is it a crime for a mother to ask her only daughter's whereabouts on the most dangerous night in Mooreville's entire history? It's a wonder the whole neighborhood didn't go up in flames."

Naturally, Fayrene has already given Mama a blow-by-blow report of the doings at Albert Gordon's bonfire. I just hope she didn't find out Lovie and I had an up-close-and-personal view. Still, Mama's exaggerating, as usual. But that doesn't mean I'd want her to see me in my present condition.

I decide to try placation. "Don't worry, Mama. My neighborhood is safe, and I'm all right."

"Then why are you going to Lovie's?"

To plot our next move is not something I want to say to Mama.

"We're having a spend-the-night party."

"Flitter."

"Mama, what does that mean?" I ask, but she has already hung up. With her, *flitter* can mean any number of things from *why didn't you include me?* to *I don't believe a word you're saying.*

"What did Aunt Ruby Nell want?"

"To be in the middle of my business."

"Cheer up, Callie. At least Aunt Ruby Nell's got good health and a lively sense of humor."

"Yeah, and most of my bank account."

Though I'll have to admit that ever since Mama left off *restorative gambling* (her words, not mine) and took up dancing with the wrong partner, I've been making fiscal progress. At the rate I'm saving money, next spring I might be able to paint a beach scene on the walls of my beauty shop, add a tanning bed and a massage table, and turn the back room at Hair.Net into a tropical spa.

The idea cheers me considerably. And so does the second big chunk of chocolate Lovie hands me.

By the time we reach the city limits, I'm almost in a good mood. It's further enhanced by the sight of the lighted snowflakes that line the streets of Tupelo and a glimpse of Christmas trees though the windows in Lovie's neighborhood.

"Lovie, is that a car in front of your house?"

She says a word that will get her on Santa's lump of coal in the stocking list. "What if the killer's not Albert? What if it's somebody else and we're his next target?"

"Duck. I'm going to drive on by. If he's looking for two people, maybe he won't notice you."

Too much snooping can get you killed. I'd take the lesson to heart if the Santa killer hadn't almost snuffed out Uncle Charlie. Whoever's waiting up ahead can forget about scaring me off. I'm a woman with two mortgages, eight animal mouths to feed, and a dangerous man in my bedroom. Nothing daunts me.

Still, I hold the steering wheel in a death grip and make myself stick to the speed limit. Approaching Lovie's house at a crawl, I get a hard close look at the car parked crooked in front of her house.

Naturally, it's a red Mustang convertible. Even if I didn't know this is just the kind of thing Mama would do—lie in wait for us—the vanity tag gives her away. *Queen Ruby 1.*

"Relax, Lovie. It's Mama." I spot her on the front porch, unmistakable in a caftan that makes her look like the queen of a small exotic country. And with her is another shadowy figure that can only be Uncle Charlie. "Your daddy's with her."

"Busted," Lovie says.

"Big time."

I park behind Mama's Mustang, take a few deep breaths, then climb down from my Dodge Ram to face the music. And you can bet it won't be "Joy to the World."

Elvis' Opinion #9 on Mooreville's Godfather, Tacky Gifts, and One Smart Dog

I guess you're wondering why Jack's sitting calmly in front of the TV eating popcorn when Ruby Nell calls to report that Callie's spending the night with Lovie. It's because he already knows my human mom is safe. Sheriff Trice didn't waste any time calling to fill Jack in on all the details of what went down at the Gordon house.

Listen, though nobody around here knows Jack's true profession except me and Charlie and now, unfortunately, my human mom, who worries too much, Jack is a cross between the Godfather and the Terminator. He's dark, dangerous, and mysterious. If you want to be "King of the Whole Wide World," that's the way to go. We may not be rolling in "Money Honey," but we've got "Respect." (I'm sure that fabulous soul sister Aretha Franklin won't mind a nod to her hit song.)

And speaking of respect, here comes that silly cocker spaniel sneaking into the den. I can smell his intent a mile away. He's trying to weasel his way into my human daddy's affections. And at Christmas, to boot.

Listen, short hairy runt. That's my job. I'm top dog around here. Numero uno. (I speak a bit of Spanish, too, I'm proud to admit.)

I bare my teeth at him and show a few hackles. If Hoyt the Lesser is looking for company, let him go back to his inferior bed and "Reach Out to Jesus."

Fortunately for his little crooked, sawed-off legs, Hoyt tucks his tail and slinks back where he came from. Listen, I'm a dog of importance. I know how to "Make the World Go Away."

One problem down and one to go. I sashay my handsome self back to Jack and make a valiant but failed attempt to leap onto the sofa. But if you're thinking I should go on a diet, tell it to "Western Union."

"Need some help, Elvis?"

Jack picks me up and settles me against his right leg, which, as far as I'm concerned is the cat-bird seat. Then he turns his attention back to the TV. QVC, to be exact.

His credit card and a note pad are at the ready, and he's taking notes and listing numbers. Well, bless'a my soul, Jack Jones is doing a little Christmas shopping.

Currently, he's listening to a stunning woman named Lisa who is making an ugly polyester blouse sound like something no woman can live without. To my horror, Jack jots down the number. I may have to heft myself off this couch, get down on paws and knees, and beg for a "Marguerita." Callie wouldn't be caught dead in that blouse. For one thing, it has polka dots, which she can't abide. For another, it's the wrong color for her skin tone.

I know a thing or two about style. What do you think I do around that beauty shop all day? Whistle "Dixie"?

I punch a paw down on the remote, and the channel switches to CNN, where you can listen to disaster all day long. Let me tell you, anything's better than a tacky, inappropriate Christmas gift.

"Cut that out." Jack switches back to QVC, where, thank "Mary Lou Brown" and "Maybelline" both, that ugly blouse is "Gone, Baby, Gone."

Now Lisa is touting a pair of pants that not even Fayrene, who has the fashion sense of Larry King, would wear. Jack's jotting order numbers like his life depends on it.

Haven't I taught him a single thing about romance? If he wants back in Callie's good graces, not to mention back in the marriage he never wanted to leave in the first place, he'll scroll through the TV menu till he finds an online shopping show that features fine jewelry.

Wrap an expensive emerald in a pretty package, take a few voice lessons from yours truly, and Jack could have Callie singing, "Today, Tomorrow and Forever."

Chapter 12

Caught Red-handed, Something Foul's Afoot, and Flitter

I hop out of my Dodge Ram primed for an argument with Mama, but to tell the truth, the little girl in me is really glad to see her. When I was growing up on the farm, Lovie and I were always getting into trouble doing things we'd been told not to. But Mama was always there with a scolding, followed by milk and cookies, a big hug, and a Band-Aid. She can skip the scolding, but I sure could use all the rest.

As I climb the steps to Lovie's front porch, I'm trying to decide whether to play defense or offense. Lovie saves me the trouble of tough decisions. Breezing past everybody, she unlocks the front door and calls over her shoulder, "Come on in. Take a load off. I'll put on the coffee."

She presses the light switch, and Mama sees all my sleuthing wounds. She narrows her blue eyes and purses her lips. I stand in front of her like a six-year-old waiting for the third degree, punctuated by umpteen "Carolinas" and "Flitters."

Instead, she hugs me for such a long time I'm close to crying. Finally she clears her throat, leads me to the sofa, and pulls me down beside her. It's like she doesn't want to be three inches from me.

"Callie, one of these days your stubborn sense of duty is going to get you killed. What in the world happened to you?"

Uncle Charlie has taken a seat in the wing chair across from us and is sitting there like a quiet, benevolent godfather, a man who will do anything to protect his family.

I start telling about Albert Gordon's Santa bonfire, leaving out a few harrowing details. Halfway through the heavily edited version, Lovie comes in with four steaming cups of coffee on a tray with cream and sugar. She's added a little chicory, and the taste reminds me of being in the French Quarter in New Orleans.

She's also bearing first-aid ointment and Band-Aids.

Ignoring her drink, Mama grabs the first-aid supplies and sets to work patching my scratches, even the ones that don't need it. By the time she's finished, I'm going to look like Frankenstein's bride. ·

At the end of my story, everybody sits in silence. This is the first Valentine Christmas marred by murder, and I think we're still in a state of disbelief about how close one of our own came to being the victim.

Mama picks up her cup and gives my cousin her famous dramatic look. "I hope you've got some Prohibition Punch back there. Before this night is over, we're going to need it."

Everybody laughs, but it's the nervous kind of laughter when you're trying too hard to see the bright side of things.

"I don't want you two putting yourselves in any more danger," Uncle Charlie says. "I've already told the Tupelo police about Albert Gordon's beef against me."

"What is it, Charlie?"

I can tell he'd like us to move on to another subject, but Uncle Charlie can never deny Mama.

"When we were in Special Forces together, Albert's temper kept him from moving up in the ranks. He blamed me."

"For Pete's sake, Daddy. Why?"

"Who knows how a mind like that works? I got the promotions and he didn't."

"Is there anybody else in Tupelo who might have a beef against you, Uncle Charlie?"

He lifts his eyebrows at me, a signal that he knows full well I'm not going to sit on the sidelines and play it safe while any member of the Valentine family is at risk.

"You might as well tell us, Charlie. The girls are pretty darned good amateur sleuths, and so am I."

Lovie's about to burst, but she has the good sense not to let Mama see how hard she's holding back laughter. As for me, I'm glad to have Mama's support. Let me tell you, any woman who can write such offbeat tombstone sayings and make a success of it is formidable.

"There's Abel Caine," Uncle Charlie says. "He did time because of my testimony."

"One of Katrina's victims?" I know him because I was one of the volunteers processing the hurricane refugees who took shelter in Tupelo's Bancorp South Coliseum. I remember him because his name is so unusual.

"Like so many of Katrina's survivors, Abel fell in love with Tupelo and stayed. He finally got a job at Mike's Tires."

"How much time did he do, Charlie?"

"Ten years."

"Holy cow. I'd say that's motive."

"Callie's right." Mama grabs a pencil off Lovie's end table and scribbles on the edge of a newspaper lying on her coffee table. "Who else wants you dead, Charlie?"

"Nelda Lou Perkins, Miss Vardaman Sweet Potato, 1966, once told me she'd rather see me dead than lose me."

Uncle Charlie's eyes are twinkling, but Mama's are not. In fact, she's so mad I can practically see sparks shooting off her.

"If Nelda Lou messes with my family, I'll send her back to
Calhoun County and put her where sweet potatoes belong.
Under the ground."

"Now, now dear heart."

"Don't you *dear heart* me, Charles Sebastian Valentine. I'm
not going to take this sitting down." Mama jerks up her car
keys. "I'm taking you back to your apartment. Then the girls
and I have some sleuthing to do."

"Ruby Nell, I strongly advise against that. This case is liable to turn nasty."

"Flitter. If you think *nasty* scares a dyed-in-the-wool farm
girl like me, you've got another think coming, Charlie."

Mama winks at me and flounces out. For the first time since
I've known him, Uncle Charlie looks helpless. It looks like
the electric shock shook him more than I had imagined.

"What am I going to do with your mother?"

I take hold of his arm. "She's right about you being home,
Uncle Charlie. I'll take you to her car, and when she comes
back here, Lovie and I will figure out how to keep her nose
out of this case."

Lovie grabs the empty cups and heads to the kitchen.
When Uncle Charlie and I step onto her front porch, the night
sky has turned splendid, like a picture postcard of winter constellations you'd want to frame.

"I know you're not going to stop until the killer is found.
But please remember, dear heart, that Jack can't be of much
help till he's out of his cast. And until I'm stronger, neither
can I."

"I know. We'll try not to repeat tonight's performance at Albert's bonfire."

"Take Jack to the farm, and let him help you with some target practice."

"You think I need to pack a gun?"

"Not until you can blow a hole in something smaller than the side of a barn."

I'm glad to see Uncle Charlie's sense of humor is still intact. I wave as he climbs into the passenger side of the Mustang, where Mama's waiting with the music turned up too loud. You can hear "Winter Wonderland" all over Lovie's neighborhood. I just hope her neighbors have enough Christmas spirit not to call the cops to report us for disturbing the peace.

I watch until the Mustang disappears around the corner, then hurry inside, where Lovie is wearing a purple robe and crown and holding her green plastic pitcher of Prohibition Punch.

"A crown?"

"Drink this. Queen's orders."

"Queen, my foot. More like the cousin who would still be stuck in Albert's window if it hadn't been for me."

"Water under the bridge."

"Amen."

We both flop onto the sofa. In Lovie's too-big clothes and a gazillion Band-Aids, I look like a refugee from a beleaguered country.

Still, I'm neck-deep in murder, and there are things I need to know. With my Prohibition Punch in easy reach, I open Lovie's laptop and educate myself on weapons.

"Did you know Albert had a Glock and a Ruger?"

She looks up from the telephone directory. "What I want to know is where Abel Caine lives."

"After tonight's fiasco, you want to break and enter again?"

"Have you ever known anything to stop me?" I giggle thinking of the many obstacles that didn't deter Lovie—a pigeon caught in her hair, a dunking in the Peabody fountain, a Mayan tribe who thought she was the Moon Goddess.

"See," she adds. "There's your answer. Besides, I sure don't want to confront him face to face."

"Neither do I. And if the Santa killer is after Uncle Charlie, I think he's the most logical suspect. But what are we going to do about Mama?"

"Give her plenty of punch."

"Not unless we're going to drive her back to Uncle Charlie's."

"We can handle that. After tonight, I'd say we can handle anything."

"Except maybe that Abel Caine character. I don't like the thought of breaking and entering the house of an ex-con, Lovie."

"Then what do you propose? There's a Santa slayer still on the loose, and you're still on the cops' suspect list."

My cousin doesn't have to remind me. Furthermore, there's a former operative from the Company sitting in his apartment over Eternal Rest Funeral Home wondering how to keep us out of harm's way (Uncle Charlie) and an active one (Jack Jones) sitting in my living room, most likely watching TV with Elvis, and he would probably chain me to the bed if he saw me now.

And I'm not talking about for kinky purposes, either.

But I'm fresh out of plans. Steam, too, it seems. All I want to do is lean my head against the back of the sofa and fall asleep.

Lovie's having the same trouble. We'd probably both have toppled headlong into slumber, where visions of sugar plums would be outnumbered by nightmares of murder, if Mama hadn't come storming back into the house.

"Ha!" She makes a beeline for the Prohibition Punch. "If somebody doesn't get me a glass in two seconds flat, I'm drinking straight from the pitcher."

Lovie prances off toward the kitchen and is back with another glass before Mama even sits down.

"The very idea." She slugs back Lovie's special recipe, which features vodka and enough other strong spirits to cure just about any ailment you can think of, except a case of hubris. Which Mama has in spades. "The nerve."

"Mama, what on earth are you talking about?"

"Nelda Lou What's Her Face."

"I don't see her at the top of the suspect list, Aunt Ruby Nell."

"Lovie's right. As far as we know, she was nowhere near the mall when Santa and Rudolph died. We don't know if she even has a connection with Steve Boone and Wayne. And having the hots for Uncle Charlie is hardly motive for murder."

"Wash your mouth out with soap, Carolina. I want that witch checked out from her knobby knees to her crows' feet."

"Mama, you don't even know her."

"I don't need to and I don't intend to. I know what I know."

I wonder where she got her information. Bobby's psychic blue eye? But I'm not about to ask. Tonight I've had enough weird happenings to last a lifetime.

I try to steer the conversation in a more sensible and productive direction.

"Abel Caine is the one Lovie and I intend to investigate. He certainly has motive, and he probably had means and opportunity."

"Flitter."

Lovie's laughing so hard her crown is crooked. "Aunt Ruby Nell, would you please explain what that means."

"It means whatever I want it to."

"Would you care to enlighten us, Mama?"

"I've come up with a plan, that's what it means. I'm not leaving Charlie's side while that heifer's on the loose."

143

"That's a wise plan, Mama. I'm proud of you." Now I don't have to worry about keeping her occupied and out of everybody's hair.

"Watching after Charlie is not what I'm talking about, Carolina. If you'll stop acting like I'm senile and in need of Depends, I'll tell you my plan."

If it's like any number of Mama's wild ideas, I don't want to know. Still, at this point Lovie and I are out of ideas, out of sorts, and almost out of chocolate.

"Tell us, Mama. Any plan is better than none." I sincerely hope those are not my famous last words.

Elvis' Opinion #10 on Normal, Taking Care of Business, and Plans That Don't Include Yours Truly

Bright and early Monday morning, my human mom and I arrive to start the week off right by making Mooreville's glitterati beautiful. Jack wasn't too happy with her when she sashayed home this morning after spending the night at Lovie's without so much as a "Love Letter in the Sand" (a Pat Boone song I could have done justice to). Still, he's a man on a mission—i.e., getting out of "Heartbreak Hotel." He knows when to express his opinions and when to keep them to himself.

He was just glad I'd be along to take care of Callie today. Forget what the uninformed think about me. Jack knows I can take care of business better than the next dog. He even got a lightning-bolt charm to put on my dog collar just to prove it.

So now here I am having a little afternoon siesta with one eye open, taking care of business.

If you want to find out everything worth knowing, spend the day in Callie's beauty shop. Everybody who is anybody (including the Tupelo mayor's wife, Junie Mae) comes to Hair.Net. While Callie's shampooing Junie Mae, I'm ensconced on another of the pink satin, guitar-shaped pillows my human mom keeps in the shop especially for my relaxation and cogitation. (Listen, contrary to a few snarky reporters, I can use ten-dollar words as well as the next singer. Better than most. When I was holed up in a hotel room hiding from fans who wanted to rip my clothes off—don't you wish!—I read the *Encylopedia Britannica* and *Webster's Collegiate*, too. I'm nobody's "Fool.")

The TV weatherman's wife, Wanda, is under the dryer, letting her permanent wave set. Darlene's in the manicurist chair, consulting the horoscope before she paints Lovie's nails. And little David is under the sinks with his Tonka truck, making sounds like a Peterbilt rig. Fortunately for everybody concerned, Darlene left that two-timing Lhasa apso William with Fayrene today. Ever since he's been making eyes at my former French sweetie, I've been laying for him.

But if you think everything is normal here at the best little beauty shop in town, then I "Really Don't Want to Know" what you think about anything else.

Lovie's not here to get her nails done. She likes to do them herself. She's here so she and Callie can finalize details on Ruby Nell's sleuthing plan. Don't think I came by this information because "I Got Lucky" either. I'm a dog with radar ears. And if that doesn't work, I stoop to any low to get the goods, including eavesdropping. That's what I did when Lovie arrived out-of-breath from catering a Christmas luncheon at All Saints Episcopal in Tupelo and the two of them hurried off to Callie's office.

I just ambled my good-looking self over to the door, lay down like I was the "Keeper of the Key," and dared anybody to cross my portly body. And bless'a my soul, did I get an earful. It seems the two cousins are going sleuthing tonight, all dolled up as former beauty queens. Not that they consider Nelda Lou Perkins a serious suspect. They're only going to placate Ruby Nell, who came up with the plan. Callie won't be packing heat, but she will be including yours truly.

Listen, I'm not a dog to take rejection lightly. Any more of this business about "leaving Elvis behind" and I'll be packing up my Pup-Peroni and howling "I'm Movin' On." There are plenty of good homes that would welcome a famous singer with a heart as gold as his records—even if I am wearing a basset hound suit.

For now, though, I wait for this evening's adventure and listen to Wanda holding forth on Albert Gordon's bonfire.

"That old toot nearly burned my house down."

"Law," the mayor's wife says, "I almost cried when I saw those burning Santas on TV."

"Most of them were just singed, Junie Mae. Butch went over there after the fire was put out and brought ours back. He's home now scrubbing Santa Claus with Ajax."

"Does anybody know why Albert did it?" Darlene asks. "The TV news didn't say."

Lovie shoots Callie a *look*, and my human mom winks.

"All I know is he had an accomplice." Wanda's holding the floor. It's obvious she considers herself an expert since she was next door to Mooreville's biggest drama since Ruby Nell hung the nude Modigliani over her dining room table. "You ought to see my hedge where they escaped. If whoever it was sets foot on my property again, he'd better watch out. Sadie can identify him by scent."

"Darlene!" Lovie speaks so loud everybody jumps. "I want ruby red on my nails."

"Your horoscope says 'Curb your impetuous nature. Caution advised.' So I'm going with the shell pink."

Wanda opens her mouth to keep her story going, but Lovie is too quick for her.

"I don't give a lump of coal what my horoscope says, Darlene. I'm going with red."

The mayor's wife, all decked out in a dress the color of

Pepto-Bismol, adds her two cents, "I'd go with the shell pink, dear. It matches everything."

"It's not Christmassy," Wanda says. "Go red, Lovie."

Around the beauty shop, everybody's business is discussed and voted on by whoever happens to be here. It's a small democracy where the majority usually rules unless Ruby Nell is here. Then we get a queen without the parliament.

"Red," Lovie tells Darlene, who has the good sense to stop arguing. I can tell from the way she pinches her nose before she grabs the nail polish that she doesn't like it. She and Bobby will probably have a long discussion this evening about people who don't take advice from the stars and the dead.

And don't think I don't know about their date. He called at lunchtime while she was having a pimento and cheese sandwich in the break room, and I heard both ends of the conversation. To keep on Fayrene's good side, those two are having to tread "Gently." Not that Fayrene's even close to losing her psychic. Listen, Darlene's been twice burned at the altar, and Bobby's not the marrying kind.

I guess I'm not either or I'd have made an honest dog out of Ann Margret before the puppies were born. "Que Sera Sera."

Here comes David, dripping ice cream down his elbows. Excuse me while I get in a lick or two before I leave with Callie and Lovie for some detective legwork.

Chapter 13

Faded Beauty, Bogus Pageants, and the Shrimp Queen

As soon as my clients leave Hair.Net and Darlene sets off with her darling little boy, I set to work on transforming Lovie into the former Kudzu Queen.

Not that there ever was such a title, but there ought to be. When the U.S. Department of Agriculture imported a bunch of Japanese kudzu in the misguided attempt to halt erosion, the foreign vine became a Frankenstein's monster that not only blanketed northeast Mississippi's pines and deciduous trees but also took over telephone poles, fences, and abandoned barns and houses. If I stood still long enough, kudzu would grow right over me and then just keep on going.

"Higher." Lovie's talking about her hair. She's got more than any two women I know, every bit of it curly and the lush golden red you can't get from a bottle, I don't care how good your coloring skills are.

I'm doing an upswept style that she says no beauty queen worth her crown would be without.

"If I take it any higher, you won't be able to walk under light fixtures."

"I'll worry about that when the time comes. I want to look authentic."

If anybody looks like a former beauty queen, it's Lovie. She's got the stature, the high color, and the big personality to carry it off. On the other hand, I'm skin and bones with sleek hair that's not going to pouf no matter what I do. I'd do well to pass myself off as a former Little Miss Mosquito. A title Lovie has already nixed.

I anchor Lovie's hair with one last bobby pin, and she starts slathering on as much makeup as I use to fix up the dead.

"Don't you think that's a tad too much?"

"TV washes you out."

"You're not going to be on TV."

"Yes, but Nelda Lou won't know that. I want to look the part."

"Did you come up with a name for me?"

"Not yet. Just zip me into this dress, and let's get this show on the road."

It takes three attempts, but I finally zip Lovie into a green-sequined evening gown so small that if she takes a deep breath she'll split its seams. I slide into a red-sequined pageant gown I borrowed from Darlene under the pretext I might need it for a Christmas party with Champ. I pride myself on honesty, but when a little white lie is the only thing that will do, I can rise to the occasion as well as the next woman.

Seized by inspiration, I tie a big red Christmas bow onto Elvis' dog collar and snap on his red leash.

"What're you doing, Cal?"

"The last time we went snooping he got out of the truck. I'm not taking that chance again. I've decided to be the former Queen of Animal Rescue and he can be my mascot. Besides, Elvis will protect us."

When Lovie looks skeptical, Elvis bares his teeth and growls. I swear, my dog knows everything I say. I guess it comes from me talking to him all the time, which is what a good dog mom is supposed to do. Furthermore, I'll be hanging a Christmas stocking for him and getting him presents.

I do my shiny hair in a quick French twist, add a rhinestone comb, and we're off for an evening of sleuthing. I hope it comes out better than our last time.

Nelda Lou lives in Highland Circle, one of Tupelo's oldest neighborhoods. Located just one block east of the busy Gloster Street, a generic north/south four-lane lined with fast-food restaurants, motels, drugstores, and service stations, the prestigious Highland Circle is tucked behind brick columns and insulated from traffic noise by ancient trees surrounding upscale houses on huge lots.

As I cruise through the neighborhood looking for Nelda Lou's house, I notice that most of the houses are dark except for huge Christmas trees alight in their front windows. Most people are shopping or going to countless Christmas parties and church pageants. Down here in the Bible Belt, you can count on seeing some version of the reenactment of Joseph and Mary following the Star of Bethlehem at least fifteen times during the holidays.

We're in luck, though. Nelda Lou's red-brick Georgian house is ablaze with lights, and there's an ancient Volvo in the driveway.

"Here we go, Lovie. Act like a queen."

"Don't I always?"

"Not if Mama gets there first."

Snapping on Elvis' leash, I get my dog out of the truck, tell him to behave, smooth down my dress, and try to channel my inner queen. This is hard. I don't think I have one. Two queens in the family are more than enough. I think of myself more as a trusted adviser. I'm just grateful not to be dressed as a man.

"Tonight I get to talk, Lovie."

"Does that mean I get to lose my life in dark basements and discover dead bodies in freezers? Whoopee, Callie."

"Sarcasm doesn't become you. We'll just play it by ear. I don't think Nelda Lou has a single thing to hide."

I just hope those are not famous last words.

Lovie prisses up the sidewalk ahead of me. As I follow along behind, I try on a beauty queen strut. Elvis makes a noise that I swear sounds like a doggie guffaw.

I'm about to punch the doorbell when Lovie's cell phone rings. She says a quick *hello*, followed by a brief pause and, "Save yourself some trouble, Rocky. I wouldn't go out with you if you were the only man on earth." Much to my dismay, she hangs up without another word.

"Is he coming here?"

"Not if he's got half a brain."

"What would it hurt to talk to him face to face? Besides, it's Christmas, Lovie."

"What does Christmas have to do with my Holy Grail?"

I'm about to answer her when the front door bursts open. The woman backlit by twinkling Christmas tree lights looks like an Amazon. Besides that, she's toting a double-barreled shot gun, and it's aimed straight at body parts I'd rather not lose.

Lovie and I both jump back, and Elvis gets his hackles up.

"What's all this racket out here?" If this is Nelda Lou, her voice hasn't lost a bit of its strength since her beauty queen days. I can picture her belting out a musical number you could hear clear to the Alabama state line.

I punch Lovie, and she leaps to the rescue. "Hello! I'm Darling Stevens, former Kudzu Queen, and this is my friend, Dimple Culpepper, former Miss Mississippi Canine Rescue with her sweet little ole mascot, Rudy."

"I never heard of that contest." The gun is still pointed at us.

"It's not well known," I say, and Lovie steps on my toes.

"It's quite elite and politically correct," Lovie adds, "which I'm sure a woman with your beauty queen record can certainly appreciate. You are Nelda Lou Perkins, aren't you?"

"I am." The former Miss Sweet Potato unbends a bit and lowers her gun, but she's still blocking the door. "What are ya'll doing out here without your coats?"

"I left my fur in the truck," Lovie says. "It's a bit ostentatious for calling on neighbors, don't you think?"

"I wouldn't know. I don't believe in wearing dead animals."

A woman after my own heart. Before Lovie makes another gaff, I step into the breach.

"Actually, we're chairing the newly formed Little Miss Tupelo Toddler Christmas pageant, and we need some expert advice."

"Why didn't ya'll say so in the first place?" She steps out of the way and motions us inside. Considering the gun, I'm thinking we shouldn't even go in. Still, Lovie barrels ahead, and I can't let her go without me. I tag along behind, keeping a tight hold on Elvis' leash. His hackles are still up and he's eyeing Nelda Lou's skinny, slacks-clad legs with the same look he gets right before he pees on my favorite shoes.

As Nelda Lou leads us into a musty-smelling room featuring Victorian furniture with faded rose satin cushions, she regales us with her history of pulchritude.

"I have the distinction of entering more beauty pageants than anybody in Mississippi. Fifty, total! I was Little Miss everything you can name. Then in 1955 I won two titles in a row. Miss Pascagoula and Miss Hospitality. It was my talent that did it. I imitated the Singing River!"

She gives us a coy smile, and I smile back. Not because I'm

impressed that she was the Singing River, but because she has finally put down her gun.

With the threat of sudden death removed, I observe my surroundings. Marble-topped tables. Lamps with fringed shades. Books with leather binders and gold lettering. Expensive Oriental wool rugs. The former Miss Sweet Potato has done well for herself.

On the bookshelves behind her sofa, I spot a line of framed photos. One of them shows her under a charity ball banner posing in a red evening gown with a man in a tuxedo who looks exactly like the newspaper picture I saw of the mall's regular Santa—Nathan Briggs. Another shows a younger, prettier version of Nelda Lou with her arm around none other than Lovie's newly murdered fiancé.

Maybe Mama was right about Nelda Lou being a valid suspect.

"That's a beautiful girl in the photo behind you," I say. "Your daughter?"

"Yes. And her husband."

"Husband?" Lovie spots her recently murdered fiance's photo and turns pale. She may be outrageous, but she draws the line at husband-stealing.

"Well, I guess you'd call him *former,* but they were seeing each other again."

Nelda Lou's lips are pursed, and her body language is tight. If she's like Mama, that's a sure sign she didn't like her former son-in-law. But did she kill him to keep him from coming back into the family?

Nelda Lou visibly pulls herself together and gives us a perky smile. "But I was telling ya'll about my titles. Once upon a time I was Miss Shrimp Queen!"

The way she says it, I almost expect drum rolls. But I'm onto something here, and I'm not about to let the Shrimp

Queen change the subject. Besides, Elvis still has his hackles up. A sign that he smells something fishy.

"How *wonderful!*" I flash what I hope passes for a beauty queen smile. "Is that Nathan Briggs with you at the charity ball? You look *fabulous!*"

Holy cow. Talking in exclamation points is harder than I'd thought. I almost choke on the second one.

While Nelda Lou preens and postures, Lovie is still in shock that her so-called fiancé was also dating his ex-wife.

"I got that gown in New York." The former queen of almost everything pronounces this *Noo Yawk.*

I've spotted something else on the credenza behind the sofa, and I discreetly kick Lovie. It takes two kicks before she comes out of her fog.

"Oh, my throat is parched," she says. "I wonder if I could have a little sip of something?"

"Forgive my manners." Nelda Lou says this as *fo'give mah mannahs.* "Can I get ya'll a little cuppa somethin' sweet?"

"Wonderful!" I punch Lovie, and she rises like a phoenix coming out of the ashes.

"Do you mind if I come along?" Lovie says. "I need to stretch my legs."

"Surely. But don't mind the house. This was the maid's day off."

Elvis curls his lips back as if to say, "It's getting knee deep in here," and when my hostess and my cousin are out of earshot, I tell him, "Amen." Then I make a beeline for the bookshelves. Earlier I'd spotted two photo albums, and I'm itching to see what's inside.

If the Shrimp Queen starts back, Lovie will send up a smoke signal. I hope.

I flip through the first album and find it's nothing more than a baby book featuring Nelda Lou's daughter, from naked infant to gap-toothed second grader to pimple-faced graduate with an unbecoming mortar board on a bad haircut.

Later this is what I'll say to console Lovie: "What Wayne ever saw in that woman, I can't imagine. You'd put her in the shade, Lovie."

And she would. That's the truth.

The second album is some sort of travelogue of Nelda Lou's treks into exotic foreign places.

"Shoot." I shove the albums back into place. Though we can connect Nelda Lou to all three Santas, we don't have a shred of evidence that proves she had a motive for murder.

Elvis growls, and I cock my ear toward the direction my cousin disappeared, but I don't hear a single thing. Old houses are like that. So well insulated a murderer could sneak up behind you and you wouldn't even hear him or her coming. Fortunately for my peace of mind, Nelda Lou's gun is lying beside the sofa. If I have to, I can get to it before she does.

Elvis growls again, and I head in his direction, squat, and put my hand on his head.

"What's the matter, boy?"

At this level I suddenly I spot the edge of a tattered-looking album through a crack in the half-shut drawer on the front of a marble-topped table. I pull it out, open the cover, and there is my uncle, sitting in his fishing boat with his old straw hat pulled down over his eyes. The next photo shows him sitting on the front porch swing at Mama's farm, both of them sipping from glasses. In another, Uncle Charlie is striding into Eternal Rest.

I flip through page after page of these photos, most of them grainy, all of them obviously unposed and probably shot with a telephoto lens.

Elvis rumbles deep in his throat, and I shove the album back into place just in the nick of time. The Shrimp Queen returns with a cup of egg nog. Lovie follows along behind her, carrying a cup and looking guilty. As well she should. She didn't even warn me. If it weren't for Elvis, I would have been caught red-handed.

"Here ya'll go." Nelda Lou presses a cup into my hands and taps hers against it. "To a successful Little Miss Tupelo Toddler Christmas pageant. Bottoms up."

I picture myself dead on the floor in this musty room in a tacky sequined gown that doesn't even flatter my complexion. The best I can hope for is that at the very least, Lovie made sure this egg nog came straight from the carton and the Shrimp Queen didn't lace it with something lethal.

I take the tiniest sip possible, though I think that's all it takes to kill you with poison. Instantly, heat rushes into my face. Any minute now I'm going to fall dead on the floor. And not even Elvis can help me.

I notice him sidling toward Nelda Lou with a leg-lifting gleam in his eyes.

"Well! That about does it!" Surprised to find that I'm still upright and talking in exclamation points, I grab Lovie's arm and drag her toward the door. "Thanks for your help, Nelda Lou. We'll be in touch."

"Oh, ya'll *do*. Beauty pageants are my *specialty*!"

We hotfoot it toward the door. Any minute our hostess could lift that shotgun and blow us to Kingdom Come. When we make it to the front porch, I grab my dog and practically toss him onto the seat of my Dodge.

Still, Nelda Lou's standing in her doorway with one hand behind her back. Is she holding the shotgun? She could blow out my tires.

"Act natural, Callie."

"I'm trying."

Instead of gunning the engine, I make myself back sedately

157

out of her driveway. Nelda is still watching. Lovie gives her a toothy beauty queen smile and even the beauty queen wave. I fear sleuthing has stolen her brain cells.

"I hope you're still pretending, Lovie."

She says a word that flattens the natural body in my hair. The sequined comb slides out and thumps Elvis on the head, and he takes umbrage by chomping it into bits.

My feathers just fall. I don't want to be doing any of this. I want to be home thinking about going down to Mama's farm to get a Christmas tree.

Finally, out of sight of the Shrimp Queen and her fishy goings-on, I shoot through the brick entrance to Highland Circle and straight into the radar of a waiting cop.

"Well, well. What are you two beauty queens up to tonight besides exceeding the speed limit?"

"Look, officer . . ."

Oh, shoot. Lovie's trying to sweet-talk my way out of a ticket. All I want is to get out of Highland Circle and out of these ridiculous sequins.

He's unimpressed by her spiel or her cleavage, and I end up handing over my license. While he calls it in, my sequins start to itch, and I'm certain I'm getting a rash.

Six years and an ulcer later, at the very least, he's back leaning in my window, handing over my license. "Miss Callie Valentine Jones. So you say you've been to a Christmas party in the neighborhood?"

I didn't, but Lovie did, and it sounds like as good a lie as any.

"Yes, officer."

"Who was at this party?"

"Nelda Lou Perkins' friends, of course."

"Did you happen to run into Nathan Briggs?"

"We didn't actually stay long enough to mingle."

"You know him?"

"Not personally. We just had a quick cup of Christmas egg nog with Miss Nela Lou Perkins."

Thank goodness neither of us had more than a sip, because this officer is definitely looking for signs of intoxication. And maybe more. Maybe he's looking for the Santa killer and thinks Nathan Briggs is the next target.

Sweat rolls from under my falling-down French twist while he scribbles on his pad. Finally he rips off a speeding ticket and hands it to me.

There goes a chunk of my Christmas gift budget. The only good thing I can say about this evening is that I'm not dead from poisoned egg nog.

As I creep off, a former Talladega Speedway driver turned snail, I tell Lovie about the hidden pictures of Uncle Charlie.

"The Shrimp Queen's been stalking Daddy?"

"Yes, but has she also been killing?"

Elvis' Opinion #11 on Gluttony, Noble Sacrifice, and Bad Plans

Once again, I saved the day. If it hadn't been for me back there in that ostentatious house with the silly, uncomfortable furniture, my human mom would be facing the business end of Nelda Lou's gun, trying to explain why she was snooping in the Shrimp Queen's private property.

Furthermore, if they'd let me handle the cop, we'd be cruising along now seventy-five dollars richer and a whole lot more cheerful. Let me tell you, in my heyday as a gorgeous, blue-eyed icon in a tight jumpsuit, I've charmed many a cop out of speeding tickets with a humble attitude and an offer of a private tour of Graceland.

I can still do *humble*. I don't like it, but I can still do it.

Be that as it may, we're creeping five miles below the speed limit along the dark streets of Tupelo now while Lovie and my human mom rehash the evening. Both agree that Nelda Lou is firmly on the suspect list, but they're still leaning toward breaking and entering into Abel Caine's house.

"When God Calls Me Home," is what I say. No canine protector worth his Pup-Peroni is going to let his human mom enter the den of an ex-con. Not while he draws a breath.

I put my handsome head over on Callie's lap while I ponder the best way to keep her out of harm. Of course, I could tell

Jack. We dogs have our ways. And my human dad is quick to read my signals. But he won't be out of his cast for a while, which means yours truly must once again come to the rescue.

While I'm cogitating, Callie and Lovie are discussing Lovie's ever-present man trouble.

"I can't believe Wayne was actually dating me and his ex-wife at the same time. Do you think that old Perkins heifer was telling the truth?"

"Even if she was, you have nothing to worry about, Lovie. While you were in the kitchen, I saw plenty of pictures. The ex-wife doesn't hold a candle to you. Her hair is tacky."

Callie crawls past the Bancorp South Coliseum and turns the truck east toward Mooreville.

"Anyhow, Lovie, what does it matter? He's gone."

"Do you think she'll come to his funeral?"

"Probably. But don't worry about it. It'll be on your turf. You can put a little extra vodka in the Prohibition Punch for the reception, and she won't even know you're there."

"Amen," is what I say. That's the way my family kicks butt. With brains and a whole lot of attitude. And I'll have to say, I'm the one responsible for the latter. Listen, when you're living with an iconic dog you learn a thing or two.

Callie finally arrives back at Hair.Net, where we all go inside to change our clothes. For me, this a simple matter of letting Callie remove the red Christmas bow from my collar. I thought about keeping it on since this is the season and all, but I decided a dog of my stature doesn't have to resort to ostentation to be noticed. My striking figure and noble nose are enough to do the trick.

"Good job, Elvis." She pats my head and rewards me with a large Milk Bone. I trot off and lie down on my silk pillow for some much-deserved rest while she and Lovie ditch sequins and return to normal garb.

Lovie doesn't even wash off her pancake makeup, but my human mom removes every trace of her evening of skullduggery. Jack can spot evidence of guilt a mile away.

As Lovie leaves, she calls out, "See you in the morning at ten. My house."

Theirs is a bad plan and it's not happening. Not on my watch. Listen, I'm a dog with a brilliant mind and an even more amazing plan. In the morning while Callie and Jack are still sleeping, I'm going to sneak into the kitchen and eat every one of the Christmas cookies. You may call it gluttony, but I call it a noble sacrifice.

My digestive tract is not what it used to be. Three years ago I could eat a bowl of dog chow, paw open a bag of Pup-Peroni and eat the whole thing, then go out in the back yard and dig up an old sandwich that stupid cocker spaniel Hoyt hadn't found, and I'd never even fart. Now, I can count on of a bunch of forbidden fat and sugar giving me a big bellyache. And with my acting skills, I can make it look worse than it is.

By the time I finish my performance, my human mom will be so concerned about me, breaking into the home of a shady character like Abel Caine won't even be on her radar.

Callie locks the beauty shop, and we climb back into her Dodge Ram for the short drive home. She sighs when she sees the house all lit up, and I can tell you, chapter and verse, what she's thinking. Before you start believing I have a psychic eye like Bobby, let me put your mind at ease. Dogs know these things about our humans. We can read body language and interpret nonverbal sounds and smell things like dishonesty, evil intent, and a body turning on itself with disease. We can even read auras. Or, as Fayrene would so famously say, *auroras*.

My human mom was hoping Jack would be in bed and she wouldn't have to explain where she'd been all evening.

"Come on, boy."

She lifts me from the truck and stops to admire the little wire reindeer glowing with tiny blue lights on her front lawn. Finally, she heaves a big sigh, then climbs the porch steps. The minute she opens the front door I smell cedar.

Callie comes to a complete halt, and I can feel her whole attitude change. Sitting in the corner of the living room, lit only by the glow of lamps, is a six-foot cedar tree, its branches bare, it roots balled in burlap just the way Callie likes.

"Oh." She just stands there, taking in the scent of Christmas.

Jack strolls into the room, his hands in his pockets, acting casual when yours truly can plainly see he's uncertain.

"Do you like it, Cal?"

"I love it." She walks around the tree, still hanging onto me like I'm the most important dog in the world. Which I am. "I can't believe it. How did you do it, Jack?"

"Jarvetis took me down to Ruby Nell's farm and dug it up for me. I can replant it after Christmas."

Jack doesn't do throwaway lines. He's checking to see how Callie reacts to the fact that he's planning to be around even after his cast comes off.

"Thank you, Jack," is what she finally says, then she puts me down and unhooks my leash.

My human mom and dad just stand there looking at each other. I'd do an impromptu performance of "Are You Lonesome Tonight," but it's a bit too obvious. Subtle dog that I am, I lick Callie on her ankle, a small reminder that every living thing needs a little TLC.

She takes the hint and strolls toward my human daddy, then kisses him lightly on the cheek.

It's not "Baby, Let's Play House," but for Jack it's enough. I

163

can see his face as he watches her climb the stairs, and let me tell you, things are looking up around the Valentine/Jones household. If this works out as well as I think it will, I'm liable to hang out my shingle: MARRIAGE COUNSELOR EXTRAORDINAIRE, ELVIS IS IN.

Chapter 14

Cookie Caper, Chocolate Trouble, and Raising Caine

I wake up in a tangled wad with my covers twisted around my waist and the nagging feeling that something is wrong. The pillow on the other side of the bed is empty, so at least *that* is okay. Last night, as much as I was tempted to scoot across the hall and make up with Jack, I shored up my resolve and refused to let a naked Christmas tree in my living room be the deciding factor on taking back a man who has made it clear he'll never be a father.

Turning on the lamp, I grab my pink plush robe and head to the bathroom. It's not until I'm finished my bath that I start to wonder why Elvis is missing. He loves to lounge on the bathroom rug while I soak in a hot tub. I think he views all that steam as a sort of doggie spa.

With Jack in the house, though, his absence is not unusual. Elvis probably padded across the hall and is curled up in bed with him. I run a comb through my damp hair, jump into a pair of navy sweats with Frosty the Snowman on the front of the shirt, then go barefoot across the hall and tap on Jack's door.

"Jack? Are you awake?"

"Come in, Cal."

He emerges from the guest bath, naked from the waist up. I

have to take several deep breaths before I can remember what
I came to say.

"Is Elvis here?"

"I thought he was with you."

"No. He's usually right by my bed on his pillow."

"What about Hoyt?"

"Come to think of it, he wasn't on his pillow, either."

"Don't worry, Cal. They're probably in the kitchen chow-
ing down. Or maybe they've already gone outside. It's a beautiful morning."

Jack's right. I have no reason to panic. Why wouldn't Elvis
and Hoyt use the doggie door? Elvis loves to sit on the gazebo
in the sun and watch Hoyt trying to play with the cats.

"I guess all that business in Santa's Court has me on edge."

I head down the stairs to put on coffee and leave Jack in his
room putting on a shirt. I hope. It would be just like him to
come bare-chested into the kitchen and take my mind off coffee. Still, having him here is reassuring, but I'm not going to
let myself get used to it. Soon he'll be getting his cast off and
leaving.

After Lovie and I see what we can find at Abel Caine's
house today, maybe we'll to go to Magnolia Manor and air out
Jack's apartment. It's not anywhere you'd want to live in the
first place. Old. Tacky. On a treeless lot. The least I can do is
let in a fresh breeze.

I round the corner of the kitchen and spot Elvis sprawled in
the middle of the floor, napping.

"I'm glad to see you, boy." He sits up, but without his usual
sass, and when I squat beside him, he actually moans. Then I
spot his distended belly and start screaming Jack's name.

"Cal!" Jack's crutches clatter on the stairs, and I figure the
next thing that happens will be my ex breaking his neck.

"I'm okay, Jack. It's Elvis."

No sooner are the words out of my mouth than Jack is standing in the doorway with a lethal weapon drawn.

"Holy cow, Jack! Put that thing down."

He ignores me. Stepping around the pile in the middle of the floor that just so happens to be me with Elvis in my lap, Jack stalks through the kitchen and around the corner to the utility room. In minutes he's back with Hoyt limp in his arms.

"Looks like these two got into the Christmas cookies, Cal."

Evidence is everywhere, a chair shoved up against the cabinet, the cookie jar overturned, crumbs scattered all over the floor. If I hadn't been so upset about Elvis, I'd have seen that earlier.

I jump up and grab the kitchen phone. "Champ? I've got two dogs who ate some chocolate chip cookies. What should I do?"

"Bring them in, and don't worry. They've probably done no harm except for a big bellyache."

The minute I hang up the phone, Jack says, "What happened to our regular vet?"

"He's old and not very cute."

I know this is not a nice thing to say, but I'm in no mood for *nice*. If Jack will care to remember, he's been gone a long time. There is no *our regular vet*. There is no *our* anything.

Besides, he knows good and well I've been taking my animals to Champ. And that lethal weapon in his hand is part of the reason. He's the one who chose chasing criminal elements over life in Mooreville deciding which vet to use.

"Are you going to stand there with a Glock in your hand or are you going to help me get my dogs to the truck?"

He glances from me to the gun as if both of us have suddenly sprouted horns. Let him wonder how I know the name of his weapon.

"You're too upset to drive." He pulls his cell phone out of his pocket and starts punching in numbers.

"What are you doing?"

"Calling Lovie."

"Stop it. She's catering a Christmas breakfast for the Civitans." I march past my ex and scoop up Hoyt. "Just get out of my way, Jack. I can take care of myself and my dogs without your help, thank you very much."

Jack picks Elvis up and storms along behind me. He doesn't say a single word till we get to the front porch.

"It's thirty-five degrees, Cal."

"When I want a weather report I'll ask for one."

"You might consider putting one some shoes."

Well, *shoot*. I forgot that I'm barefoot. Totally ignoring him, I step onto the cold frost-covered grass. But I refuse to shiver.

"Unless you're partial to frostbite." He's chuckling. I ought to slap him.

"For your information, if I get frostbite in the next three minutes I'll go down in the Guinness World Records."

Besides, my concern is not my feet; it's my dogs. Stashing Hoyt on the seat, I race past Jack, who is placing Elvis in the truck. In the house, I step into cute L.L.Bean wool clogs, grab a blanket, and race back to the truck. Jack is still there, leaning over my pets and reassuring them with such tenderness I almost weep.

Why? That's what I want to know. Why did everything go wrong between us? Why did we come to this, adversaries sparring over the dogs?

Jack spots me and acts as if he hasn't been talking baby talk to Elvis.

"Tell the vet . . ."

"His name is Champ."

". . . that the cookies contained chocolate and the dogs ate at least a pound."

"I know what to tell him."

"If he needs to keep them overnight, he should put them in the same kennel so they won't get lonesome."

"He knows that."

"It won't hurt to remind him." Jack opens the door for me, and I climb behind the wheel of the Dodge Ram. "Drive carefully."

"I know how to drive."

"When you're upset, you speed."

"Good grief."

I slam the door and drive off while Jack's still standing in my front yard, probably thinking up more bad advice. Giving my dogs reassuring pats, I head north on Highway 371 toward Mantachie. As soon as I'm satisfied that Elvis and Hoyt are still doing okay, I whip out my cell phone and call Lovie.

"How was the Civitan breakfast?"

"A roaring success. Everybody there bought a copy of my cookbook."

"See. I told you they'd love it." Quickly I brief my cousin on Elvis' cookie caper. "And poor Hoyt. Whatever Elvis does, he tags along. I'm on the way to see Champ now."

"This means you won't be breaking and entering this morning."

"Unfortunately, no. And neither will you."

"Why not?"

"You need backup."

"Caine won't be there. I'm the one who picks the locks, anyhow. I can do this without you."

"Don't even think about it. I don't want you alone in the house of an ex-con. We need to come up with another plan."

"I could be a Welcome Wagon lady and take him a basket of cookies."

"He's been in Tupelo too long. We need a different plan."

"If he consulted the horoscope and wore fingernail polish, we could offer him a free manicure with Darlene."

"I think you're on to something, Lovie."

"A manicure? You've got to be kidding."

"No. A free haircut."

"He's going to be suspicious. How'd he win it?"

"How about this? He's one of four winners in a Christmas extravaganza giveaway at Hair.Net. We did a random pick from the telephone directory."

"I hope he's not bald."

"It's been a long time since I've seen him, and I think he was wearing some kind of baseball cap."

"Atlanta Braves?"

"Holy cow, Lovie. I can't remember that far back. What difference does it make?"

"I can't see an ex-con coming to a beauty shop for a free haircut. Offer him a massage, too."

"You're right. Darlene also does massages."

"People talk on the table."

"I'll rent a massage table and set it up in that empty back room I'm planning on turning into a south of Mooreville spa. But how are we going to get Darlene to ask the right questions without letting her in on what we're doing?"

"*I'll* do the massage."

"You don't know anything about massage, Lovie."

"I've had my hands on more male bodies than any masseuse in Lee County. If I can't fake it, nobody can."

"All right. But I don't plan to leave you in the room with him alone. And I plan to be packing heat."

"Then you'd better practice, Annie Oakley."

"Oh, hush up. I've gotta go, Lovie. I'm at Champ's."

He's waiting for me in front of his clinic. I'm so happy to see him I almost burst into tears. I pride myself on being an independent woman, but when things go wrong it is very reassuring to know there's a good man waiting to give you a helping hand.

Champ helps me unload my two pets, and I follow him into the clinic. Poor Elvis gives me this hangdog look that has guilt written all over it.

"I'm not mad at you, boy. Just get well. We'll talk about forbidden cookies later."

He understands every word I say. And anybody who tries to tell me any different will be cut off my Christmas card list.

Elvis' Opinion #12 on Pills, Pushups, and Pillows

Thanks to my clever plan, my human mom ditched her silly plan to break and enter into the house of a dangerous man. Soft touch that she is, she's not even miffed that I broke the cookie jar, ate all the cookies, and conned that foolish cocker spaniel into getting belly deep into big trouble.

When you're planning something illegal, it's always best to have a fall guy. If worse had come to worst, I could always blame Hoyt for instigating the great cookie heist.

As it turns out, both of us are now back at home on our pillows. Mine's bigger and made of silk, a clear indication that I'm top dog around the Valentine/Jones household. And of course, mine is right next to Callie's bed. Hoyt's was, too, but I shoved it over in the corner where it belongs. One snarl from me, and he didn't even try to drag it back. If you're going to be the boss, act like it, I say.

Callie has already made her phone call to Abel Caine, but so far he hasn't called back. Meanwhile, I've spit out all the horse pills Champ gave me; my belly is back to normal, but I'm still milking my convalescence for all it's worth. Listen, eating too much chocolate for the cause is not as easy as it sounds. I'm still not interested in being Santa Paws. I'm can't even get my hackles up about that bushy-tailed William acting like Casanova and trying to steal my personal French poodle. The way I see it, it's Ann Margret's loss.

In other developments here in the heart of beautiful downtown Mooreville, the police have questioned Callie again about the Santa murders, Wayne's body was released and she's already fixed him up, and she's been down on the farm shooting holes in trees. Naturally, I was the one she took with her.

Let me tell you, Callie doing target practice is not a pretty picture. She narrowly missed a milk cow or two, and if that .38 bullet had come two inches closer to Ruby Nell's old bull, my human mom and I would be singing "All I Want for Christmas Is My Two Front Teeth" and a few other body parts I'd rather not live without.

Suffice it to say, we got back into her Dodge Ram in the nick of time and hightailed it out of the pasture with that old bull ripping and snorting behind us. He even got close enough to put a dent in her back bumper.

When Jack said, "How'd you get that dent," she said, "Beats me," and that was that.

Her secret's safe with me. I'm not a dog to tattle. I don't even indulge in gossip unless it's the juicy kind.

Well, bless'a my soul. Who's this coming through the front door but Jack's personal physician? That just goes to show Jack's status. Doctors don't make house calls anymore unless you're the King (that would be me) or a man of great importance (that would be my human daddy).

"Are you ready to get that cast off?" the doc says, and my tenderhearted human mom tears up. She won't let Jack know, though. That's how stubborn she is.

And he won't let her see how grateful he is to finally get rid of the plaster that's been holding him back. That's how much pride he has.

My work's cut out for me. Getting these two back together is going to be harder than a peace settlement in the Middle East.

With the plaster off, Jack's doc pronounces him "good as new."

That means he could be moving back to his apartment any time, a little fact Jack and Callie are careful not to discuss.

After the doc leaves, he picks up his crutches and say, "I guess I won't be needing these anymore," and she says, "Not anytime soon, I hope."

And then he says, "Why don't I grill steaks for supper?" and she says, "That sounds great."

He wanders out to the grill, and she wanders upstairs to pull a box of Christmas ornaments out of her closet. I trail along behind Callie, of course. A dog knows which human parent needs him the most. I can smell her regret and uncertainty a mile away.

She's sitting cross-legged on the carpet holding a Radko ornament Jack gave her on their first Christmas together, a quarter moon in a midnight-blue field of stars. He got it at the Christmas Store down in Tampa where they'd spent an idyllic week together.

I lean my handsome head in her lap and tell her *It's okay to cry.* Don't tell me good human moms can't read their favorite dog's thoughts.

She cuddles me close and says, "Elvis, I wish I knew what to do."

Dogs have instincts about these things, but humans have washed out, drowned out, preached out, and legislated out their natural instincts. They twist and turn with every one of life's storms. They get lost, start over, pray, agonize, discuss, debate, and rationalize till it's a wonder a single one of them ever finds his way to peace and happiness.

If I could have one wish granted this Christmas, it would be that human beings would become more like dogs. We always listen to our instincts, are happy with leftovers, and almost never pee on anybody's shoes.

Chapter 15

Cops, Jazz Funerals, and Dashing Through the Pearly Gates

Abel Caine hasn't called yet to take me up on my offer of a free haircut and massage, but that's probably for the best. Right now, I'm up to my ears in giving my customers new Christmas hairstyles and making preparations for Wayne's jazz funeral.

Lovie is ecstatic that he'll get the jazz funeral, Uncle Charlie is feeling fit and back in charge, and Mama's raring to show her musical chops with a roaring rendition of "When the Saints Go Marching In." Though I can't say I think Wayne was any saint, especially since I found out he was dating my cousin and his ex-wife at the same time.

Still, the Valentines never shirk when it comes to sending the dearly departed through the Pearly Gates. Or in the other direction, as the case may be.

I finish putting Elvis' pink bowtie on his dog collar, his regular getup for funerals, and am in the midst of pulling on the black Stuart Weitzman boots I prefer for winter funerals when Lovie calls.

"Where are you?"

"Still at home."

She says a word that would discolor teeth. "Wayne's ex is acting like she's lost the love of her life, that crazy old Opal

Stokes is wearing her sweet little cookie lady face, and somebody's stalking me. I'm fixing to arm myself."

"Don't do anything rash, Lovie. I'll be headed to the funeral home in five minutes. Tops."

"If you're not here soon, I won't be responsible for what I do."

"Stay in the kitchen till I get there, Lovie. Nothing's going to happen with Uncle Charlie around. Have a cup of Prohibition Punch."

"I already tried that. It's not working."

Jack suddenly appears in the doorway, looking far too handsome and too much like he belongs in this house. He's made such fast progress with his therapy, you'd never know he was recently in a cast.

"Cal, which tie looks best with this shirt?"

"Do I hear Jack?"

"Yes," I tell Lovie, and to Jack, I say, "Wear the navy one." He winks, then heads back across the hall.

"I can see why you're late."

"You can see nothing of the sort, Lovie."

"Then why is he still there?"

"It's Christmas." She giggles, and I get defensive. "It would be just plain tacky to send him back to that ugly apartment to spend the holidays by himself. Besides, with the Santa killer still out there, I need Jack here to help out."

Lovie says a word that would melt the North Pole.

"Don't start with me, Lovie. I've said all I'm going to say on the subject of Jack."

"It's not Jack. It's that heifer." I don't even have to ask to know she's talking about Wayne's ex. "She looks like a strumpet. If she gets anywhere near me, I'm liable to skewer her and serve her up as kabobs."

"Holy cow, Lovie. Hide."

"Where?"

"I don't care. Anywhere. Just don't go near her till I get there."

I yell for Jack, brief him on the dangerous love triangle and the possible stalking. Then the three of us—Jack, Elvis, and me—race off to Eternal Rest in his silver Jag.

We arrive in less time than it takes me to put up a French twist. The parking lot is filled with squad cars.

"Stay close." Jack grabs my hand, I hang onto Elvis' leash, and we weave our way through a bevy of cops both outside and inside the funeral home. Naturally, they're out in force. The killer often shows up at the victim's funeral. For what purpose, I don't know, and I don't want to know. I just want him caught so I can decorate my tree and finish my Christmas shopping in peace.

We make our way to the first parlor, where, thanks to my skills, Wayne is laid out looking as if he might sit up any minute and ask for a piece of pecan pie.

I scan the crowd for Lovie, but she's nowhere in sight, thank goodness. Nelda Lou is up front near the casket, and though she's in a black pantsuit that suggests deep mourning, she's not looking a bit happier to see her former son-in-law dead than she did when she talked about him alive. I make a mental note to keep an eye on her.

So do the cops, it seems. Two of them are standing in the corner near a potted peace lily. One has his eyes peeled on Nelda Lou; the other has a bead on the mall's manager, Cleveland White.

Uncle Charlie is also near the casket, resplendent in a crisp black pinstriped suit and looking fully recovered, I'm happy to say. He's talking to none other than Nathan Briggs, the mall's original Santa.

Fayrene is also near the front, wearing Christmas-tree green from head to toe, but Mama is nowhere in sight. That doesn't concern me, though. When she's in charge of the music, she always heads to the chapel early to make sure everything is in order.

My phone vibrates, and Lovie's name pops up on the ID. I lean over to whisper to Jack, "I've got to find Lovie."

"Stay sharp."

"Don't worry about me. You just make sure Uncle Charlie is safe."

Ordinarily he'd have insisted on coming with me, and I'd have put up a huge fuss. It has been like this ever since his cast came off, though. We're more considerate of each other. And neither of us has broached the subject of when Jack's leaving.

Mindful that the eyes of the Tupelo Police Department are also on me as a possible suspect, I stroll casually out of the viewing room and into the hall. It's packed. Some of the people I know, but most I don't. Who'd have thought Wayne had so many friends?

Or maybe they're enemies.

In my eagerness to avoid cops, I almost run over Opal Stokes. She's left her tough, Santa-slaying persona behind and is back to looking like the sweet little old lady you'd never dream would enter Santa's Court and dispense cookies laced with Ex-Lax.

She gives me a big smile and leans down to pet Elvis. His hackles come up, and I scoop him off the floor.

"He's having a bad day," I say, then hurry off before she recognizes me as the "boy" she ordered to clean up her kitchen floor.

As soon as I'm out of sight of the funeral crowd, I whip out my cell phone and call Lovie.

"Where are you?"

"Downstairs. Your room."

She means the room where I make up the newly deceased. Keeping a tight rein on Elvis, I head down the stairs. His hackles are still up, and I have the creepy feeling I'm being followed. Whirling around, I glance back up the stairs and glimpse a shadow slipping back into the hall. The dark pants could be either male or female. But the shoes looked like men's footwear.

I'm torn between racing back upstairs to see who was following me or continuing down to rescue Lovie. My cousin wins. Besides, by the time I'd get back upstairs, whoever was skulking along behind me would have vanished into the crowd.

I push open the door to a room that's as familiar to me as Hair.Net. Lovie is sitting on the sofa with a cup in one hand and a butcher knife in the other.

"What in the world?"

"Prohibition Punch." She nods toward another cup and a pitcher on the end table. "Have some."

If ever I needed something to pick me up, today is the day. I pour myself a cup of Lovie's cure-all and sit down beside her.

"I'm talking about the knife, Lovie."

"Somebody's been tailing me ever since I got here."

"Me, too." I tell her about spotting the shadowy figure at the top of the stairs.

"It's probably Abel Caine," she says.

"How do you figure that?"

"I saw him earlier, and he's wearing a black suit just like the stalker. Cleveland White's wearing gray, and Albert Gordon's in jail for burning Santas."

"Still, that doesn't mean Abel Caine is stalking us."

"Why do you think he hasn't called about the free haircut and massage?"

"I haven't got a clue."

"If he tried to kill Daddy, he's bound to know who we are. He wouldn't just waltz into your shop knowing you're Daddy's niece."

"You have a point about that, Lovie. But Nelda Lou Perkins is also wearing a dark pantsuit. And now that I think about it, she had on lace-up shoes. Very masculine."

Lovie says a word that would parch peanuts. "If it's that old biddy, I'll serve her liver as canapés."

Upstairs, the organ strikes a big chord—Mama, signaling the service is about to begin.

"We've got to get upstairs. Are you going to be all right, Lovie?"

"Just stick by me and keep that ex-wife witch out of my way."

"You can count on me. Put the butcher knife down, Lovie."

"What if I keep it hidden in the folds of my skirt?"

"No. Besides, Uncle Charlie and Jack are here. Not to mention two dozen cops. Nothing bad is going to happen today."

I sincerely hope I'm right. Actually, it's not a catfight between Lovie and Wayne's ex that worries me. It's the horses.

This is only the second jazz funeral we've had at Eternal Rest. The main feature of a jazz funeral, of course, is the cortege to the cemetery. The last time we had used nice, friendly horses from Mama's farm to pull the hearse. This time, though, the family wanted all-white horses.

Miraculously, Uncle Charlie and Bobby found six white horses, but they came from a two-bit circus camped over in Pontotoc County for a Christmas performance. Apparently, they agreed to one last show before they made their way to winter quarters in Florida.

Although we're only five blocks from the cemetery, we're dealing with a lot of unfamiliar elements. Too many cops, two jazz trumpets, two rivals (one already showing the effects of too much punch), and too many strange horses.

On the way up the stairs, I pray to the Heavenly Father, the Holy Mother, and Mother Earth. Just to be on the safe side, I add a little plea to Oprah.

Elvis' Opinion #13 Funerals, Faulty Planning, and Farts

Nobody asked my opinion about this funeral. If they had I'd have told them the way dogs do it is much more dignified. No fuss, no eulogies, no public displays. Just go off into the woods, lie down on a soft bed of fragrant pine needles, close your eyes, and say *sayonara*, which means till we meet again. And if it doesn't, it ought to.

Dogs know we'll be coming back around again. If we get lucky we might make it back as a famous singer, and if we don't, we could come back as a cat. Still, there's always next time.

But I will have to say in defense of my Valentine family that they know how to put on a funeral. Ruby Nell's making that organ walk and talk with her jazzy spirituals. Backed by Charlie's superb trumpet and Bobby's shaky one, this funeral sounds like it might be taking place in the heart of New Orleans.

Which is where Charlie spent many of his early years. His shady past, I call it. Let me tell you, he picked up a few skills besides trumpet playing, and not all of them you'd want to whistle along to. Strip away his fine suit, his Southern manners, and his community spirit, and he's not the kind of man you'd want to cross.

The easy part of the funeral is winding down. That would be the indoors part where I get to sit on the pew between my human mom and my human dad with two rows of policemen in the back watching over the proceedings. Looking for a killer.

The Santa killer is here, all right. It didn't take me three minutes to pick up that scent. It's the same one I picked up in the robing room at the mall. The killer stalked my human mom and was probably the one stalking Lovie, though I wasn't here when that happened.

If they'd turn me loose, I'd have the Santa killer collared before the first stupid white horse lets out a fart. And it's sure to happen. You mark my words. When you're dealing with big dumb animals, you can expect to get your shoes dirty.

Now if Charlie had found some nice big Saint Bernards to pull the hearse, or even some of those lanky Great Danes, he wouldn't have a minute's trouble. But like I said, nobody asked me.

They're saying the final prayer now, and the pallbearers are putting poor old Wayne up behind a bunch of crazy circus horses. The mourners file out and take their places in a motley parade somewhere south of the business end of the horses, and we clomp off toward the cemetery.

Wayne's ex starts bawling like a newborn calf. If looks could kill, the one Lovie shoots her way would fell her on the spot. The next thing I know, Lovie has pulled out a handkerchief and is trying to out-bawl the Queen of Mourn.

All over the neighborhood, dogs take up the howl. If I weren't so busy taking care of Callie and trying to keep order on the street and keeping my nose to the ground for the scent of a killer, I'd march my iconic self across a few fences and teach those lesser dogs a lesson. They've got such a poor grasp of funeral protocol, this is either their first time around or they've been reincarnated from cats.

"Do something," Ruby tells Charlie, and he puts his trumpet to his lips to drown out the dogs with a rip-roaring rendition of "Swing Low, Sweet Chariot."

I guess circus horses are used to this kind of ruckus, because for two blocks they lead this jazz funeral as smoothly as I led my former recording sessions.

Looks like I'm going to have to eat my words.

Suddenly shots ring out. Or so everybody seems to believe. Mourners scream, and Jack pulls Callie and Lovie to the pavement. Then he and the cops take off in the direction of the shots.

The horses rear up on their hind legs, the hearse tilts, and the deceased shoots out the back door. Bless'a my soul. There goes Wayne rolling down the street in a runaway casket. Who knows? Maybe he didn't like jazz as much as Lovie thought.

Mourners leap out of the way, and Lovie says a word that's going to get her on the prayer list of every church in town, while Charlie tries to rein in the horses.

"I've got him," Bobby yells.

With his lanky legs pumping double time and his psychic eye jumping, Eternal Rest's assistant undertaker single-handedly collars the late mall Santa Claus. Who'd have thought it?

Ruby Nell leads the applause. Then as Charlie and Bobby load Wayne back into the hearse, Lovie says, "That Wayne! What will he do next? He was always a show-off."

Laughter ripples through the crowd, Wayne's ex gives Lovie the evil eye, and yours truly helps herd everybody back in line so the procession can continue. Callie helps, of course, but I'm the one in charge.

One of the things I do is prance around Wayne's family (not

his silly ex-wife, but his only brother and his ancient mother). Looking adorable and cuddly, I frolic around them long enough to satisfy myself they're not going to sue Charlie. If I have to, I'll be the first one to remind the family that this jazz funeral was free.

Meanwhile, my human mom keeps searching the crowd for signs of my human daddy. She might as well settle down and enjoy the rest of the show. Jack won't be back till he's collared the one who fired the so-called shots.

With Charlie and Bobby on either side of the horses doing a trumpet duet of Dixieland jazz and making sure there are no further incidents, we finally arrive at the cemetery. Mostly in one piece, though I imagine Wayne's attempted getaway has him "All Shook Up."

As the crowd gathers around the open grave, Fayrene can be heard all over the block telling Ruby Nell, "The infirmament is my favorite part."

Let the malapropisms roll is what I say. Anything to keep Callie's mind off the fact that Jack and most of the cops are still missing and the crowd's collective mind off the fact that there's a murderer loose in the graveyard.

The scent is coming from the direction of a massive monument featuring an angel comforting Jesus in the Garden of Gethsemane. If Callie would let me off this leash I'd corner the Santa killer, and everybody could go back to shopping and baking Christmas cookies and bickering over whose turn it is to feed the in-laws.

Well, bless'a my soul. Here comes Jack. Callie perks up like she's been trapped in a dark room and he knows the whereabouts of the only light.

He takes her elbow, then leans down to whisper, "Kids with firecrackers."

ELVIS AND THE BLUE CHRISTMAS CORPSE

I could have told them that in the first place. Discharged guns don't smell a thing like firecrackers. But nobody bothered to ask me.

If I'd come back as Marie Antoinette, I'd say, *Let them eat cake.*

Now I say, *Ignorance is not bliss.* But it takes a dog of my intelligence to figure that out.

187

Chapter 16

Bogus Massage, Free Cuts, and Suspecting Caine

After yesterday's fiasco at the jazz funeral, I let myself in early at Hair.Net. I like to have time to relax and center myself before my clients start arriving.

I love the small rituals of morning. First, I make coffee in the break room just the way I like it, dark with a touch of New Orleans French Market–style chicory, plenty of cream added, no sugar. While the coffee is brewing I select a stack of Christmas CDs to set the mood.

I love to collect coffee mugs, so the next part of my ritual is selecting exactly the right one for the day. Today's mug features a Native American sacred white buffalo and the advice to listen to my inner voice.

I pride myself on doing that, but it's always good to have a reminder. I settle behind my desk with my special mug of coffee and the newspaper while Elvis settles onto his pillow nearby.

An item in the police report section leaps out at me: *Police foiled an attempted burglary at Nathan Briggs' home at 613 Highland Circle. Nothing was reported stolen. The culprit fled and was not apprehended.*

Was the so-called burglary a cover for a killer after the mall's original Santa? Is Uncle Charlie still in danger?

I'm getting ready to call him when the phone on my desk rings.

"Abel Caine," a deep voice says. "May I speak with Miss Jones?"

I'm so startled I almost drop the phone. One, that he's finally calling. Two, that he sounds like a Southern gentleman instead of an ex-con.

"Speaking."

Abel wants to come in for his free haircut and massage. Today, if possible.

I don't have time to consult Lovie. Racking my brain to think of her catering schedule, I tell him, "Two o'clock."

If my cousin can't be here to do the massage, I'll do it myself. After all, Darlene will be here to oversee my shop full of clients. Among them will be Mama, coming in to get her hair dyed red for Christmas. She changes hair color more often than some people change socks.

Thank goodness, her appointment is not until four. Abel Caine will be long gone by then.

If necessary, I can ask Jack to spend an hour or two at Hair.Net. He and Uncle Charlie are the only two people who can keep Mama in line. Besides, he'd be handy if Abel has more on his mind than a few freebies.

Lately, I've been seeing how Jack is handy for many things—running a hot tub, making Mayan chocolate, bringing in the Christmas tree. But I'm not going to dwell on that.

I'm also not going to dwell on the fact that he's accessible because he's still at my house. I'll think about that someday when catching a killer has not just shot to the top of my to-do list.

As soon as I hang up after my chat with Abel, I call Lovie with the latest development. She lets forth a string of words that would measure way up there on the Richter scale.

"It can't be that bad, Lovie."

"I was going to be cooking casseroles for tonight's city-wide preachers' dinner."

"That's okay. I can handle this."

"Forget it, Lone Ranger. All I need to keep a bunch of preachers happy is a long-winded blessing and plenty of fried chicken. I'll be there."

I'm relieved. No matter what kind of trouble Lovie and I get into, we're always in it together.

The bell over my shop door tinkles, and I go up front to greet my first client, Roy Jessup from Mooreville Feed and Seed, who says he's looking to change his style.

He's either out to impress his fiancé or he's broken up with her and is out to impress somebody new. But since he's close-mouthed and I don't pry, it will remain his secret. Unless one of Mooreville's gossips arrives to ferret the truth out of him.

My shop bell tinkles again, and in walks Mama.

"I thought I'd come early."

If Roy weren't sitting in my chair, I'd point out that seven hours before her appointment is not Mama being early. It's Mama being nosey. She can sniff out my plans faster than I can make them, especially if they're something I don't want her to know. She ought to be a basset hound.

Still, there's something reassuring about the thought of Mama swooping around in her gold caftan while an ex-con is loose in my shop. Especially if Abel Caine has murder on his mind.

"Just make yourself at home, Mama." As if she needs an invitation.

She gets a stack of magazines, ensconces herself on my hot-pink loveseat as though it's her personal throne, then proceeds to grill Roy about his love life.

He turns out to be full of surprises. It turns out he's "split the sheet with Trixie Moffett," his words, and is "catting around," a direct quote. Who would have thought Mooreville's mild-mannered feed and seed guy was such a Romeo?

Around noon, black thunderclouds turn the shop gloomy, so I go around switching on all the lights. In spite of the impending storm, everybody who comes in for my beautifying touch is full of Christmas spirit and the latest gossip. By the time Lovie arrives, I've almost forgotten our appointment with a suspect.

"What are you doing here, Lovie?" Trust Mama.

"Same as you, Aunt Ruby Nell. Looking for trouble."

I give Lovie a high five behind Mama's back. It might be my last victory for a long time. Abel Caine has just walked through the door. Though I haven't seen him since Katrina, I'd know that arrogant swagger and pock-marked face anywhere.

Abel Caine looks like disaster walking. His nose has a hump in the middle, probably where it was broken, and sits slightly off-center. His eyes are small and too close-set, and he has a haircut so ugly it would make less-talented hair stylists cringe.

Both Elvis and Darlene's little Lhasa Apso William get their hackles up. If I were a dog, I'd have mine up, too.

I nod to Lovie, who whisks the pets off and shuts them up in my office. The last thing I need is Elvis picking a fight with a man who looks like he could break a dog in half with one hand and rip out his liver with the other.

Thank goodness, Lovie stays in the back. It won't do for Abel to become suspicious of her even before she starts masquerading as somebody who knows her way around a male body for reasons that we will not talk about.

"I'll want my massage first," he says.

Mama's eyebrows shoot up, and I escort him toward the back before she can open her mouth. Thank goodness, Lovie has turned the lights down low, lit candles, lined up the scented oils, and is waiting beside the rented massage table.

I think we'd pass for the real deal.

"I'm going to leave you in the capable hands of my masseuse," I tell him. "Afterward, I'll see you in my chair for your free haircut. Just give a yell if you need anything."

He says, "Okay," but I'm talking more to Lovie than to Abel Caine.

I'm reluctant to leave her alone and even more reluctant to face the music with Mama.

"Since when do you have a masseuse?" she says the minute I get back up front.

"Didn't I tell you, Mama? Before I decided what all I'm going to do with the back room, I'm experimenting with a rented massage table."

"No, you did not."

"Well, I thought I did."

"Carolina, if you're implying I'm senile, you can just get off that high horse right now."

Darlene is all ears. And so is Wanda Jenkins, who obviously came in for her manicure while I was in the back with Lovie and Abel. Before Mama and I started our argument, Wanda was holding forth on Mooreville's semi-famous TV weatherman as if her husband was God's gift to meteorology.

Now she says, "Oh, I like the idea of a massage table, Callie. That way I won't have to drive all the way over to Tupelo."

"I know somebody who does body art." Darlene is dead serious.

"I can't picture any of my clients wanting a tattoo."

"Who's the masseuse?" Mama says.

If I'm not careful, she's going to blow this undercover operation before it even gets started. I turn my back squarely toward Darlene, who is now consulting today's horoscopes, and Wanda, who is bound to want something different no matter what the stars say.

"Mama." I speak so loud Mama drops her magazine. I bend over and get it off the floor, and when I hand it to her, I wink.

She's nobody's dummy. She winks back and announces in a tone that queens would do well to imitate, "You need to come with me to the kitchen and make me a snack. That pimento sandwich I had for lunch is long gone."

Mama's up to something. She knows her way around my beauty shop kitchen as well as I do. When she's here, she fixes whatever she wants to eat, anytime she wants it.

I follow her into the kitchen, put my fingers over my lips, and close the door. There's no sense taking chances that private information will fall on the wrong ears.

"You and Lovie are barking up the wrong tree with that Caine character."

"Why do you say that, Mama?"

"Because Nelda Lou Perkins is the killer."

Mama could be right. Nelda's secret photo album of Uncle Charlie, her dislike of her son-in-law, and her ease with a lethal weapon point strongly in that direction. Still, we have no hard evidence.

"Do you know something I don't, Mama?"

"I know plenty you don't, but you never bother to ask my advice. You're bullheaded, just like Michael."

Michael Valentine was my daddy and the love of my mother's life. He died when I was just a little girl, and no man will ever hold a candle to him in my book or Mama's. Of course, we don't include Uncle Charlie in the comparison. He and Daddy were brothers, both beloved for their own reasons.

"Well, I'm asking now, Mama. What do you know about this case that I don't?" I open the refrigerator door and find a pack of Twinkies, one for Mama and one for me. Lunch was rushed and all this stress is making me hungry.

"I heard everything Charlie told the cops."

"When was this?"

"After he got out of the hospital. They came to his apartment to talk to him."

"And you eavesdropped?"

"Naturally."

"You go, Mama." I give her a high five.

"Get this. Nelda Lou hated Ruldolph the Red-Nosed Reindeer's guts."

"Steve Boone? Why?"

"It's a long story with no substance, and it goes all the way back to when her husband had an account with Tupelo Hardware. She's a grudge holder. Always has been, always will be. And get this, her husband was an electrical engineer."

"She could have picked up a few pointers. She could be a Miss Sweet Potato who knows how to hotwire Santa's throne."

"Furthermore, a while back she called Charlie to come over for Thanksgiving dinner and has been calling him ever since. He said *no*, of course."

"The jilted lover."

"They were never lovers."

"How do you know, Mama? Uncle Charlie's a good-looking man and Aunt Minrose has been dead a long time."

"Flitter."

If I laugh, Mama will probably cut me off her Christmas

card list. I hold in my mirth and store it away for when Lovie and I can compare notes on today's doings.

"I'll have to say I'm impressed with your eavesdropping skills, not to mention your powers of deduction."

"You just earned yourself a bigger Christmas gift, Callie."

It seems Nelda Lou had reasons to hate every one of the men killed in Santa's Court, as well as the one who didn't die.

"Mama, if she did kill her ex-son-in-law and the man she claimed did her husband wrong at the hardware store, she could still be after Uncle Charlie."

"I've already thought of that. Now that Santa's Court is closed, Fayrene and I have come up with a plan to lure her out into the open."

"Do I even want to know?"

"We're going to have an open house at Gas, Grits, and Guts for the séance room."

"I can just hear what the Baptists will have to say about your séance room. And a few Methodist won't be too happy with it, either. Nobody will come to that open house except Episcopalians."

"For Pete's sake, I wonder why I didn't think of that."

"It's a good plan, Mama. It just needs a little refining, that's all. If you call it a Christmas open house at Gas, Grits, and Guts, and then invite all the suspects plus anybody who had anything to do with the charity event at the mall, it just might work."

"It could have been anybody in that crowd."

"We'll all put our heads together and try to come up with a list. Tonight at Uncle Charlie's?"

"No. Lovie's."

"You didn't discuss your plan with Uncle Charlie?"

"Do you tell him everything you're going to do?"

"Of course not."

"What he doesn't know won't kill him."

"Let's hope not, Mama."

About that time, all the lights go out in Hair.Net and somebody screams.

What if Mama's wrong about Nelda Lou and the killer is right here in my beauty shop?

Elvis' Opinion #14 on Body Building, Fake Massages, and Dog Heroes

If my human mom thinks I'm going to stay shut up in her office with the likes of that silly-looking dog of Darlene's, she's barking up the wrong tree. William promptly goes over and tries to mark his territory by hoisting his leg on Callie's desk. What Ann Margret ever saw in him, I don't know.

I prance my iconic self over, look down my famous nose at the Lhasa Apso who thinks he's the Dalai Lama, and snarl. He changes his tune in a hurry. Listen, if he knew how silly he looks with that little sawed-off leg hoisted in the air, he'd squat to pee. Dogs without real legs ought to know better than to show off. Especially in front of the King.

Once I show that Lhasa Apso who's boss, I put my front paws on the office door and proceed to "Shake, Rattle, and Roll." The latch pops open, I sneak out, and push the door shut behind me. I don't intend to share my freedom with a lesser dog. Especially one who's been courting the mother of my puppies behind my back.

The crazy, self-styled Dalai Lama sets up a howl. Fortunately, my human mom is too busy arguing with Ruby Nell to notice.

Taking a kingly stance, I sniff to find out what's cooking.

Smells like "T-R-O-U-B-L-E" to me. And it's coming from the direction of Lovie and the ex-con.

I head that way, and fortunately, the door to the so-called massage room is not fully closed. All it takes is a little nudge to open it a crack and prance right in. The lights are low, and it takes a while to get the lay of the land.

There's a pile of men's clothes on a chair, a big hulk on the table that I take to be the ex-con, and Lovie, in black toreador pants and a tight green sweater that shows more peaks than Mount Rushmore.

A woman after my own heart. If you've got it, flaunt it, I say.

She sees me and grins. Lovie and I have a pact. I don't tattle on her and she doesn't tattle on me.

I lay my handsome self down near the Himalayan salt lamp Callie installed just for this occasion. It's putting out so many negative ions, I feel like I'm lying on a beach. Which was smart thinking on Callie's part. With all that sea-breeze-like tranquillity, who's going to notice that the masseuse doesn't have a clue what she's doing?

"Man, that feels good," Abel Caine says.

"I'm so glad you like it."

Lovie grins at me and then slathers enough oil on his big, ugly, hairy body to enter him in a greased pig contest. Smart girl. What she lacks in skill, she's making up in the externals. Too much scented oil. Music that will put you to sleep if you're not careful. Soft lights. And this beachy lamp that's got me so relaxed I'm already yawning.

"My, what muscles." Lovie sounds like a character in a fairy tale. And I guess this is a fairy tale of sorts. Two of the nicest amateur sleuths I know trying to catch a killer. "You must work out."

"Six days a week. It's my religion."

"Does that give you time for friends?"

Lovie's trying to find out if killing is also this man's religion. I sniff the air for clues. I could tell her a thing or two, but she's too busy trying to find out what Caine knows about the Santa murders to consult a smart dog.

"I keep to myself," he says.

"A man who entertains himself has to be very resourceful."

"I guess you could call it that." His laugh is as big and ugly as his body.

When Lovie lifts the sheet so he can turn onto his back, I find out more about him than I ever wanted to know. She's discreetly hidden behind the sheet, but I'm on the open side. And let me tell you, Abel Caine without his clothes on is not a sight you'd want to encounter in the dark. With his over-pumped muscles, he looks like a cartoon figure of a superhero.

And when I say cartoon figure, I'm not kidding. You know how Disney and Pixar draw those heroes? Neutered. No embarrassing body parts that would get their movies rated X.

If I was so underendowed, even I might go on a rampage against Santa Claus. Fortunately, I have Ann Margret to attest to my many charms.

Lovie upends the oil bottle onto him. If she's not careful, he's going to slide right off the table.

But when she starts up with her questions again, he sidesteps as smoothly as a man dancing the tango. She's going to learn nothing from this man. I could have told her and Callie.

While they're playing cat and mouse with an ex-con, the real killer's out there planning another move.

That's not to say they're in no danger. This man is nobody's fool, and his aura has turned nasty. It wouldn't take much to push him to violence.

It's not happening under my vigilant eye. If I can keep said eyes open.

I'm nodding off when all bedlam breaks loose. The lights go out, the hulk rises from the table, somebody screams, and Callie bursts through the door, hollering for Lovie.

This situation calls for a real hero. Elvis the Incredible to the rescue!

Chapter 17

Bravery, Bedlam, and Beauty

When I march into the faux massage room, I almost faint. Lovie's backed into the corner with my Himalayan salt lamp raised like a weapon, Abel Caine's hulking over her in a sheet, and Elvis is tugging at its corner and growling like he's going to eat somebody alive.

"What's going on in here? Lovie, was that you screaming?"

Believe me, I might sound like somebody in charge, but I feel like a quivering bird trying to cling to a high wire in a bad wind.

"Not yet, Cal."

"You sure you're all right, miss?" Abel says. "I thought it was you."

Is this man kidding? Did he really think Lovie was the one who screamed and him right here in the room with her?

Elvis has grabbed hold of Abel's sheet, and the way he's hanging on, he's not going to let go till Christmas. Something's afoot. My dog is never wrong about people.

"Who turned out the lights?"

Holy cow. It's Mama standing in the doorway, flicking the light switch.

"They won't work, Mama. Something tripped a switch."

In the front of the shop I can hear Wanda yelling "What's going on?" and Darlene trying to calm her down.

"If you'll call off this dog and let me get my clothes back on," Abel says, "I can fix it."

"Are you sure?"

I'm the one who's not sure. Is he saying that so Lovie will put down her weapon and I'll collar Elvis, and then he'll be free to do his meanness? Or is he sincere?

"If you're going to fix it, you'd better hurry," Mama says. "I've already called Charlie."

Abel suddenly goes very quiet. Does he still harbor a grudge against Uncle Charlie?

Finally he makes a sound that passes for laughter, and the tension eases a bit.

"I'll be quick, ma'am. Now if you'll excuse me."

I tear Elvis away from the sheet, then we all file out and leave Abel Caine shut up in the dark. Hopefully putting on some clothes.

I motion for Lovie and Mama to come into the break room, then shut the door behind us, and we get in a huddle.

"Did you really call Uncle Charlie?"

"No, but I'm fixing to."

"Wait a minute, Aunt Ruby Nell. I don't think Abel Caine's the killer."

Mama purses her lips, which could mean any of a dozen things, none of them good.

"Why, Lovie? What did he say?"

"It's not anything he said, Cal. It's just a feeling I have. And you know I have good instincts about men."

That's debatable, but I don't want to get into that subject with Lovie. Mama doesn't have the same self-control.

"If we stake our lives on your instincts about men, we'll all be dead."

"Not if I have anything to say about it." Lovie opens my cutlery drawer and pulls out a paring knife. "Wonder Woman to the rescue."

Suddenly she gives me a warning nudge, and I turn around to see Abel Caine, who has invited himself inside without knocking. The only good thing I can say about this situation is that he's wearing clothes. He's also staring at the knife in Lovie's hand.

"Oh, there you are, Mr. Caine." I try for cheerful but come off a little ragged around the edges. I give Lovie a help-me-out poke in the ribs.

"I'm making sandwiches," she says, then whirls around to the counter and jerks up a loaf of bread. "What would you like, Mr. Caine? Pimento or ham and cheese."

"Neither, thanks. I'm looking for the switch box."

If he'd said ham and cheese, I might have had to kill Lovie. There's nothing in my refrigerator except a box of Mrs. Weaver's pimento cheese, a bag of questionable lettuce, and a pitcher of Prohibition Punch.

"Behind the last cabinet door on the right," I tell him.

When he walks past, I try not to scrunch in closer to Mama and Lovie. I don't care what my cousin's instincts say, I don't trust this man.

A big clap of thunder makes us all jump, and a torrent of rain slashes against the windows of my little beauty salon. *It's a good time for murder*, is what I'm thinking. Though, of course, it's daytime, and I'm not in the middle of a scary story. I'm in the middle of wishing I was somebody else. I'd have a nice quiet mama who stays home and bakes pies instead of spending my money in the casinos over in Tunica, and a less flamboyant cousin who would never think of ditching a perfectly good man who loves her to get engaged to a soon-to-be-dead Santa.

When the lights come back on, I nearly jump out of my skin.

"All set." Abel is back in my kitchen looking only slightly less threatening in the light than he did in the semi-darkness.

"Thanks. Are you ready for that free haircut?"

"You bet."

I head out to the front of my salon with Abel in tow. Lovie follows with Mama close behind. I notice my cousin has fixed two sandwiches. She's scarfing down one, and Mama's nibbling on the other. Lovie may have the worst instincts about men since Little Red Riding Hood got fooled by the Big Bad Wolf, but she knows how to set the stage for everything, including catching a killer.

"Callie, I think I know why the power went out." Darlene comes from behind her manicure table, holding her nail dryer. "When I plugged this in, the lights went out."

"If you ladies will allow me," Abel says, "I can have that fixed in no time flat."

"Great." Darlene hands over the nail dryer while I try to send Lovie a signal she either doesn't get or has chosen to ignore. Her sandwich already finished, she's on my loveseat with a copy of *Entertainment Weekly*.

Trying to act natural and in charge, I ease her way and flip through a copy of *Southern Living*.

"The washer and dryer will be on now," I tell her.

"Oh, goodness." She puts the magazine back in the rack. "I guess I'd better head back, then, and get the table ready for my four o'clock."

Why didn't she say *five o'clock*? If Abel doesn't hurry up with that nail dryer, he's still going to be in my chair at four, and I don't take him for a fool. He's bound to notice if nobody comes through the door for a massage.

Lovie has already gone to the back, so I can't signal her

again. And I don't want to leave Mama and Darlene, not to mention Wanda, up front with this man. No matter how helpful he is. His handyman persona could be a front.

Still, this is a perfect opportunity for me to do a little detecting on my own. I stroll to the manicure table, where Abel is seated on the frilly pink client's stool with the nail dryer in pieces.

I lean down as if I'm inspecting his work. "My goodness, you're handy."

"Yep."

"Are you an electrician?"

"Of sorts."

"There's a big renovation project going on down at the mall." I leave room for him to make up his own mind whether I'm prying or just being friendly. His stare chills me.

"Been on that job myself. Too bad about poor old Steve Boone."

"I doubt there's a soul in Tupelo who hasn't been in his hardware store. Everybody will miss him."

He doesn't comment either way, just hands the nail dryer back to Darlene, says, "All fixed," then goes to sit in my chair.

While Wanda slides her nails back under the dryer for the finishing touch and Mama's on the loveseat pretending to be interested in magazines, I pick up my scissors, thinking that at least I have a weapon. And if push comes to shove, I know where to plunge the blade for maximum damage.

Next I drape him with the pink plastic cape, my signature color, and fasten it around his bull-like neck. The whole time, he's watching me in the mirror. I'm having a hard time keeping my hands from shaking.

"I probably should get capes in a different color for my male clients."

"I don't care what color the cape is, as long as you know

what you're doing." He gives me another heebie-jeebie-inducing stare. "I'm told you do."

So he's checked up on me. I wonder if his interest had to do only with hair or if he had other reasons.

"Good cuts are my best advertisement."

He stares at my reflection in the mirror for so long I tighten the grip on my scissors.

Darlene finally finishes Wanda's nails, and Wanda prisses out of the shop. Which is a huge relief. If Abel Caine goes on a rampage, I'd prefer he not kill my paying customers. I feel a trickle of sweat roll down the side of my face. Finally, Abel says, "I've been ugly all my life. Do you think you can improve on me, Miss Callie?"

"I've never seen a beauty challenge I couldn't conquer."

Forget murder. I lift the scissors and set to work doing what I do best.

Halfway through Abel Caine's hair makeover, Fayrene breezes through the door.

"I hope I'm not too late for my massage," she says. "I try to be punctuated."

I never thought I'd see the day when I'd be glad to see Mrs. Malaprop coming to my rescue.

Elvis' Opinion #15 on Gold Lamé, Christmas Surprises, and Aging Gracefully

Take it from a dog who knows more about style than any canine in Lee County: my human mom's hair makeover on the ex-con is nothing short of spectacular.

When he leaves the shop, he hands her a tip big enough to ensure that I get plenty of Pup-Peroni in my Christmas stocking. And if I play my cards right, I'm liable to get the gold lamé doggie suit I've been hankering for.

Every time we go into Pet Smart, I drop the hint with a subtle performance of "Blue Christmas." I say subtle because I'm not one to pull out all the stops for shoppers who are paying more attention to birdseed than they are to the King.

So far, Callie hasn't bought the gold outfit. I know because I've sniffed out all her hiding places and torn open a few boxes. I even had a little sample or two of the doggie treats she's saving for my stocking. Which I sincerely hope she doesn't discover unless Jack is in the house. Having my human daddy around makes everybody more mellow.

Now I'm not saying the suit makes the man. When I was putting every song I recorded on the charts and bringing millions of fans worldwide to a screaming frenzy, it was my pipes and my charisma that did the trick, baby. Not the costume.

Still, it would be nice to dress in a gold dog suit and lord it over this crooked-legged little Lhasa apso. I'm glad when closing time comes and Darlene scoops him up and leaves Hair.Net.

Callie sinks onto the loveseat beside Ruby Nell, and Lovie bursts out of the so-called massage room with her fake client right behind her, who is not a sight for the faint of heart. Fayrene is still wearing her towel, showing more of herself than I ever wanted to see. Take it from a worldly dog who's been around and knows these things: women trying to age gracefully are better off leaving most things to the imagination.

"Talk about the elephant of surprise," Fayrene says. "If Lovie decides to leave catering behind, she can make a living giving massages."

Our Lovie doesn't take offense at being called an *elephant* instead of an *element*. She just says, "Thank you," and goes on about her business of heading back to the break room for a pitcher of Prohibition Punch and a bunch of glasses.

"I don't know if I ought to get started on this punch." Ruby Nell's protests don't mean a thing. She fills her glass to the rim and chugs a fourth of it down in one gulp.

Fayrene and Lovie follow suit, but Callie declines. My human mom knows better than to count on yours truly as the designated driver. No opposable digits and my hind legs won't reach the gas pedal.

"Since we're all here, there's no need to gather at Lovie's," Mama says, and Fayrene says, "Amen," and refills her glass.

Then Ruby Nell tells her to put on some clothes. I'm so relieved by this development I almost forget myself and look around for that annoying Lhasa Apso to give him a high paw.

While Fayrene's dressing, my human mom outlines the new Christmas open house plans for Lovie. Then Fayrene comes back wearing enough green to sod a lawn.

208

"Bobby's psychic eye is working again," she says. "I really want to do a séance. It'll be my chance to show Jarvetis he didn't know what he was talking when he said we didn't need the séance room."

My best friend Trey (Jarvetis' favorite redbone hound dog) told me all about that argument. Jarvetis told her, "Half the folks in Mooreville don't speak to each other. What makes you think they'll talk to the dead?"

And Fayrene told him, "You go right on with your silly idea to build business by giving away potted Canadians and a hand-knit African, but I'm the one who's out in the manure, here."

I howled so loud at that I scared an alley cat out of at least eight of his lives. He was going through the Gas, Grits, and Guts garbage at the time, and my full-bellied mirth sent him running into the woods behind the store.

Trey got Fayrene's caladiums and hand-knit afghan, but I had to interpret *out in the manure (entrepreneur)* for him.

Now she's holding forth with such passion about her séance and Bobby's rejuvenated psychic eye that Callie says, "All right, Fayrene. Go ahead with the séance. But please don't advertise it. We don't want pickets out front."

"I'll do the catering," Lovie says.

"Jarvetis wants to serve our speciality."

"That's fine, Fayrene," Lovie says. "I can throw a few sprigs of mint around the platter and nobody will even know they're eating pickled pigs' lips."

"I'm not worried about the food," Callie says. "It's the guest list."

Lovie grabs a notepad and pen out of her purse, and they all start suggesting names.

"Put Nelda Lou Perkins at the top of the list." Ruby Nell hates that woman's guts.

"Don't forget that old biddy who served Ex-Lax cookies." Lovie despises seeing people ruin good recipes. "I think Opal Stokes is running neck and neck with Nelda Lou as the prime suspect."

"Don't forget Albert Gordon," Ruby Nell reminds them, and Callie tells her mama, "He's in jail."

"Not anymore. He's out on bail."

"How do you know?"

"Eavesdropping on Charlie."

"Mama, someday Uncle Charlie's going to catch you."

"Flitter."

"Put Albert Gordon down," Callie says. "Abel Caine, too. And don't forget Cleveland White."

"He's not guilty," Ruby Nell says.

"Mama, you don't know that. Put him down, Lovie. And add Corky Kelly and Nathan Briggs."

"Former Santa and his helper? What have we got on them?" Lovie writes them down anyhow.

"Nothing yet. But if we're going to do this right, we need to invite anyone who has a connection to Santa's Court."

"Don't forget the mayor," Fayrene says. "Besides, if Junie Mae's not invited she'll go into a swoon on that fancy sexual sofa she's so proud of."

Junie Mae would faint at that moniker for her sectional sofa. Still, with Tupelo's mayor and his wife in attendance, the Christmas open house at Gas, Grits, and Guts is shaping up to be Mooreville's social event of the year.

In a town with a population of just over six hundred and fifty, the premier social gathering of the year is usually Ruby Nell's annual hog roast.

They finally move on from the guest list and start talking decorations when Lovie's cell phone rings. With my radar ears, I hear none other than Rocky Malone on the other end of the line. He's in a nostalgic mood, and he wants to fly to Tupelo to see Lovie for Christmas.

"You've seen all of me you'll ever get to. I don't hand out second chances."

Rocky changes the subject to ask about Lovie's folks. He's not a man to sit up and beg. I like that about him. If he were a dog, he'd be a noble basset hound.

Instead of hanging up, which she usually does, Lovie talks to her ex-boyfriend a while longer. I don't know if time and distance have softened her or if she's had too much Prohibition Punch.

When she finally tells Rocky goodbye, everybody starts dishing out advice. Most of it bad.

"If you want to get him back," Fayrene says, "I can suggest a Mayan ceremony. Or we can have Bobby consult the spirits."

"Flitter. I know what men want. A lap dance will do the trick."

"Holy cow, Mama, since when do you know what men want?"

"That's for me to know and you to find out."

Callie jerks her car keys out of her purse. "I'm taking you home before you can come up with something else outrageous."

"I can drive."

"Not today, Mama."

Callie herds Ruby Nell and Fayrene to her Dodge Ram and sets off to deliver them safely home while I wait at Hair.Net with Lovie.

"Why does love have to be so complicated, Elvis?"

She rubs my head, and I howl a sweet rendition of "Have I Told You Lately That I Love You."

"You're a good boy, Elvis. Come on. I could use a little snack, couldn't you?"

With me cutting a handsome swath behind her, she proceeds to the break room, where she makes me a big fat sandwich with extra pimento and cheese. That song gets her every time.

You might call my tactics sneaky, but I call it taking care of business.

Chapter 18

Christmas Ornaments, Hair Mistake, and Salem Witches

When I get back to Hair.Net, Lovie's in no shape to drive home, emotionally or physically. And I'm more than happy to take her to my house. Jack's still staying in my guest bedroom, but I'm not making any rash promises to myself about how long that will last. My unfortunate attraction has been making itself known with depressing regularity. I blame it on the Christmas season.

Take tonight, for instance. When I go inside, he's got a box of ornaments on the floor, two mugs of hot chocolate on the coffee table, and the lamps turned down low. To top it off, he's playing Elvis' love ballads. If there's anything sexier than the King's voice crooning about love, I don't know what it is.

Jack helps Lovie and me out of our coats, then hangs them in the hall closet.

"I thought we'd trim the tree tonight, Cal."

The last thing I want tonight is to be reminded of all the years Jack and I spent trimming the Christmas tree—those great years when hopes were high and dreams were bright.

Lovie is no help at all. She just shrugs her shoulders and heads for the stairs.

"Wait, Lovie. We haven't had dinner."

"I made myself a sandwich while you took Aunt Ruby Nell

and Fayrene home. I just want to crawl in a tub of hot water and have a long soak."

" 'Night, Lovie." Jack's just full of good cheer. I wonder how fast he'd wipe that smile off his face if he knew I'd been up to my neck today in the murder investigation.

"I'm tired, too, Jack. I don't think this is a good time to trim the tree."

"You need a little dose of Christmas, Cal." He starts to massage my shoulders. It feels so good, I ought to hire him as a masseuse for Hair.Net. It would be one way to keep him from getting shot at.

Or maybe not.

"Besides," he adds, "I can put the star on top."

He could always put the star on top, and I'm not just talking about trees. I can feel myself caving in when my cell phone rings.

It's Champ, reassuringly down-to-earth and full of stories about Mantachie's mayor who brought her cats, twin Siamese named Puss and Boots, to his clinic today.

"She didn't have them crated, and they both got loose. Boots climbed the Christmas tree, and Puss grabbed the garland. Before I could corner them, my patients got hog-tied with forty feet of garland, and the tree had crashed down onto Mr. Simpkins' Great Dane, who took off after the cats."

I plop onto the sofa, lean my head back, and laugh till tears roll down my face. It feels so good, I keep on chuckling, even after Champ has ended his story and is asking me out to dinner tomorrow night.

Somewhere in back of the sofa, I hear Jack moving around. Is he putting ornaments on the tree? I close my eyes and rub my temples and simply lose myself in the soft cadence of Champ's ordinary conversation.

A click from front door catapults me from the sofa, and I

race to the window in time to see the taillights of Jack's Jag disappearing down my street.

Should he be driving so soon? Where is going? And is he coming back?

"I'd like to see you tomorrow night, Champ."

"Great. I have a surprise for you."

My appetite gone, I head up the stairs to see Lovie. She's out of the tub and going through the stack of books on my bedside table. One I've already read, two I'm trying to read but can't get interested in, and one I'm saving for a weekend when nobody is being shot at or poisoned or electrocuted and I have the luxury of sitting in my rocking chair with a cup of hot chocolate and a little blaze in my Victorian-style gas heater.

"Trying to take your mind off things, Lovie?"

"Yeah, but I don't think it will work tonight."

"Me, neither."

We look at each and simultaneously say, "Popcorn," then head to the kitchen to make a popper full, cooked the old-fashioned way, served up in a big blue bowl, and dripping with butter.

"Where's Jack?"

"Gone."

"Where?"

"I don't know."

"Do you want to talk?"

"No, do you?"

"Nope."

"Good." I head up the stairs with Lovie right behind me. We sit in the center of my bed with the bowl between us. Elvis plops on his pillow beside the bed, Hoyt yawns and stretches from his pillow in the corner (I don't even want to know how it got there), and I breathe, simply breathe.

Sometimes, the best way to solve a problem is to keep quiet and just sleep on it.

I wake up to the smell of coffee and the sound of laughter. The bedside clock hands point to eight, and my first appointment is at nine. I can't believe I overslept.

Grabbing my robe, I race down the stairs, pass by my poor naked Christmas tree, and hurry into the kitchen. Lovie and Jack are making waffles and bacon.

"Good morning, sleepyhead." Jack smiles at me as if nothing happened last night. Come to think of it, nothing did, really. I was on the phone and he left to get supper. Or take a drive. Or shop. Or help catch a killer. It could be any one of those.

"Guess who sent a Christmas card?" Lovie nods toward the table, where the morning mail is in a stack beside the newspaper. "Jill Mabry."

I grab the envelope with a Tennessee postmark and open it to find a note from the cute little kitten-like former Miss Paris (Tennessee, not France) that Lovie and I took under our wing in what we now call the Memphis mambo murders.

My divorce from Victor is final, she writes. *Yay! And I'm back in school working on a degree in medicine. It's harder than I'd thought. I'll probably be in Depends before I finish. (Grin) I just wanted to thank you and Lovie for being so nice to me in Memphis. Without you, I'd never have had the courage to change my life. I'd like to come down and thank you in person. Maybe sometime during the holidays?*

"This is wonderful, Lovie."

"I know. Makes me feel all Oprahish."

"I don't think that's a word."

"It ought to be."

Jack's filling a plate with buttery waffles with syrup and a side of bacon. He sets it on the table in front of me.

"I don't have time to eat, Jack. I've got to dress and run."

"Eat. I'll go open the shop and put the coffee on." I open my mouth to protest, but he says, "It's not negotiable," then he grabs my spare shop key off the key rack on the kitchen wall and walks out whistling.

What can I say? I'm starving, so I dig into breakfast.

Lovie studies me over the rim of her coffee cup. "He'd be a hard man to let go."

"I know."

"You do?"

"Yes." I put down my fork. "Lovie, Champ's getting ready to propose."

"Nothing wrong with that man, either. But I'd take a test run before I bought the car."

"I'll leave the test runs to you."

"Way to go. If you keep on, you're liable to grow up and be a smart mouth just like me."

"I don't want to grow up."

"Nobody does."

"I just want to make up my mind."

"Good luck, kiddo."

My cousin knows when to offer advice and when to merely lend support. Good friends always do.

She turns on the small kitchen TV, refills her coffee cup, fills her plate, and joins me at the table. On the local morning news, a reporter gives an update on the murders at the mall and announces that no suspects have been arrested.

"Not yet, but wait till Aunt Ruby Nell and Fayrene have their séance. The dead are going to show up at Gas, Grits, and Guts to point out the killer."

It feels great to start the day with laughter.

"I agree about the futility of a séance, Lovie, but the open house might work."

217

"Not unless we can learn more than we already know. I'm about ready to turn in my detective badge."

"What badge?"

"The one I'm going to have tattooed near the Holy Grail."

"You're kidding. Right?"

"Just think of the confessions I'll get when I flash my badge."

I toss my napkin at her, and she bursts out laughing.

The TV camera cuts from the mall to a roving reporter standing in a residential neighborhood in Tupelo.

"In separate incidents in Highland Circle," he says, "two residents were mugged while they were jogging at night. The mugger, believed to be a male of average height, has not been caught."

"People ought to know better than to jog in the dark." Lovie gets up to add more waffles to her plate. "They ought to know better than to jog, period. It's bad for the knees."

She reaches up to turn off the TV.

"Wait a minute." I scan the area behind the reporter. "That's six thirteen, Lovie. Nathan Briggs' house."

"That doesn't mean Nathan was mugged."

"What if he was? Or even if he wasn't, why was the mugger in that neighborhood? They have really tight security."

"You're saying he was more than a mugger?"

"Maybe this so-called mugger is the killer." I get up to rinse my plate and put it in the dishwasher. "Think about it. First, a break-in at Nathan Brigg's house, and now two muggings in his neighborhood."

"No such thing as coincidence," we say at the same time, then high-five each other.

"Lovie, I think the killer is after the mall's original Santa."

"What about poor Wayne and the attempt on Daddy?"

"They were in the perfect disguise. If you hadn't known they were going to be in Santa's Court, would you have recognized the man behind all that fake hair and beard?"

"You've got a point, Sherlock."

"What's on your schedule today, Watson?"

"Besides baking ten of my famous butterscotch cream pies for the Christmas party at the Wellness Center, I think I'll be finding out who had a beef against Nathan Briggs."

"You're serving cream pies at the Wellness Center?"

"They wanted broccoli bites with low-calorie dressing, but I'm fixing to show them the error of their ways. If those exercise nuts don't put on a little weight, they're all going to dry up and blow away."

"I've got to get dressed, Lovie. Call me if you find out anything."

"My van's at the beauty shop. Remember?"

Actually, I didn't. With everything that has been going on, it's a wonder I remember my name.

Though I love to soak in a leisurely bath and take my time dressing, I'm a woman who can be showered, changed, and fully made up in fifteen minutes flat.

Fortunately, so is Lovie. And Elvis is always ready to go. We hop into my Dodge Ram and head to Hair.Net. Lovie bids us goodbye outside, then drives off toward Tupelo.

I push open the door and walk into my domain, where all the lights are on, the lamps are glowing, the thermostat is set exactly right, and the coffee is already brewed.

I'd like to thank Jack, but his Jag is not in the driveway, so I know he has already left. One of the nicest things about living in small-town Mississippi is that it's still safe to leave your door unlocked.

I walk straight to the kitchen and pour myself a cup of coffee. There's a note by the coffee pot: *Cal, I thought you needed some privacy last night, so I spent the night at my apartment. XOXO Jack*

Hugs and kisses. Plus breakfast every morning, hot chocolate nearly every night, and a live Christmas tree I can replant.

Right now, though, I can't think about the many ways he's trying to please me—and why?—because the bell over my shop door just tinkled.

"Come on back and grab a cup of coffee, Mabel."

Mabel Moffett, here for a trim, likes to be the first client of the day. She joins me in the kitchen and helps herself to the coffee.

"I'm so excited about Fayrene and Jarvetis' open house. I've got to go to the mall after I get my hair done. I don't have a thing to wear."

Mabel Moffett could start a clothing store with her used evening gowns. She goes over the top at Mooreville's social events, always wearing long gowns with too many fake pearls, even at Mama's annual hog roast. And she thinks it's a sin to be seen in the same gown twice.

Still, I'm glad the word's getting out about the open house, and I'm glad Mama and Fayrene have thought to invite Mooreville's glitterati. After our tangle with the law at Albert Gordon's Santa barbecue, it won't do for the Lee County sheriff to figure out what Lovie and I are up to. The last thing we need is a long line of uniforms.

If there's one thing I've learned from my unexpected involvement in murder, it's that no killer is going to tip his hand in front of a bunch of cops.

We finish our coffee and head up front, where I drape Mabel in a pink cape and take out my scissors.

"I had to stop by the post office to mail a Christmas package to my sister in Atlanta," she says. "Did I see Jack leaving your shop?"

"He volunteered to open up this morning."

"He seems like such a nice young man."

"He is."

"I told my daughter, I said, 'Trixie, forget about marrying Roy Jessup. He's nothing but a fertilizer and manure man. If Callie's divorce is ever final, you need to set your cap for that handsome Jack Jones.' "

I cut off a chunk of her hair as big as Texas. Accidentally, of course. It never occurred to me that if I didn't want Jack, women all over Mooreville would be clamoring for him.

"You look funny, Callie. Did I say something to upset you, hon?"

"No. I suddenly remembered I've got to pick up a roast for dinner." I make myself smile at her reflection in the mirror. "Jack likes meat and potatoes."

It's better for Mabel to chew on that for a while than to know I'm doing some creative styling behind her back. Holy cow. I never make a miss-whack with the scissors. If I don't learn to keep my personal feelings under wraps, I'm going to ruin my reputation as the best stylist this side of the Mississippi River.

At mid-morning, Darlene comes in, and we both get so busy I barely have time to think about my quandary over Jack. Around four, Mama drops in, which usually spells trouble. But I'm so glad to have an excuse to take a break, I don't care if she's come to say she needs the rest of my Christmas gift money for a little restorative jaunt to the casinos over in Tunica.

"Callie, come outside. I've got to show you the decorations we're putting in the séance room."

221

Leaving Darlene with one customer in her manicurist's chair and another waiting, not to mention my dread of instant holiday poverty, I head to my small parking lot, where Mama's Mustang is taking up two spaces. Yesterday's storm has blown over, the weather has turned unseasonably mild, and she's driving with the top down.

The red convertible is overflowing with gold garlands, strings of lights shaped like snowflakes, and an assortment of hang-from-the-ceiling Christmas characters. Santa's there with Mrs. Claus and Frosty the Snowman, plus all his reindeer and Rudolph, too.

"Holy cow, where will we put the guests?"

"Jarvetis is going to put all this stuff in the store." Just as Lovie drives up, Mama reaches into a pile of silver bells and pulls out a crystal ball and a gypsy's scarf decorated with red roses. "*This* is what I'm talking about for the séance room. It's the genuine article."

"Do I even want to know where you got that?"

"It belonged to a real witch. I got it at that little antiques and junk store down at Richmond."

"If she's still able to straddle a broomstick, invite her to the séance open house, Aunt Ruby Nell." Bound for Lovie.

About two miles south of Mama's farm is the tiny farming community of Richmond. It features Richmond Baptist Church, a hole-in-the-wall store called Junk and Stuff that has a beauty shop attached, and a convenience store that Fayrene says won't hold a candle to Gas, Grits, and Guts. I feel the same way about their beauty shop. Though Richmond would love to be as uptown as Mooreville, they don't even have a post office, let alone a salon as cosmopolitan as Hair.Net.

"How do you know it's genuine, Mama. I never heard of a witch in Richmond."

"I've personally met one or two," Lovie says.

"Be nice," I tell her. "It's Christmas."

"This belonged to one of the Salem witches," Mama says. "Her crystal ball got handed down from generation to generation and ended up with a descendant in Richmond."

"That's a little far-fetched, Mama."

"I showed it to Bobby to verify that the crystal ball is real." Mama stuffs it back into her car. "You'll see."

With that dire prediction, Mama drives off.

"Holy cow!" I say, and Lovie deadpans, "And pig, too!"

"What did you find out about Nathan Briggs, Lovie?"

"Not much. Five years ago, he was Tupelo's Man of the Year. He's a deacon at First Baptist and has a wife named Wendy and two daughters in college."

"You need to make sure Wendy is invited to the open house."

"Why me?"

"I've got to do something I should have done when we got back from Mexico."

Lovie gives me this searching look. She knows. I swear, sometimes I think we can read each other's mind.

"Do you want me along for support?" she asks.

"No. I'll be fine. I'm taking Elvis. Just go over to Gas, Grits, and Guts and make sure Mama and Fayrene are not planning something with that crystal ball that will scandalize Mooreville."

Lovie leaves in her van, and I go inside to tell Darlene to lock up when she leaves. Then I freshen up in the cute bathroom featuring my salon's signature pink, load Elvis in my Dodge Ram, and head toward Mantachie.

Elvis' Opinion #16 on Breaking Up, Great Pies, and Mean Cats

If you're wondering why Callie would take a dog as moral support for a breakup, you've got a lot to learn about human nature. The best moral support is not somebody who will talk your ear off and tell you how you ought to do it and afterward tell you what you did wrong.

It's a smart canine who keeps his mouth shut, puts his head in your lap, and holds in his noxious gas till he gets out of the truck. Listen, there's a lot to be said for a canine head on your lap. It gives you a warm and fuzzy feeling, a sense that you're not alone and that you are totally loved, no matter how bad you mess up.

My human mom keeps her hand on my head all the way to Mantachie, but she doesn't say anything, just drives with more caution than she usually displays when she's behind the wheel. She's in no hurry to get there. And who can blame her? Champ's a good man and a doggone good vet.

If a disaster came along and I ended up without Jack, I could get used to a substitute who can give a vaccination so easy you don't feel it.

But Jack's still here, and nobody can take his place. Callie's finally realized this. Still, that didn't make her decision any easier or what she's about to do any less difficult. I smell regret and pain all the way to Champ's clinic.

When we go inside, his secretary tells her the vet is in his office and to just go on back. Naturally. Nobody keeps the King waiting.

"Callie?" Champ acts surprised to see her, but I can see he's putting on a front. The vet's a smart man. I've read his aura and his body language. He's been expecting this ever since my human daddy ended up at Mooreville in Callie's house.

My human mom is gentle as she tells Champ she can't keep giving him false hope, that it's not fair to any of them, that all along she's been fooling herself.

"Champ, what I feel for you is the deep respect and loyalty of a good friend."

"I understand, Callie. I just hope we can remain friends and that I can remain your vet." Luke Champion shows why he's called Champ when he gives my human mom a genuine smile and gives me a big old pat on the head. "I'd miss seeing the King, here."

"I'm so relieved you said that. I'd hate to lose you, too."

Callie doesn't even know she's crying till Champ hands her a tissue. She wipes her eyes and gives him a hug, then we're off for our little cottage in Mooreville.

But if you think this is one of those old movie classics where the heroine walks straight home into the arms of her true love, you don't know real life from Pup-Peroni.

Jack calls to say he has some things to do, that he'll be at his apartment if she needs him, and we settle in to decorate the Christmas tree. Everything but the star. Callie can't reach the top, and I wouldn't be climbing a ladder even if I did have digits. Too many chances my portly self might take a large tumble and do major damage to my handsome face.

Be that as it may, at least we have a mostly trimmed tree, complete with colored lights. It keeps us company over the next few days while Jack is on his mysterious errand and my human mom helps get ready for the Christmas open house at Gas, Grits, and Guts.

When the big day arrives, I get all gussied up in my four-legged red suit as the one and only Santa Paws and set out with my human mom to put Mooreville on the map.

Gas, Grits, and Guts is popping with lights and filled to the brim with guests. Looks like nobody turned down the chance to hobnob with Mooreville's answer to Lucy and Desi. Fayrene, looking like a stalk of asparagus in her green velvet suit, has even talked Jarvetis into wearing a vegetable green tie.

But I'll have to say if Macy's ever needs a new decorator, Fayrene and Ruby Nell would fit the bill. Santa and Mrs. Claus, hanging from the ceiling just inside the door, greet guests. Lights are strung on every shelf in the store, with extras surrounding the disco ball Fayrene and Jarvetis won at the Memphis dance competition. A special display has been set up near the entrance to the séance room: Ruldolph and Santa's sleigh, suspended over the pickled pigs' lips.

Along the back wall of the store, a table is filled with holiday treats from Lovie's Luscious Eats: her famous pies—butterscotch cream, Hershey, and pumpkin pecan—her Happy Holiday Kiss Kiss Eggnog, and enough other goodies to keep a dog who knows the art of the con busy the rest of the night.

Though everybody wants to stop and pet a beguiling basset in a Santa paws suit, I don't waste any *ho, ho, hos* on the crowd. I reconnoiter before heading for the food.

Up front, Callie greets guests and hands out door prizes, another way of saying she's checking out all the suspects. They're probably checking her out, too. In a silver sequined blouse, black skirt, and the extravagant spike-heeled black calfskin designer boots I wouldn't dream of peeing on, even in a snit, she looks like the kind of woman who wouldn't be caught dead in a store with "Guts" in the name.

Charlie is keeping a low profile while he keeps an eye out for trouble. So is my human daddy, though he mostly has eyes for you know who.

If they want to see trouble, they'd do well to cast their attention in my direction.

Just when I'm getting ready to con the mayor's wife out of a piece of pie, Darlene waltzes through the door. And while she's got sense enough to realize you can't take a Lhasa apso out in public and expect anything except embarrassment, she's apparently got a blind spot about cats.

That stupid cat she calls Mal is with her. In a little cat carrier, granted, but how long does she think it takes a mean cat to get out of cat prison?

She sets the carrier in the corner and makes a beeline for Bobby Huckabee. The minute she turns her back, that ridiculous pox on the animal kingdom reaches toward the latch with a vicious claw.

I'd march over there and scare him out of about seven of his sorry little lives if I didn't have pressing business with the mayor's wife.

One more adorable basset grin in her direction, and she sets a paper plate on the floor with half a piece of pie.

"Here, you cute little Santa. I don't need the calories."

I start lapping up butterscotch cream, but don't think I'm not still in charge. I know the minute Bobby leaves the front of the store. He's going to get ready for a séance in the newly renovated back room, and he'll be using the crystal ball of a genuine Salem witch.

I also spot that sneaky cat creeping out of his cell, heading in my direction. If he keeps on coming, I predict that the only dead who will show up for Bobby's séance will be Darlene's cat.

If the odious Mal puts one claw on my Santa suit—or my pie—he's going to become the third Christmas corpse.

Chapter 19

Killing Miss Sweet Potato, Lethal Spaghetti Sauce, and Armageddon

It turns out that the open house at Gas, Grits, and Guts has lured some of the suspects, but not as many as I had hoped. Over the last fifteen minutes I've spotted Cleveland White, Nelda Lou Perkins, and Opal Stokes. Still, it's early, and not everybody likes to be among the first arrivals at a party.

According to plan, Mama, Fayrene, Lovie, and I are spread out so we can cover the crowd. If we spot anything suspicious, our signal for help is to say in a very loud voice, "Has anybody seen Elvis?"

It's sure to bring laughter among those who don't know he's a dog, and a search party of locals who know he is.

The signal was Fayrene's idea, which surprised me. Her contributions are usually bizarre. But she said this would be a good way to "alert each other without giving anybody a Cadillac arrest."

Well, there you go. Who wants to do CPR at a party? Especially on a Cadillac.

What I also don't want to do is find myself alone with Jack. I haven't told him about my breakup with Champ and don't intend to. Whatever happens next is up to him. I don't intend to act like a desperate woman who flits from one man to the next.

Independence, that's my motto. If Jack comes back into my life, it will be for the right reasons. Not because I'm available, or lonely, or scared. And certainly not because I want to have children before my rapidly shriveling eggs start looking like raisins. I've learned the hard way that the desire for a family is not reason enough to plunge into a relationship.

I spot Uncle Charlie near the front door and head that way. When I'm a feeling a little blue, he always cheers me up.

Out of the corner of my eye, I see Nelda Lou Perkins also steaming toward my uncle. In full beauty queen mode, she's wearing a gold lamé dress with matching shoes. The heels are so high, she's tilted forward. I expect her to topple at any minute. If the shoes don't do it, the makeup will. She's loaded it on so thick it looks heavy enough to slide right to the floor—and her with it.

For once, I don't even mean that in a nice way. Anybody who gives Uncle Charlie a hard time does not deserve my good wishes.

Unfortunately, before I can reach them I get stuck in a wad of people between the canned peas and the potato chips. Still, Nelda Lou is so loud I could hear her if I were out in the parking lot.

"Charlie! You look *so handsome!*" She slides her arm through his, and though I can tell he'd like to shake her off, he's too much of a gentleman. "I've got something you have *got to see!*"

"I'm afraid I'll have to decline, Nelda Lou." He smiles to take the sting out of his rejection. Uncle Charlie goes out of his way to be nice to everybody, whether they deserve it or not. "Jarvetis and Fayrene have asked me to help them host. I can't leave my guests."

"They can do without you for *one little minute.*"

She starts trying to drag him through the front door, and

short of embarrassing her in front of a crowd, what can he do? Still stuck in canned goods, I yell, "Has anybody seen Elvis?"

Amid general laughter, one wag says, "Yeah, but you're looking in the wrong grocery store." A reference to the famous *I saw Elvis at the Piggly Wiggly* comment.

I'm beginning to think none of my cohorts in crime heard me when I see one heading my way. Unfortunately, it's Mama.

Considering her animosity toward Nelda Lou, I consider not even motioning toward Uncle Charlie. But somebody has already tried to kill him once, and the former Miss Sweet Potato is a suspect. At least, in the Valentine book.

I nod toward the door. Mama glances in that direction, goes all squinch-eyed and evil-looking, then barrels after Uncle Charlie and Nelda Lou. Still stuck in the clump of people who have now inched down to the green beans, I try to extricate myself. To no avail.

I have to get outside before Mama kills Miss Sweet Potato.

Where is Jack when I need him? Head and shoulders taller than everybody else, he's easy to spot in a crowd. But a quick glance confirms he's nowhere in sight. Does he know something about the Santa killer that I don't?

Suddenly an unholy screech followed by a string of words only Lovie could use comes from the back of the store. Abandoning all social graces, I elbow my way out of canned goods and race in my cousin's direction.

Darlene's cat appears out of nowhere and streaks past me, yowling as if the hounds of hell are after him. But it's not the hell hounds: it's Elvis in a total snit and the mayor's wife in a squashed-looking, marshmallow-pink suit and a mood to kill.

I've never seen Junie Mae move that fast. Furthermore, she's screaming, "Come back here, you little scamp." I don't know whether she's bent on doing bodily harm to my dog or Darlene's cat. Or both.

I spin around to go after Elvis. Lovie can take care of herself. I hope.

My abrupt change in direction catapults me straight into the arms of my almost-ex. And I don't want to think about how good it feels to be in his solid presence.

"I've got Elvis and the cat under control, Cal. Go see what's up with Lovie."

"What about Uncle Charlie? He's outside with Mama and Miss Sweet Potato."

Chuckling, he puts his hands on my shoulders and points me in the direction of the séance room. "Charlie and Ruby Nell can handle that. Scoot."

As I charge toward my cousin, I'd be grateful I no longer hear screeching if I weren't now hearing what sounds like the battle of Armageddon.

Though Jack would never send me off toward danger, I grab the nearest weapon—a jar of Prego spaghetti sauce.

Holding my weapon aloft, I skid to a stop underneath Santa's sleigh. I'm sorry to report that Ruldolph and the reindeer have been knocked askew and are now dangling from the ceiling and into Lovie's bowl of Prohibition Punch.

Standing in front of the punch and clutching a bottle of Kaopectate, Lovie is squared off against none other than the cookie lady/Santa thief. In the perimeter, a crowd starts to gather.

"That's mine," Opal Stokes screams at Lovie. "Give it to me."

"I'm going to give it to you, all right, you hag from hell. If you take another step in the direction of my punch, I'll sit on you and personally pour the whole bottle down your throat."

"Lovie, let's remain calm. I'm sure Mrs. Stokes is open to reason."

Seizing the opportunity, Opal lunges for freedom. But she

doesn't count on me and my Prego. I tap her upside the head with the spaghetti sauce. Not hard, though. I love justice as much as the next hair stylist, but I draw the line at clocking a senior citizen . . . even if she does steal Santas and put a laxative in the Christmas goodies.

And I certainly don't intend to get tomato sauce all over my Christian Louboutin boots. Besides, I have an audience.

"Way to go, Cal. That'll teach her to tamper with my Prohibition Punch." Lovie grabs the culprit on one side and I grab her on the other. Then she turns her considerable charm on our growing audience. "It's all over, folks. The punch and cookies are safe. Enjoy!"

With Opal sagging between us, we hustle her into the darkened séance room. I can't get her out of sight fast enough. Fortunately, I see Uncle Charlie heading our way to smooth-talk the crowd.

I kick the door shut behind us, then lean weak-kneed against it. Opal still has not made one little peep.

"What if I killed her?"

"Good riddance."

"I'm serious, Lovie."

"So am I." She shoulders Opal's weight. "I've got her. Turn on the light. Let's see what's going on with this mean old heifer."

I flick the light switch. In the sudden wash of brightness, Opal looks as white as Santa's beard. And on the other side of the room, Darlene and Bobby look like two people who have been caught making out.

"Don't tell Mama," Darlene says, confirming what I already suspected. There's more going on with my manicurist and Uncle Charlie's assistant than sharing horoscopes.

Bobby clears his throat and tugs at his Christmas tie, bright red with sequined snowflakes, probably a gift from Darlene.

I've never seen him wear anything that would call attention to himself.

"Darlene's been giving me some moral support."

"One euphemism is as good as the other." Lovie winks at Bobby and Darlene—who winks back. Meanwhile, Opal still droops like a blowup Santa that has sprung a leak.

"It looks like Opal won't be talking for a while, Lovie."

"Is there a closet in here?"

"Holy cow! We can't just stuff her in the closet."

"I don't see why not."

"For one thing, she may need medical attention."

Lovie says a word that makes Bobby blush. "You keep forgetting everything she's done, Cal. I think she's capable of murder."

Darlene's eyes go wide. In spite of Fayrene being up to her asparagus green zippers in murder, her daughter has been clueless about our sleuthing shenanigans. Until now, of course.

"Don't tell Jack," I say.

"Tell me what?"

I jump as if a bomb has detonated under my designer boots. Jack has sneaked in behind me and he feels like a mountain, one brewing up a snowstorm if not an avalanche. Furthermore, he scalds the back of my neck with the hottest kiss this side of X-rated movies.

I melt into my boots, but fortunately Lovie retains her starch.

"Jack, Opal Stokes is the Audubon Christmas thief and the one who served up laxative-laced cookies at the mall. She went after my punch and Callie beaned her with the Prego."

"Did you, now?" He winks at me, then whips a little vial out of his pocket and holds it under Opal's nose, and she sputters to life. "She's not the Santa killer."

When Jack throws her over his shoulder as if she weighs no

more than a snowflake, Opal barely squeaks in protest. "I'll take care of this. Fayrene's about to announce the séance."

"What about Elvis and the cat?"

"Safely stowed, Cal." He leans down and kisses me as if we have bassinets in our future. "You stay put."

I couldn't move if fifteen wild elephants were stampeding my way. Which is not a bad description for the crowd that pours into the séance room shortly after Jack disappears out the back door and Fayrene blares over the loudspeaker up front, "Everybody step right this way. The séance is about to *convince.*"

I'm convinced, all right. I'll never get over Jack Jones, no matter how many divorce lawyers I hire.

Elvis' Opinion #17 on Sweet Revenge, Getting Busted, and Doing Time

I've been busted. But it was worth it to see the look on that stupid cat's face when he thought I was going to rearrange his tacky fur coat. Sweet revenge for trying to steal my cream pie. That asinine feline was actually relieved when Jack collared him and locked him back in his cage.

Being confined to the cab of Callie's truck for the duration of the party is not so bad, considering what happened to my arch enemy. Jack hustled that stupid cat to Jarvetis, who took the whole kit and caboodle back home. The odious Mal is now doing hard time.

Take it from a dog who knows. Jarvetis is a redbone hound dog man. His favorite hound dog, and my best friend, Trey reports there's no love lost between his human daddy and Darlene's evil-eyed cat. I'll bet Jarvetis didn't even give Mal any catnip to ease the pain of prison.

Unlike my human daddy, who apologized profusely for putting me in Callie's truck and eased my pain considerably with a big hunk chunk of ham and biscuits from Lovie's refreshment table.

"It won't be for long, Elvis. I promise. Just behave yourself for a little while, don't try any tricks, and we'll all go home together. I promise."

Now there's a promise you can hang your hat on. Forget "All I Want for Christmas Is My Two Front Teeth." All I want is my family back together . . . and the biggest pile of gifts under the Christmas tree.

Listen, I'm no Solomon, but whoever said *less is more* ought to have to spend one night under a bridge in thirty-degree weather. Or try to stretch one bowl of rice over six mouths. Or bathe in a river full of crocodiles.

As I scarf down my ham and biscuits, I'm as thankful as the next dog that I'm warm and dry and safe from sharp-toothed predators. After I root out the crumbs that dropped and lick the remainder off my muzzle, I ensconce my fabulous but grateful backside on the jogging coat Callie sometimes leaves in her truck and watch the crowd as they continue to stream into Gas, Grits, and Guts. There goes Nathan Briggs, the mall's original Santa, and a good-looking dark-haired woman I'm betting to be his wife, Wendy.

Don't think I don't know this guest list from top to bottom. If Jack would let me out of the truck, I'd not only behave myself, I'd have the killer collared before Bobby could bend over his crystal ball and say, "Abracadabra" or whatever incantation he uses to raise the dead.

Hold the fort. Look who's hiding behind the gas tanks.

In the shadows, Nelda Lou Perkins lights up a cigarette. Her anger is so palpable it might as well be Pup-Peroni.

Ruby Nell's instincts are good. It will do to keep an eye on Miss Sweet Potato.

But what's this I smell? Corky Kelly, the mall's former elf, the one my human mom and I saw the first day of Santa's Court. He doesn't see me, but I could pick up his scent in the middle of the tundra. My hackles stand straight up as he slides through the front door of Gas, Grits, and Guts.

And who's this creeping up from the woods behind the

store? It's hard to see his face behind all that camouflage paint, but I smell that scent every time Callie and I jog past his house. It's Albert Gordon, the Santa bonfire man. And he's loaded to the hilt with weapons.

I'd set up a howl if I thought it would do anything except get me shot. But Jack doesn't need any warnings. Now that his cast is off and his rival is out of the picture (don't think Jack doesn't know that Callie broke up with Champ), my human daddy can handle anything Gordon throws at him.

Well, bless'a my soul. What's this I hear? Sounds like backup, to me. Barreling in this direction in his big, bad truck (I heard the engine many a time coming to the little cottage on Robins Street) is none other than Rocky Malone. It doesn't take a betting dog to know he's coming to crash the party.

I'd give up one of the bones buried in my back yard just to see the look on Lovie's face when her ex-boyfriend walks through the door.

Fortunately, I don't have to. Nobody's going to open this truck door, and my human daddy is on the job. So I settle back on the coat that holds my favorite scent, eau de Callie, and wait for the fireworks that are sure to come.

Chapter 20

Raising the Dead, Jilted Lovers, and Whodunnit

"**E**verybody, right this way. There's always room for one more." Mama sounds like the barker at a side show, which is probably a good description for this so-called séance. Though Bobby is a good man and a capable undertaker, I don't hold out much hope of his resurrecting the dead.

The Baptists are proving me wrong by pouring into the séance room. Are they here to talk to the dead or to take names for their prayer list? After our public scene over the Prohibition Punch, Lovie and I will be at the top of the list.

On the heels of the locals comes Cleveland White, the mall's manager. As he files past with Mayor Getty and Junie Mae, Lovie pokes me in the ribs.

"Psst. Over there."

I look in the direction of her nod and see Corky Kelly in a jovial mood as he chats with Nathan Briggs and a woman who must be his wife. For one thing, Nathan has his arm around her waist. Nathan's an average-looking man with hair that could use a good trim and a belly that's beginning to sag. Who'd have thought his wife would be a knockout?

Coming in behind them are Mabel Moffett and her daughter Trixie, all gussied up in red taffeta ruffles and blush that clashes. After her recent jilt from Mooreville's fertilizer man, she looks like a woman on the prowl.

"If Trixie thinks she's going to get her claws into Jack, she's got another think coming."

I know whispering in public is a tacky thing to do, but I don't think announcing you're looking for a killer is socially correct, either.

"Grrr," Lovie says. "Go get her, tiger."

"Smarty pants."

"Yeah, well. If the britches fit... I'm not talking about Trixie. Albert Gordon is here."

Fayrene is already at the light switch, turning the dimmer, but I study the crowd again. Just before the lights get too low to recognize anybody's face, I spot Albert Gordon skulking around the perimeter in full camouflage.

"He's got a gun, Lovie," I whisper. The room is now jampacked, and even if I yelled, "Has anybody seen Elvis?" it's now too dark for any of my conspirators to see what I'm talking about.

I grab Lovie's arm and head in Albert's direction.

"What are we going to do if we catch him?" she whispers.

"Improvise."

"I left my Moon Goddess outfit in the jungle."

I'm glad to see Lovie's sense of humor is intact. Especially considering that at any minute, we could become Christmas corpses number three and four.

Latecomers are still crowding into the séance room, trying to find a space to stand. As my cousin and I push toward Albert, nobody pays us any attention.

Is Albert after Uncle Charlie? Or Nathan? Or both?

We're close enough now to smell the grease of Albert's camouflage paint.

"Have you still got the Prego, Cal?"

"Yes, but I don't think I can take Albert down with a whack from a plastic bottle."

Lovie jerks it out of my hands, holds it like a gun, then steps behind Albert, and pokes the plastic cap hard into his back.

"Freeze, sucker," she snarls in his ear. "I've got a gun, and I'm itching to use it. Make my day."

Holy cow. Who does she think she is? Clint Eastwood? Any minute now I expect Albert to turn around and blow my cousin to Kingdom Come.

Over my dead body.

I step beside Lovie, jerk a bobby pin out of my French twist, and ram it against the side of his throat.

"If you don't think I'll slit your throat with this stiletto, think again, buster."

"Are you broads crazy? I can take both of you out with my bare hands."

I notice he's not trying. I'm still congratulating myself on how tough Lovie and I are when Uncle Charlie and Jack materialize right in front of Albert.

"Don't even think about it," Jack tells him, then he and Uncle Charlie hustle Albert out without even a scuffle.

"I think I'm going to wet my pants," Lovie says as they slip out through the back door.

"Not on my designer boots."

"Shut up."

My cousin and I collapse against each other in relief. Now that the killer has been caught, we can enjoy the rest of the show.

"Ladies and gentlemen . . ." It's easy to see why everybody

says Fayrene once considered going into show business. She
has a voice that can carry all the way to the Alabama state line.

"Close your eyes," she says. "Let yourself slip into Bo-
livia."

A few out-of-towners titter, while the Mooreville crowd remains respectful. Fayrene is their beloved Mrs. Malaprop.
They know *oblivion* when they hear it.

Suddenly the crystal ball in the center of the room lights up.
In the eerie glow, Bobby looks almost majestic.

"I present to you . . . psychic extra-ordinarily . . . *Bobby Huckabee!*"

As he raises his hands, a hush falls over the crowd. Something hangs over this séance room that puts little shivers along
the back of my neck. Lovie squeezes my hand, a signal that
she feels it, too.

"Spirits of the universe . . ." Bobby begins to chant in a
fluid, ethereal voice that doesn't sound like the shy young
man who rarely strings two sentences together. "Speak to us.
Speak to us now."

The silence feels like a wool cloak. It's too warm in here,
and I'm starting to sweat.

"We implore the dead," he says, "any old dead."

I make a mental note to remind him to polish his patter.

Bobby clears his throat. Where are his psychic powers when
he needs them most?

"Any old dead will do." He begins to falter, then I see a
hand descend onto his shoulder. Fingernails glowing with silver Christmas stars. Darlene.

"Particularly the newly Christmas dead." Bobby has re-
gained momentum, and his voice sweeps over us like Moses
commanding the Red Sea to part. "Talk to us, Ruldoph the
Red-Nosed Reindeer! Speak to us, Santa!"

"Win-dy." As the hoarse whisper hangs in the overheated

room, I'm wondering why the dead would send a weather report. But, frankly, I could use a little breeze.

"Windy," the whisper says again, "Briggs."

Holy cow. That's no crazed spirit talking about the weather. That's a possible killer talking about Wendy Briggs.

I punch Lovie, and we both start creeping in the general direction of the voice.

"Speak!" Bobby's shouting like a hellfire-and-brimstone preacher at a tent revival. Apparently, success has gone to his head.

"Wendy, you married the wrong man," the disembodied voice says. "Leave Nathan Briggs before it's too late."

Somebody bolts toward the door—probably Nathan with his wife, Wendy—followed by fifty other people who suddenly realize they are not hearing the voice of the dead. It's bedlam in the dark.

In the noisy stampede, I'm torn away from my cousin. Groping for her hand, I make contact with flesh.

"Lovie?"

"Guess again." Arms trap me from behind, and suddenly I'm a hostage of the Santa killer. As all the puzzle pieces fall into place, I don't know whether to scream or wet my pants. Fortunately, my social graces rise to the surface, along with the last grain of bravery I have.

"You don't have to do this, Corky."

"You're too smart for your own good, Miss Jones." As he wrestles me toward the door, who's to notice in the rest of the chaos?

"Why did you kill Steve and Wayne?"

"Nathan was not supposed to be home with the flu."

"And you didn't know who was behind the beard?"

"Bingo, Miss Jones. Or should I say Mrs.?"

I see my future as being six feet under while Jack walks this life in eternal regret that he left me for a Harley Screaming Eagle.

Still, if I can keep Corky talking till we get outside where the lights are on, somebody will see us and stop him. I hope.

"But why Nathan?"

"He stole her," Corky screams. "My cousin and best man stole my fiancé at the altar, then rubbed salt in my wounds for fifteen years. Always complaining that I was a bad elf."

We burst from the shadows of the séance room into the Christmas lights and disco ball trophy brightness of Gas, Grits, and Guts. Mama yells, "He killed Santa and Rudolph. And now he's got my daughter!"

She picks up a six-pack of Coors Light and charges our way. Never underestimate the power of familial love.

Neighbors and guests grab purses and jars of pickled pigs' lips, car keys, and kegs of beer—whatever weapon is handy—as they race to my rescue.

Still, Corky is gaining the door, with me as his shield, and who is to stop him once he gets outside? And where is Jack when I need him?

There's a roar like a wounded bull, and charging to the front of the vigilante group is the man I'll never allow to become my ex.

"Corky, halt!" He's pointing a gun, but even a crazed Santa killer knows Jack Jones will not try to shoot while I'm in the line of fire.

Waving her Coors, Mama catches up with Jack. Uncle Charlie and Lovie are right behind her, and my cousin's brandishing a meat cleaver. I don't even want to know how she got that.

Jack blocks them with his left arm.

"Stay back. You'll make it worse. Everybody stay back."

Somewhere in the parking lot behind me, Elvis is barking

like crazy. In front of me, half of Tupelo and Mooreville are frozen behind Jack with their motley assortment of weapons. We must look like a shoot-out scene from an old TV western. Where's the cavalry when you need them?

I try to dig in my heels, but Corky is strong for a small man. I feel myself being dragged irrevocably backward. If he ever gains his car, this will be my last Christmas.

Over my dead body.

In the tight grip of Corky's arms, I start easing my hands toward my back.

"I'd suggest you stop right there and let Mrs. Jones go."

Rocky Malone!

I don't even pause to wonder how Lovie's former boyfriend got here. Seizing the distraction, I grab a handful of Corky's Christmas decorations—a euphemism my Valentine grandmother would surely approve—and give a big yank.

With a yowl, Corky goes down. Jack and Rocky are on top of him before he can even surrender. With his knee in Corky's decorations, Jack grins up at me.

"Nice move."

"Thanks."

"Don't ever try it on me."

"I won't. As long as you promise to behave."

"The only promise I'm making is to put the star on your Christmas tree."

I smile at him. Jack Jones can put the star on my Christmas tree any time.

Elvis' Opinion #18 on the Star Restored, Stuffed Turkey, and a Merry Christmas to All

With Corky behind bars, the crazy cookie lady and the deranged Santa barbecue man under psychiatric care, Miss Sweet Potato cooling her jets back in Highland Circle, and the singed Santas restored to their rightful rooftops, Christmas in Mooreville is back to normal. That means the chaos is almost manageable and yours truly, basset hound extraordinaire, reigns supreme.

Of course, I could have caught the Santa killer long ago if they'd turned me loose. I picked up Corky's scent in the robing room at the mall. And when Fayrene said that he couldn't possibly be a suspect, that everybody called him *good old Corky, always lending a hand*, I figured out how he turned Santa's throne into an electric chair.

Turns out I was right. (Listen, don't ever doubt the instincts of a dog with my intelligence, not to mention charm.) According to Jack and Charlie, years of being the man who could fix anything paid off when Corky Kelly turned his mind to murder. In hard hat and tool belt, he blended right in with the work crew making repairs at the mall. It would have been easy for a handyman to create a leak over the robing room, ensuring that when Santa sat on the throne Corky had rigged up as Old Sparky, his wet clothing would guarantee a quick trip to his final resting place.

But all's well that ends well, as Charlie and Shakespeare would say. Charlie's spending Christmas on the farm with Ruby Nell, who is up to the neck of her sequined caftan in preparations for the Valentine Christmas dinner. She vows that if Miss Sweet Potato shows up with her long-lens camera, she'll end up in the oven covered with marshmallows.

Speaking of cooking, Lovie took Rocky Malone back to her pink house in Tupelo, presumably to stuff the Valentine Christmas turkey. Though the mood they were in when they left Gas, Grits, and Guts, I'd say the archeologist stands a better than average chance of discovering the National Treasure.

Fayrene has invited Mooreville's new séance king, Bobby Huckabee, to her house for Christmas dinner. Of course, Darlene and cute little David will be there. Probably that silly-legged Lhasa Apso, too, but I'm not betting on the black-hearted cat.

If you think I forgot the most important people, you'd be mistaken. I'm a discreet dog. All I'm going to say about my human parents being back together is that the star is on the Christmas tree and I'm keeping the seven stray cats and that silly cocker spaniel in line so Callie and Jack can enjoy making up in peace.

When I'm not taking care of business around the Jones household and stockpiling steak bones in the back yard (Jack is a man who loves to grill), I'm busy laying my own plans.

But they're not about to include a French poodle who got the "Fever" for a dog with a useless tail. As soon as I finish burying this bone and talk that dumb Hoyt into helping me dig the escape hole, I'm planning to cruise around the Mooreville Truck Stop. My best buddy Trey says there's a beagle babe hanging out there just looking for "T.R.O.U.B.L.E."

Look out, baby. Santa Paws is back in town.

Elvis has left the building.

Lovie's Luscious Eats

Holiday Sweet Treats and More

Alice Virginia Daniel

These four recipes are from Alice Virginia Daniel, of Tupelo, Mississippi. A flamboyant redhead who knows her way around the kitchen, Alice is the author's friend and the inspiration for Lovie.

Butterscotch Cream Pie

4 T. flour
2 T. butter
1 cup brown sugar
3 egg yolks, well beaten
¾ c. Pet milk, diluted with 1¼ c. water
1 t. vanilla

Mix above ingredients in top of double boiler, stirring occasionally, until thick; then add vanilla. Put in a pie shell already baked till just before it turns light gold. Top with meringue (recipe below) and bake in preheated oven at 350 degrees till meringue is golden. Refrigerate.

Meringue

Beat 3 egg whites and 6 T. sugar till stiff.

"This is a 100-year-old family recipe passed down with the spirit of heavenly flavor."—Alice (Lovie)

Happy Holiday Kiss Kiss Eggnog

6 eggs, beaten
¾ cup sugar
1 pint whipping cream
1 pint bourbon
1 jigger rum
Nutmeg
1 cinnamon stick

Beat yolks separately with ¼ cup of sugar. Beat whites with ½ cup of sugar. Whip cream. Fold whites and cream into egg yolks. Add bourbon. Last, pour in rum, stirring constantly. Pour into two festive pitchers. Top with dash of nutmeg and chill until ready to serve. Pour into punch cups or mugs. Stir with a cinnamon stick. (Option: a teaspoon of vanilla ice cream added is so creamy and tasty.) Serves 8–10, but it all depends on the size of the cup. When in doubt, serve it in a beautiful punch bowl.

"Now get your honey bun, stand under the mistletoe, raise your cup high, and kiss, kiss!"—Alice (Lovie)

Aunt Louise's Hershey Pie

6 chocolate almond bars
18 marshmallows
⅔ cup milk
½ pint cream

Put the first three ingredients in a double boiler and dissolve thoroughly. Cool well. Whip cream and fold in. Put into a large graham cracker pie crust (recipe below). Refrigerate overnight or at least 8 hours before serving.

"OMGosh, so fine!"—Alice (Lovie)

Graham Cracker Pie Crust

1½ cups graham cracker crumbs
2 T. sugar
1 stick butter, melted

Mix all ingredients and press into the side of a pie pan. Cook crust at 350 degrees approximately 15 minutes. Cool before adding pie filling.

Peggy Webb

Gum Drop Squares

1⅛ c. brown sugar
2 eggs
1 c. self-rising flour
½ c. nuts (pecans or walnuts), chopped
1 t. vanilla
pinch salt
½ lb. orange gum drops

Slice and chop fine the orange gum drops. Drop pieces into flour and toss. Cream eggs and sugar, vanilla, and salt. Add flour, gum drops, and nuts. Mix well. Bake in 8x8x2-inch pan, well greased and floured. Bake at 300 degrees for 30 minutes. Cut into squares while hot. Dust with powdered sugar.

"Prepare for yummy comments, especially from your honey bun."—Alice (Lovie)

Peggy Webb

This next recipe is original with the author and one of her favorite comfort drinks after a day of writing.

Jack's Mayan Hot Chocolate

3 squares of Ghiradelli Intense Dark 60% Cacao (Evening Dream, All Natural)
1 T. water
1½ packets Splenda or to taste
¾ cup 2% milk
Dash each of cinnamon and red pepper or to taste

In a small heavy-bottomed pan over a simmer burner or in a double boiler, melt the chocolate squares in 1 T. of water. Stir constantly. Do not let the chocolate come to a boil. Remove from heat and stir in Splenda, cinnamon, and red pepper. Return to very low heat and slowly pour in the milk, stirring constantly. Heat till warm, but *do not* let the chocolate milk reach boiling. Boiling spoils the flavor.

"Pour into a mug then curl up in a rocking chair in front of a fire with your favorite book. You'll want to keep a spoon handy while you drink, because the bottom of the mug is likely to have a lovely chunk of thick, melted chocolate." —Peggy, who is the voice of all the characters, especially Elvis!

Darlene Hayes

The next two recipes are from Darlene Hayes, of Pensacola, Florida. A tall, charming blonde who drives a Dodge Ram with a Hemi engine, Darlene provided inspiration for Callie's manicurist as well as her truck. Darlene is a good friend and next-door-neighbor to the author's son and his family.

Peggy Webb

Pumpkin Pecan Pie

Pumpkin layer

1 cup Libby's 100% pure pumpkin
⅓ c. sugar
1 egg, beaten
1 t. pumpkin pie spice

Combine pumpkin, sugar, egg, and pie spice. Spread over the bottom of a baked pie crust.

Pecan layer

⅔ c. light corn syrup
½ c. sugar
2 eggs, beaten
3 T. melted butter
½ t. vanilla
1 c. pecan pieces

Combine corn syrup, sugar, eggs, butter, and vanilla. Stir in the nuts. Spoon over pumpkin layer. Bake in preheated 350-degree oven for 50 minutes or until a knife inserted in the center comes out clean.

"I also add cinnamon and cloves to my taste to this recipe. Happy holidays!"—Darlene (Darlene Johnson Lawford Grant)

Veg-All Casserole

1 large can of Veg-All, drained
1 can cream of chicken soup
2 medium onions, chopped
1 can water chestnuts, drained and chopped
1 cup mayonnaise
1 cup grated cheddar cheese
1 stick butter, melted
1 stack Ritz crackers, crushed

Preheat oven to 350 degrees. Mix the first six ingredients and pour into a casserole dish. Mix melted butter with Ritz crackers. Spread the topping over the casserole and bake 30 minutes or until bubbly.

"This is my family's favorite holiday side dish."—Darlene

Trey Webb

The following two original recipes came from the author's son, Trey Webb, of Pensacola, Florida. A dog lover, a world-class cook, and the world's best son, Trey was the inspiration for Jarvetis' favorite redbone hound dog, who is Elvis' best friend.

Peggy Webb

Italian Chicken Soup

3 chicken breasts (boneless, skinless)
1 medium onion, diced
1 medium bell pepper, diced
1 lb. can diced tomatoes
1 T. minced garlic
¼ stick butter
3 quarts chicken broth
½ t. each salt, black pepper, and Cajun seasoning
½ bag egg noodles
Dash each of dried oregano and basil

Boil chicken in broth and Cajun seasoning till done. Remove chicken from broth, cool, and pull into slivers. Add salt, pepper, and garlic to the onions, then sauté in ¼ stick of butter. Just before the onions are done, add the bell pepper and finish cooking. *Note:* you want the bell pepper to still be firm at the end of this process. Add this mixture to the broth. Add the can of tomatoes with its juice, the basil and oregano, and the slivered chicken to the broth. Cover and simmer on low for at least 1 hour. Before serving, bring back to a slow boil, add the egg noodles, and cook till done. Remove from heat and serve.

Collards (Soul Food)

1 smoked hog jowl
2 lb. collard greens, washed and cut into squares
4 t. salt or to taste
4 t. black pepper or to taste
4 t. sugar or to taste

Cut hog jowl into 8 to 10 large chunks, add to a large pot, and cover with about 2 inches of water. Add salt, pepper, and sugar. Cover and slow-boil for about ½ hour. Then add the collards, cover, and let slow-boil for 10 to 15 minutes more. Reduce heat to low, and let cook for about 1 hour. Serve with 2 or 3 pieces of fried hog jowl and Southern cornbread.

"Friends and family frequently request my collards at potluck suppers."—Trey

Debbie Turner

Debbie Turner, one of the best cooks in Tupelo, Mississippi, provided these two recipes. Debbie is the author's friend and the wife of the author's webmaster, Roy Turner.

Chicken Pesto

1 lb. boneless chicken breast (or chicken tenders)
3 to 4 cloves garlic, chopped
1 lb. box farfalle pasta
1 c. frozen English peas
Olive oil, as needed to coat chicken
Salt and pepper to taste
2 to 3 T. Classico pesto sauce or your own Alfredo sauce (recipe below)

Preheat oven to 350 degrees. Put chicken in a roasting pan. Sprinkle chicken with olive oil, salt, pepper, and chopped garlic cloves. Cover with foil and bake approximately one hour or until chicken is done. Let chicken cool and shred with a fork. Set aside.

Alfredo Sauce

1 stick of butter
2 c. grated parmesan cheese
1 c. whipping cream

In a small sauce pan, slowly melt the butter and parmesan cheese. Use very low heat and stir constantly till melted. Whisk in 1 c. of whipping cream. Set aside.

Cook pasta according to directions. Drain and put in pasta dish. Top with shredded chicken, frozen peas, and Alfredo sauce or 2 to 3 T. of prepared pesto sauce.

ELVIS AND THE BLUE CHRISTMAS CORPSE

Debbie's Chocolate Chip Bundt Cake

⅔ c. chopped pacans
¼ c. butter, softened
2 T. granulated sugar
2¾ c. all-purpose flour
1 t. salt
1 t. baking soda
1 c. butter, softened
1 c. packed brown sugar
½ c. granulated sugar
1 T. vanilla extract
4 large eggs
1 c. buttermilk
1 12 oz. bag semisweet chocolate mini-morsels
Whipped cream and cherries, for garnish

Preheat oven to 350 degrees. Stir together first three ingredients in a small bowl, using a fork. Sprinkle in a greased and floured 12-c. bundt pan. Whisk together flour, baking soda, and salt. Set aside.

Beat butter, brown sugar, granulated sugar, and vanilla at medium speed with a heavy-duty electric stand mixer for 3 to 5 minutes or until fluffy. Add eggs, one at a time, beating until just blended.

Add flour mixture alternately with buttermilk, beginning and ending with flour. Beat at low speed just until blended after each addition, stopping to scrape bowl as needed. Beat in chocolate mini-morsels. Mixture will be thick. Spoon batter into prepared pan and bake at 350 degrees for 50 to 55 minutes or until a long wooden pick inserted in the center comes out clean. Cool pan on a wire for 10 minutes. Remove cake from pan and let cool on wire rack for approximately one hour before serving.

"These are family favorites."—Debbie

Marie Hussey

The recipe grand finale is Marie Hussey's original Southern cornbread dressing. During her lifetime, she prepared this dressing at every Thanksgiving and Christmas holiday meal on the farm in Mooreville, Mississippi. Marie is the author's beloved mom and the inspiration for Callie's feisty, opinionated mama, Ruby Nell Valentine.

Mama's Southern Cornbread Dressing

2 large pans baked cornbread (recipe below)
½ large loaf of sliced white bread, best if at least a day old
4 large onions, chopped fine
6 sticks butter
3 to 4 T. black pepper (or to taste)
5 or 6 cans chicken broth, more if needed
1 can cream of chicken soup
12 to 14 eggs, beaten

Bake cornbread and crumble in a large mixing bowl. While it is still hot, stir in 5 sticks of butter. Sauté onions till golden in remaining stick of butter and add to cornbread mixture. Crumble loaf bread fine and add to mixture. Next add black pepper to taste, cream of chicken soup, and beaten eggs. Heat chicken broth, then add it slowly to the cornbread mixture, stirring well. The mixture will be soupy when finished.

This mixture makes at least two large pans of dressing. You may want to freeze some to bake later.

When ready to bake, spray a large baking pan or CorningWare baker with Pam. Fill the pan not quite to the top, allowing for expansion during the cooking process. Bake in a preheated 350-degree oven until dressing stands apart when spoon is inserted. This dressing should be moist and not firm like cornbread. Serve with turkey and giblet gravy.

Mama's Southern Cornbread

2 c. self-rising Sunflower or White Lily Cornmeal Mix
2 eggs, beaten
Approx. 1 cup buttermilk (or whole milk)
¼ c. canola oil, or to taste

Combine cornmeal mix, eggs, and buttermilk. Stir well. This mixture will be the consistency of cake batter and will pour easily; add more buttermilk if it is too thick. Put oil into a 10-inch cast-iron skillet and heat on top of the stove until the oil begins to sizzle. Turn off the burner. Pour most of the oil into the cornbread batter and stir well, leaving only a thin coating of oil along the sides and bottom of the skillet. Immediately pour batter back into the hot skillet (mixture will sizzle), and bake at 400 degrees until golden brown. This bread is equally good used as the basis for cornbread dressing with giblet gravy and served hot with black-eyed peas.

"If these directions seem vague, it's because Mama rarely recorded her recipes. My two sisters and I have tried to re-create her famous dressing. Jo Ann is the only one who gets it right. Happy Holidays!"—Peggy, who remembers her own mama saying, "Flitter!"